THE LAST REQUEST

BRANDON BARROWS

BLOODHOUND
— BOOKS —

CHAPTER ONE

The little plane looked promising before I boarded. It was freshly painted in glossy white, with a dark-blue stripe from nose to tail. Walking across an airstrip and climbing what was basically a ladder to board a plane was a new experience, but the attendant was friendly and smiling. "Welcome aboard Arctic Airlines flight 201," she said. It gave me a good feeling.

The moment I was inside, though, that feeling evaporated. The carpet down the aisle was ragged and stained; most of the seats sported electrical-tape repair jobs and one of the six rows of six seats was roped off with a handwritten sign that just said OUT OF ORDER. I turned back, but the attendant was disappearing into the cockpit. I don't know what I would have said to her anyway. My ticket was paid for and this was the only way to the town of Foster's Place that wouldn't require days on the road – and that was if I wanted to rent a car and drive myself. This feeder line was the only mass transit that serviced the place.

There were already six or seven people seated, most of them with a half-row to themselves on one side of the aisle or the other. I found a seat in the second-to-last row. The inner two seats were empty, but across the aisle, there was a heavyset woman with skin a rich copper color and dark, shiny hair that looked so soft I was envious. Her hands were clasped across her middle and her eyes were closed. She looked like she was already asleep even though we only boarded a couple of minutes ago.

The flight to Foster's Place was a little over an hour and reading on a plane gave me headaches, so I try to find people to chat with whenever I have to fly. It's something my mother taught me when I was a little girl. "Little while friends" she called them.

"Hi," I said, shrugging out of my parka.

The woman opened one eye, glanced at me and nodded, before closing it again.

"Don't bother."

I turned and saw a man somewhere in his middle thirties, about ten years older than me, twisted around in his seat two rows up and across the aisle. He was wearing a tweed suit that looked like it was slept in more than once. His eyes found mine as he continued. "Miriam's been on this flight every time I've taken it the last two years and I've never heard her say a word."

"Oh," I began, wondering how he knew her name if that was true, but then the captain's voice cut in over the loudspeakers, announcing takeoff. A moment later, there was the roar of engines, only barely muffled by the cabin's walls, and the sudden press of gravity as we were pushed back into our seats by the force of the thrust.

I've flown at least a dozen times in my life, but it was the first time I was ever scared. I'd never been in such a small plane before and maybe it was my imagination, but the sound of the engines seemed to have a raspy, almost asthmatic quality that brought gruesome images to mind. I glanced at the woman across the aisle; her eyes were still closed, her hands still clasped. The way her chest rose and fell, she might really have fallen asleep this time. I squeezed my eyes shut and tried to follow her lead.

Within a couple of minutes, the plane leveled out, and the

engine noise faded to a constant throaty rumble. When I opened my eyes, the plane was surrounded by mist, pressing in against the nearby window as if trying to enter the cabin. Seconds later, we popped out of the cloudbank and into brilliant blue sky, clearer than I ever saw before.

I shifted over to the window seat for a better look and as soon as I did, I heard a rustle of fabric. I turned; the man who spoke to me a moment ago was settling into my aisle seat. "Nice," he said, but I had the feeling he didn't mean the view. He stuck out his hand and smiled. The smile, the suit, and something in his eyes all combined to give me the impression of a salesman, the kind people deal with because they have to, but will never warm up to. "Charlie Shelton."

"Holly Shaw." I brushed my fingers against his, half expecting him to grab them and hold on, but he didn't.

"First time in Alaska?" Shelton asked.

I nodded. "Yeah."

Shelton smiled again. "Like it?"

I lifted my shoulders. I hadn't really seen anything but the airports in Anchorage and Fairbanks and except for their size, they could have been just about anywhere.

"On vacation? Out for a little adventure?" The way Shelton said it set off warnings in the back of my head. He must have seen something on my face because he held up his hands. "Sorry, was that out of line? Don't know what'll provoke people these days with all that 'wokeness' bull or whatever. I meant it's just unusual to see a woman traveling alone way out here. A non-native, I mean. This commuter line only makes the trip to Foster's Place once a week and there's not much out there except the refinery."

"I'm visiting family," I said. "My great aunt. Maybe you know her – Lydia Orlov?"

Shelton said nothing for a moment. Then he collected himself, saying, "I should have known." He stood, nodding once, as if dismissing me. "Nice meeting you, Miss Shaw. I hope you have a good visit." Without another word or a backward glance, he went back to his original seat.

It was strange. I know I'm not bad-looking, and like any woman, I got used to dealing with men early on in life. This was the first time a guy ever gave up so quickly or easily, though, and I was sure it didn't have anything to do with me. Shelton was pretty clearly working up to something, right until I mentioned Great Aunt Lydia. I'd never met the woman, didn't really know anything about her except that she'd raised my dad and was supposedly really rich, but I doubted she was all that scary.

Whatever. Maybe Shelton had something personal against her.

Without anything better to do, I tugged my carry-on from under the seat, unzipped it and dug out the registered letter I'd received the week before. The creases were starting to loosen where the paper was weakened from being folded and unfolded so often. I'd read it so many times I had it memorized, but I read it again anyway.

Grandniece, it began. *I would like for you to visit me in my home, in Foster's Place, Alaska. I am dying and I assure you that a visit will be well worth your time. Enclosed you will find a check for travel expenses.* It was signed, *Your Great Aunt, Lydia Orlov,* and when I first received it, a check for a thousand dollars was paper-clipped beneath the signature.

Before I got the letter, I hadn't thought about Lydia Orlov in years—not since I was a kid. I'd never met her, never even saw a picture of her, and because of that, she wasn't really a person who existed in any real sense. She was just some relative, a name I'd heard a couple times, mentioned as the woman who raised my father. Maybe if Dad was alive, it would have been different, but he was killed in a car accident when I was four and Mom never had much contact with his family. I barely even remembered my father and I hadn't seen his brother or sister, or their kids, since the funeral. The only real connection I had with them was my name, 'Shaw', and Great Aunt Lydia didn't even have that.

I guess I'm naturally the suspicious type, but it's hard not to be intrigued by something like that. The letter came to my work, which didn't go over too well with my boss; I had her breathing down my neck the rest of the day because of it. The moment I got home, though, I hopped on the computer and tried to find whatever I could about Lydia Orlov.

There wasn't much. Using what I knew about my dad and where he grew up, I found a name and a birthdate—Lydia Anne Shaw, August 24th, 1945, Philadelphia, Pennsylvania—and a notice from 1989, in Seattle, Washington: the marriage of Lydia Anne Shaw and Piotr Orlov. That gave me another angle, so I tried looking up Orlov. There was a lot more about him, but none of it really useful. The important parts were that he was some sort of Russian businessman who'd fled the Soviet Union when it fell apart and ended up in Alaska, running a mining operation and later an oil refinery. That, at least to me, said money.

I wished Mom were alive so I could ask her about all of this family stuff. I never even gave a thought to it before receiving that letter and now it seemed impenetrable. It was almost two years too late, though; ovarian cancer is a bitch. At least I still had her old address book.

In the book, I found listings for aunts, uncles, and cousins on both sides of the family. My dad was the youngest Shaw sibling, and his brother and sister were several years older than him, so their kids were probably older than me. If I remembered correctly, the closest to my age was Jonathan. By some miracle, the number Mom had for him was still good.

"You got a letter, too?" was the first thing he said after we got greetings out of the way. He'd already heard from both his older brothers, Marcus and Blair, and Blair had spoken with our mutual cousins. All five of them had received letters identical to mine.

"You're going, right?" Jonathan asked.

"I don't know. Alaska in February? To visit a relative I've never even seen a picture of?"

"Lydia's rich, dear." There was a small note of superiority in Jonathan's voice, but Lydia's money, if she had any, wasn't his accomplishment, so I didn't get it. "You like money, don't you?" he added.

I liked money. Who didn't? But it was all too strange, like something out of an old movie—the kind where everyone ends up dying.

CHAPTER TWO

Obviously, I decided to go and now, the tiny plane was soaring high over snowfields dotted with clusters of scruffy little trees, the morning's light glaring off the white expanse, making it glow like a second, ground-bound sun. I looked at my phone, and assuming the time zone was updated correctly, it was just after nine o'clock in the morning. I'd been traveling for almost sixteen straight hours, but it was almost over.

I closed my eyes, just to rest them, and the next thing I knew, the uneven, sickly engine sound was back, vibrating the wall of the cabin. I jerked upright in the seat. Other passengers were gathering their stuff together, getting ready for landing. I must have fallen asleep. Even with all the stuff in my head, I guess the body does what it has to.

I leaned over to look out the window. The scenery had changed. It was still pretty flat, but there were a lot more trees now. A long, narrow strip of asphalt snaked its way through them and in the far distance, I could see a tiny cluster of what must have been buildings.

Without warning, the captain's voice crackled above us,

announcing we would be landing in Foster's Place, where the local temperature was a balmy twenty-two degrees, in just about three minutes. The plane began to descend even as he said it. I closed my eyes and braced myself. The landing was sudden and bumpy, but when I opened my eyes again, we were all in one piece and on the ground.

The flight attendant appeared at the head of the aisle. "Please remember to take all of your belongings," she chirped, as bright and friendly as when she greeted me back in Fairbanks. "And thank you for choosing Arctic Airlines." I realized I hadn't seen her since the plane took off. I guess hellos and goodbyes were all she was there for.

I climbed down the steep boarding ramp to the ground, shivering inside my parka. Twenty-two degrees in February was pretty mild back home in Ohio, but here, in the middle of nowhere, it seemed colder. Most of the few other passengers were already off the plane and now they headed towards a small lot where a dozen or so cars and trucks were parked.

The Foster's Place airport was even smaller than the one in Fairbanks. It was really only a single runway, a hanger, and a building marked TERMINAL. A man wearing a blue jumpsuit and a wool hat came out of the terminal building, pushing a luggage cart. His arms were bare to the elbow and the cold didn't seem to bother him at all.

"This way," a voice next to me said. I turned and saw the woman Charlie Shelton called Miriam. "They'll bring your bags in." She was pointing at the terminal.

I smiled. "Thanks." If Charlie Shelton never heard her speak, it was probably because she didn't think he was worth talking to.

It was warm inside the building, but that was about all it had to offer. There were half a dozen chairs, a rack of old magazines, a coffee pot, and a desk. A door in one corner was labeled TOILET. Another was labeled EMPLOYEES ONLY.

"Holly Shaw?"

The voice startled me and I backed away a step as I turned. A man, a couple of years younger than me, stood just inside the doorway. He was about five-ten, with a café-au-lait complexion, and eyes so dark they were nearly black. His hair, too, was black and a little curly, even though it was cut fairly short. He was wearing a brown leather bomber jacket with a fur collar; a big watch with the shine of real gold peeked out of the left sleeve. He was smiling and he was very, very good-looking.

"H-how do you know my name?" I stumbled over the words a little, surprised and wary. I thought of what Shelton said on the plane, that it was unusual to find a woman traveling alone up here. When I was in college, I traveled all over the country, both in groups and by myself a few times, and never really worried. Alaska was part of the United States, but they call it 'The Last Frontier' and all of a sudden, it felt like I was in a foreign country.

The man—boy, almost, though he wasn't much younger than me—held up both hands, palms outwards. "Whoa! Sorry if I scared you. I'm Rick. I'm your ride."

My brows came together. "Ride? Wait, you were expecting me?"

"Sure, six folks, all guests of Mrs. Orlov, coming from the lower forty-eight. The rest got in yesterday as a group on a private charter, and you're the only one off the plane I don't recognize, so you must be Holly."

"You know my aunt?"

Rick laughed. "Everyone knows Mrs. Orlov." He stuck out his hand. "Anyway, it's nice to meet you."

When I didn't take it, he retracted the hand and then held both of them up again. "I get it. Strange guy just comes up to you, you're suspicious." He smiled again, wider this time, showing me his teeth. "But I'm harmless. Promise."

"Yeah, okay," I told him, not a hundred percent convinced. He said he was my ride, but the town couldn't be that big. I was pretty sure I could find my own way to Aunt Lydia's place.

Rick turned to the window. "Here comes Pete with the bags. Once we've got your stuff, I'll toss 'em in the Explorer and we'll get going."

"No thanks."

The young man turned, a question on his face. "What do you mean?"

"I'm not getting in a car with you."

"Then how're you gonna get out to Dacha Orlov?"

I tugged my iPhone from my coat pocket. "I'll get an Uber."

Rick laughed, loud and hard. "Oh, that's good." He lifted a hand as if wiping away a tear. "Where do you think you are?"

The door opened, letting in a blast of cold air. The man in the jumpsuit wheeled the cart in; it only held my two suitcases. "Shaw?" the man asked. I nodded and he set the luggage down on the floor.

He started to push the cart back outside, but stopped when I said, "Excuse me, sir—is there a taxi service?"

The man nodded at Rick and said, "Right there."

I looked back at Rick; he was smiling again, but now it was like a little boy who'd just showed up all the adults.

"So can I get those bags now?" he asked.

"I guess I don't have a choice, do I?"

He was already picking them up, one in each hand. "Not unless you want to walk."

Slinging the strap of my carry-on over my shoulder, I followed him out to the parking lot, trying not to show my embarrassment. He stopped at a black Ford Explorer, at least ten years old, opened the back seat, set the bags he carried inside, and then took the carry-on from me, too. When he stepped back to close the door, I put my hand on the edge. He asked, "You wanna sit in the back? When there's just one, passengers usually sit up front with me so I can show 'em the sights."

"What's there to see?"

10

"You ever been here before?" he asked, even though he knew the answer.

"No."

"Then it's all new to you." He grinned again.

I gave up and went around to the front passenger-side door. We climbed into the truck. Rick put the key in the ignition, but didn't start it. After a moment, I asked, "What's wrong?"

"Nothing," he said. "Just savoring the feeling. I've never had a girl as beautiful as you in my car before."

"I'll ride in the back," I told him, opening the door again.

"Hey, hey." I felt a touch on my shoulder, very light through the parka. I looked back, one leg already outside. "It was just a compliment. I'm sorry if I offended you."

His voice was soft, but there was a sort of intensity in it all the same, and there was a look in his eyes that matched. Charlie Shelton, back on the plane, made me wary, but not afraid. Somehow, I was a little scared of this boy, Rick. I didn't want to go anywhere with him, but short of hitchhiking or walking, I didn't know how else I'd get to my aunt's.

"Really. I'm sorry," Rick said.

I pulled my leg in and closed the door. "If you know who I am, you know why I'm here."

"Sure," he agreed.

I gave him my sharpest look. "So do you really think I'm in any mood to be picked up when I'm here to visit my dying aunt?"

"Point taken." He turned the key in the ignition; it started with a rumble that reminded me of the airplane. Then he spun the wheel and we were out of the parking lot and heading away from the little airport.

Rick drove fast. Within a minute or two, we were in what must have been the actual town of Foster's Place. Little stores and houses lined the street, cars and trucks—mostly trucks—jammed up against the curb. Except for the huge mountains in the distance, it could have been a tiny town back in Ohio or anywhere else in the Midwest. No, that wasn't quite right. There was one more difference: everything looked old and run-down. It wasn't just the airplane or Rick's SUV, everything seemed like it was from fifteen or even twenty years ago and nothing was changed since.

"Is this the whole town?"

"Pretty much," Rick said, without taking his eyes from the road. "Except your aunt's place and the refinery, and they're both a ways out of town."

"What about all the sights you said you'd show me?"

Rick smiled. "That was it."

Before I could think of a response, we were back out in open, snow-covered prairie, following a cracked, asphalt highway towards the nearest of the mountains. Even though I knew it must be miles away, it was still huge. I could make out individual trees and rocky crags jutting out from between them in detail, like I was looking at it through a telescope. I'd seen mountains before, in California and in Colorado, but nothing like this.

"How far is it to my aunt's house?"

"You mean Dacha Orlov? About nine miles, but then we have to go up the mountain."

"Up the mountain?" I slid down in the seat and craned my neck, trying to get a better view of the huge mountain. "What's its name?"

"Foster's Peak."

I turned in my seat. "No."

"Yep. Family named Foster used to own this whole area— mountain and town included."

"I guess that explains the name. I didn't know you could own a mountain though."

"Ha," Rick barked. "You can own *anything* with enough money."

"So who owns it now then?"

Rick glanced at me. "Who else? Your aunt."

I looked out the window, watching the open space close in around us as we entered the foothills. Snow-covered trees replaced the snowy fields. "So she really is rich."

"Very."

"Do you know my aunt?"

He shrugged. "As well as anyone who doesn't live in that house, I guess."

"Which means...?"

Rick only shrugged again.

I thought for a moment, then asked, "Did my cousins tell you anything? You drove them out to the house, right?"

"Just that they were going to meet your aunt. The big one, Marcus, hoped to go home rich."

"He told you that?" I tried to remember Marcus, but the only time I ever met him, I was barely more than a toddler. I could picture a group of cousins, but they were all older children or young teenagers and I didn't know what names belonged with which face.

"Not in those words, but it was pretty plain."

The SUV slowed. The road was bumpy here, full of potholes, and beginning to angle upwards. When he got past the worst of it, Rick said, "Your aunt's dying, supposedly. They told me that, but I already knew."

"How?"

Rick's lips twisted into a tiny, knowing smile. "I get around." He glanced at me and the smile disappeared. "It's a *really* small town, Miss Shaw. There aren't many secrets."

I doubted that, but I didn't see any point in saying so.

By then, the road was much steeper and we were climbing into the true mountains. Trees still grew up alongside the road, but the ground was rockier and there were huge boulders at intervals, like they were just pushed aside when the road was laid down. After a while, we came around a bend and the trees fell away suddenly. Overtop the trees around the base of the mountain, I could see clear across the snowfields to the town. Further away, hulking like some black monster, was what must be the refinery.

I realized my ears felt plugged and worked my jaw, trying to pop them. I wished I had some gum.

"That's a sight to see, huh?" Rick asked. It was the first thing either of us said in a while.

"How high are we?"

"About twenty-five hundred feet now. Dacha Orlov is at just over three thousand. The mountain itself is a little over five."

"What's 'dacha' mean?"

"Russian for 'fancy house' or something like that. Your uncle named the place." He glanced over. "Or, your aunt's husband, if you prefer."

Piotr Orlov. I read about him, but didn't give him much thought. I knew he was dead, I picked that much up from Google, and I knew he was past sixty when he married my aunt. And she was forty-four when they got married. I didn't think about it before, but I doubted they had any children. Maybe that explained why Lydia was so anxious to meet all of her grandnieces and nephews.

The road curved, winding through a narrow gap cut directly into solid rock. We came out in a dense stand of trees and then, all of a sudden, they disappeared and I got my first look at Dacha Orlov. It was huge, rambling, made of some light-colored wood. It had three stories, and two attached wings, one made all of glass, and it backed almost up to the edge of a precipice, beyond which I couldn't see anything but sky.

Rick swung the Explorer around the circular gravel driveway, coming to a stop at the bottom of a wide set of wooden stairs leading to a porch the width of the entire front of the house. He was out of the car before me and by the time I climbed out, he'd already set my bags on the bottom stair. I reached into the inside pocket of my coat for my wallet and asked, "How much is the fare?"

"Zero dollars and zero cents." He smiled. "Your cousin Blair tipped me well enough yesterday that I'd feel bad taking any more of your family's money."

I didn't know how to feel about that. Thinking about what he said when I first got into his car, I kind of doubted that was the real reason. "Well... thanks for the ride then," I told him.

"My pleasure." He dipped his head. "And I hope I'll get a chance to chauffeur you around again. Maybe I can show you a little more of Foster's Place."

"I'm here on a family matter," I told him, trying to put a bit of ice in it. "I'm not a tourist."

"If you were, you'd probably be the first this town ever got this time of year." He grinned. "But I hope you'll give me a call anyway. Your family have my number, and who knows? Maybe you'll need a friend sometime."

"What does that mean?" I asked, but all he did was smile, climb back into the SUV, and take off back down the mountain.

CHAPTER THREE

There was a brass-plated doorbell next to the wooden double doors of the huge house. I didn't get a chance to press it, though, before one of the doors swung open. Someone must have seen or heard Rick's car coming up the driveway, which wasn't unusual. That didn't prepare me for the person who appeared from the house though.

I never saw a bigger man in my life. He was tall enough that I was sure he'd have to stoop to get through the doorway and his shoulders were so broad that he did have to turn sideways with only one of the doors open. Unconsciously, I stepped backwards, keeping my distance from the man—more out of surprise than anything else.

His skin, stretched over high, jutting cheekbones, was pale except for a smattering of old, reddish pit-scars. His hair was dark, making his skin seem even whiter in comparison. He wore it a little long, and combed to one side; a sharp parting showed a contrasting line of chalk-white scalp. His eyes, too, were dark, almost black, and sunken deeply in the sockets. If I only saw the man's face, I would guess that he had been sick for a long time.

His body put the lie to that, though—he must have weighed three hundred pounds and none of it looked like fat.

The man stepped forward and bowed slightly from the shoulders. When he straightened, somehow he seemed even larger than before. My first guess at his height was about six-foot-four, but I revised it up to at least six-six. I noticed his clothing for the first time: a dark, conservatively cut suit, with a plain white shirt and black tie. Examining his clothes, my eyes were drawn to his hands: the wrists were strangely thin, and the hands huge, but boney. They didn't seem to belong to the rest of this powerful man.

I must have seemed rude, staring so long, probably with my mouth hanging open. I was about to apologize when the man said, "Miss Holly Shaw?" His tone was flat, but his voice was deep and rumbling; it reminded me of a video I saw once of an avalanche and the sound it made, as the wave of snow tumbled down the side of a mountain.

"Y-yes," I said. "I'm Holly Shaw. This is my great aunt, Lydia Orlov's house?"

"Yes." He nodded, just a dip of the chin. "I'll take you to the missus."

I turned and reached for my luggage, but the huge man was suddenly beside me, and then the bags were in his hands. "I will take them, miss. Come." He sidled through the open doorway and into the house.

Stepping inside, I said, "Thank you. Um... you work for my aunt?"

"Yes." He motioned with his head for me to follow.

Following wasn't as easy as it sounds. He was so huge, I felt like a kid trying to catch up to her father. I couldn't really remember what my father looked like, but I knew it was nothing like this man, and I was glad for that. He was perfectly polite, but he gave me the creeps.

We marched through a high-ceilinged entrance hall with

marble flooring and an elaborate chandelier set directly over the middle of the room. It was a little chilly from the door being left open and that, plus the stone floor that seemed to radiate cold, made me shiver inside my coat.

The butler, or whatever he was, led me through an open archway into what I guess was a sort of reception hall. The flooring was hardwood, polished to a warm glow, and the walls and ceilings were cream-colored. The ceiling was laced with wooden beams and the walls were decorated with paintings and photographs. A fire burned in a hearth on the far side of the room, and between it and the archway were comfortable-looking chairs and a small sofa. There were several doors off the room, all closed.

I hoped we would stop here, at least long enough to enjoy a little of the fire's warmth, but the man kept right on going, turning through another archway that let out into a short hallway ending in a broad stairway, each step plushly carpeted in the same cream color as the walls. Without checking to see if I was still following, he went up the stairs. His long legs let him take them two at a time without any trouble. I had to hurry to keep up, again feeling like a small child.

He paused at the second-floor landing and waited for me. He set my bags down. "I'll put these in your room later, miss." He held out a hand. "Your coat, please."

For an instant, I didn't understand what he meant, and felt foolish when I realized. I shrugged off my parka and handed it to him. He folded it carefully and draped it across my bags, then gestured towards the stairs leading further up. "The master bedroom is on the third floor." He resumed his climb.

The stairs ended in a long, airy hallway that must have run the whole length of the house. There were only a few doors off the hall, all of them closed, but the ceiling had skylights at regular intervals and both ends of the hallway had tall windows that must have caught the sunrise on one side and the sunset on the other. The result was almost like being out under the open sky. We were so high up the mountain, and higher still on the third floor of the house, that I imagined the view must be as close to being a bird as any person ever got without actually flying.

I followed the butler down the hall, and as I did, the unreality of it all began crawling around inside my head, making my stomach churn. I was so focused on just getting here, to this massive house in the middle of nowhere, that I never really spent much time thinking about *why*. I came a long, long way to meet a relative I barely even knew existed and now I was about to see her face to face for the first time.

The man stopped at a door exactly halfway down the hall, knocked gently, and took a listening stance, his head cocked so one ear was close to the door. I didn't hear any response, but the butler must have, because he opened the door, then stood aside, and nodded for me to enter. Again, there was nothing I could do but obey. I realized then how little say I had in anything that had happened to me since the moment I got off the plane in Foster's Place.

I nodded at the man, because it seemed like the thing to do, and then stepped inside. I don't know what I expected—maybe a darkened room, filled with humming and beeping medical equipment, the smell of medication, antiseptic, and death hanging in the air. There was nothing like that at all. The room was as bright and airy as the hallway and gave me the same feeling of lightness as those skylights and the two big windows did, and if the room smelled of anything, it was a faded memory of lilacs.

The door clicked shut behind me as a soft voice said, "Do come in."

I moved towards the bed, hesitant now. The room wasn't scary at all, but I still didn't know what to expect of Great Aunt Lydia.

The bed was on the far side of the room, between a pair of

windows so huge it was almost as if that entire wall was made of glass, except for the solid strip in between, where the bed was. The bed itself was massive, an old-fashioned four-poster of dark, polished wood with a canopy that looked like silk. It didn't match the lightness of the room at all.

A queen's bed. The thought just popped to mind, but it fit very well when I got a good look at my aunt.

Lydia occupied only a small space in the center of the bed, propped up on a mound of pillows. A sheet was pulled up to her waist, but her upper body was covered by a white, lacy gown so loose she seemed almost lost in it. She was a tiny little lady, probably under five feet tall, though it was hard to judge with her in bed. I wondered if she was always this small or if it was a result of her illness.

"Hello, I'm Holly."

"Yes," the older woman said. "I suppose you must be."

Her voice was rich, cultured, and strong. Despite her letter, and even though she was apparently bedridden, Aunt Lydia didn't seem close to death. She didn't seem sick at all, really. Her hair was snow-white, and beautifully styled, and her face, if not really pretty, was handsome, without many lines for a woman of her age. It held the kind of power that usually takes people pretty far in life. Her eyes were blue, very clear, and intelligent. I got the sense she was studying me without being as obvious about it as I was in studying her. I tried not to stare, but it was difficult—it was like my eyes were just drawn to her.

"Am I what you expected?"

Heat came to my cheeks. I tried to look away, but wasn't sure where else I should be looking. Not looking at my aunt would be as rude as staring. "I didn't expect anything. Not... exactly."

"Not exactly, no," Lydia said, amusement in her voice. She was enjoying my embarrassment. "But you must have had some idea in mind. You've never met me, but you've heard my name, and

I'm sure you tried to find out all you could before you decided to come up here."

"Why do you say that?" I asked.

"Because you look like an intelligent girl and it's what I would have done in your place."

"Well." I shifted under the gaze of those blue eyes; it felt like they were actually looking *through* me. "I guess I did, but I couldn't find much."

"Don't guess," Lydia said sharply, startling me. "Own up to everything you do and never be ashamed of anything you've thought out beforehand. Trying to learn whatever you could was the right decision." She paused and a slow smile came to her lips. "You didn't find much, though, did you?"

"No," I admitted.

"So then," Lydia said. "What *do* you think of your old aunty?"

"You're a very attractive-looking lady."

The old woman's eyelids lowered; she had dark, heavy lashes. "I was beautiful once," she said. "I wouldn't have caught the eye of Piotr Orlov if I wasn't." She took a deep breath through her nose, then opened her eyes. "I realize you're just being polite though. I'm a wasted old sack of bones and I know it. But enough about me. My letter clearly interested you, as did the cashier's check. It didn't cost you the full amount to get here, did it?" Her eyes met mine and there was something calculating in them, as if I'd just walked right into some sort of trap.

"No, it didn't. It was very generous, thank you."

"But you hoped there was more where that came from, and now that you've seen my home, you know there is. Don't try to deny it."

I felt a little guilty and I knew the color in my cheeks must be getting deeper and brighter. I wasn't really embarrassed anymore, though, so much as I was insulted. "I'm not going to apologize for anything I thought. You must have known what

21

that letter would make us all think. You did say it would be 'worth our time', didn't you?"

Great Aunt Lydia smiled and nodded. "That's a good answer, and you didn't have to think too long about it, so I know it's at least close to how you really feel." I opened my mouth, but she held up a hand. "Don't ruin it by saying something defensive now. I've decided I like you, Miss Holly Shaw, so try not to change my mind."

She caught me off-guard. "You like me?"

"Why not?" She lifted thin shoulders. "You're intelligent and you're very pretty. That's more than can be said for most people."

I looked down at myself; the dark, skinny-cut slacks that hugged my hips were wrinkled from so many plane rides, and the soft, long-sleeved white blouse probably had stains under my arms. I hadn't seen myself in a mirror since the day before and I couldn't imagine what my hair looked like.

"I don't feel very pretty right now," I said. "Or even presentable."

"Oh, I'm sure you'll be gorgeous once you've had a chance to freshen up, but I told Elijah that I wanted to meet you the moment you arrived—there was never any doubt in my mind that you'd show up sooner or later—before you could compose yourself and put on another face for your dear, old aunty. And trust me, Holly, when I tell you I never lie. I told you that you're pretty and I mean it. I didn't expect you to be blonde though," she added.

"Well, I was adopted."

"So I've been told. You must know that the Shaws are all dark, with black hair and usually dark eyes. Black Irish stock. Pirates and ne'er-do-wells, the lot of them. With my blue eyes, a rarity in this family, I always wished I was a blonde. I dyed my hair for a while when I was young, in fact. When I still had the time to care what I looked like."

She narrowed her eyes and I felt her gaze roam over me. "In

fact, you're very much the way I pictured my ideal self when I was about your age. Pretty, well-dressed, good figure."

I was blushing again. "Thank you."

"Don't thank me. Thank your own good fortune and whoever gave you your genes. When I was your age, clothing was cut so it could hide the little imperfections, but somewhere along the line, the fashion industry decided that nice clothes were only for girls with good bodies.

"You aren't married," she said, abruptly changing the subject. "Or did you just keep your maiden name?"

"I'm not married," I answered, wondering what it mattered and sure she already knew the answer anyway.

"Any prospects?"

"No."

"How old are you again?"

"Twenty-four."

"Well." She pressed back against the pile of pillows, squirming as if trying to find a more comfortable position. "You don't have to settle or accept the first man who asks, but you better hurry up before all the best men are spoken for. Take my advice. I know what I'm talking about and I wish someone told me the same when I was your age."

"Okay," I said. "I'll get married as soon as possible."

Craftiness came into the old woman's eyes. "To make me happy?"

I shook my head. "To put your good advice to use."

Aunt Lydia smiled again, genuinely this time, I thought. It brought a little warmth to her face and I thought I could see some of the younger woman she once was. "Holly, I think you're going to be my favorite relative. Sit down, let's have a serious discussion."

There was just one chair in the room: a straight-backed, wooden chair without any sort of cushion. It was to one side of the nightstand closest to where I stood. It didn't look very comfortable, but I was suddenly tired and decided I would be glad to sit for the rest of this interview—or whatever it was.

I pulled the chair away from the wall, set it close to the head of the bed, and sat.

For a moment, we just looked each other, then Aunt Lydia said, "Now, tell me: why didn't you come up here with the rest of your family? They all arrived as a group yesterday and when I asked, none of them knew a thing about your plans."

"I have a job, and I couldn't leave any sooner than I did. My manager didn't want to give me the time off at all with such short notice."

"Even though my letter said I was dying?"

"Well..." I considered a moment. I didn't tell Kara, my manager—"team leader", she preferred—about why I suddenly had to go to Alaska, only that it was a family matter. We didn't really get along beyond the bare minimum needed to work together, and I didn't think it was any of her business. I knew Aunt Lydia wouldn't care about that though. "I didn't want to leave them short-handed. I left as soon as I could."

"My letter said the trip would be worth your time. Why worry about a job you may never have to go back to?"

"I had no idea what 'worth my time' meant."

"But you hoped it meant a lot of money."

"I did," I agreed. "But hope doesn't pay the bills. I wanted to make sure my job was still there waiting for me if I needed it."

Lydia faked surprise. "My, how very practical."

We just looked at each other for a moment, then she asked, "Would you like to know how much I'm worth, dear?"

"If you want to tell me."

Lydia's brows came together. "No, I'd rather you continued to sit there and pretend you don't give a damn one way or the other." The sharpness was in her voice again.

"Aunt Lydia—do you mind if I call you Aunt Lydia?"

"Not at all. I *am* your aunt."

"Okay. Aunt Lydia, your letter was purposely meant to pique our interest and our greed. Anyone could see that. So why are you upset that it did exactly what you obviously wanted it to do?"

The old woman sighed and slowly shook her head. "You're a clever girl, Holly." She looked me dead-on again. "Perhaps, though, I hoped some of you Shaw children would be different than I expected."

"I don't believe that for a second. You've lived long enough to know what the mention of money does to people. And," I added, "your letter also said you were dying. I don't think I believe that either."

"Well, now you're just being rude. What, exactly, does a dying person look like? Should I be hooked up to a lot of machinery? Should I be writhing and wailing in agony?"

I smiled, feeling like I finally won a point in our debate. "Maybe I am being rude, but I'm just telling you what I think. I thought you liked that about me."

Aunt Lydia leaned back against the pillows, her face to the ceiling. She must have been thinking about me or something I said or this entire situation she created, but I couldn't tell what was going through her head. Her face was totally blank and the room was silent.

After a couple of minutes I said, "I think you brought us all here to play some sort of game, Aunt Lydia, and I don't know if I want to play it. Maybe I should just go back to Foster's Place. Maybe the plane back to Fairbanks hasn't left yet. If your man—Elijah, you said?—if Elijah can give me that taxi-driver Rick's number, I'll call him and see if he can come get me. I have a round-trip ticket, so if the plane hasn't left, I'm sure I can work something out."

I stood, moved the chair back to where I found it, and started towards the door.

"Holly Shaw!"

I turned. Aunt Lydia's body was in the same position, but her face was tilted towards me and her eyes were bright—so bright, they almost seemed to glow. She was excited now. "Holly Shaw, I forbid you from going home when we've only just met."

"I'm sorry, Aunt Lydia, but you have no right to tell me what to do. I've been my own woman for a while now."

"You aren't interested in the money?"

"Of course I am, but I don't want to get into all of that again."

"I'm talking about a lot of money, Holly. I'm a very wealthy woman, and some of that wealth could be yours."

I didn't say anything. I just watched her. Our eyes locked. Lydia wasn't smiling now and the craftiness was gone. The only thing left was the excitement, and it was a feverish kind.

We both knew I was interested in the money—I was a human being, living in a society that revolved around the stuff. Literally anyone would be interested, because rich or poor, everyone wants more than they already have.

"Does ten million dollars interest you, my dear?"

"Yes," I told her. "I'd be interested in ten million. I'd be interested in even a fraction of that, if I'm honest."

Lydia's smile returned, but it was so tiny now, I wasn't sure if I was imagining it or not. "Then you better forget about calling Rick. Elijah will show you to your room." She rolled over onto her side, facing away from me, ending the interview.

CHAPTER FOUR

Slowly, I crossed the room. The nervousness I first felt at meeting Aunt Lydia was gone, replaced by a different kind of worry, and more than a little confusion.

Elijah, the huge butler, must have been standing in the hallway with his ear pressed to the door, listening for some cue, or maybe just nosey, because before I reached the door, it swung silently open, and there he was, almost completely filling the entryway.

He waited for me to join him in the hall, then gestured for me to follow and lumbered off without a word.

We went back to the second-floor hallway. Elijah brought me to the last door on the left. He opened the door, stepped inside. When I followed, he gestured to the bed, where my bags sat, then to an old-fashioned corded telephone sitting on the dresser. "If you need anything, just lift the receiver." Then he bowed slightly and disappeared into the hallway, closing the door behind him.

The room was lovely, as open and airy as Aunt Lydia's, though nowhere near as big. It was on the side of the house that faced the precipice the building clung to, and the view from the huge picture window was stunning. It was like a photo in a travel magazine, but close enough to touch. I got out my phone and snapped a picture, but when I tried to post it on Facebook, I discovered there was no signal at all. I frowned, waved the phone around a little, turning it different directions and couldn't get even a single bar. I turned on the wifi and there were no networks in range. "Figures," I grumbled.

I turned back to the room. There wasn't much in the way of furnishings. An area rug that covered most of the hardwood floor, a double-sized bed, a nightstand, dresser, and a single chair. The furniture was all in a style that looked rustic at first glance, but that even a layman could tell was actually very high quality, built by a master craftsman. Overall, the effect was of a high-end hotel room meant to look like a tourist's idea of Alaska. I wondered if Aunt Lydia picked the decor herself.

I unpacked my suitcases, hanging some things in the closet, where my parka was already hung, hoping the wrinkles fell out, and putting the rest in the dresser. Afterwards, I opened one of the smaller windows set aside the picture window. The room was directly above a patio area, and beyond that, was the steep drop of the cliff-face. I wondered if it went straight down the whole three thousand feet Rick mentioned.

The window was screen-less. It was a casement window and didn't open very far, but I stuck my head out into fresh, crisp air and inhaled deeply. I could feel the coldness working its way down into my lungs. Now that I'd been in the warm house for a while, it was invigorating, and made me feel a little more like myself.

I started to get cold after a minute or two; I closed the window and went into the room's private bath. It wasn't large, but it had a tall window that made it as airy as the bedroom. Stripping out of my grimy, travel-soiled clothing, I ran a hot shower and spent a long time under the stinging needles. When I was done, I toweled off and put on the least wrinkled of the dresses I hung in the closet.

And then I didn't know what to do with myself. I went back to the big window and looked outside, but nothing was changed. I sat down on the bed, wondering if Aunt Lydia had anything planned for the afternoon, if maybe I should go back upstairs and ask or just dig out the book I never even cracked open on any of the planes and try to relax.

A knock on the door saved me from having to make a decision.

I was certain that I would find Elijah on the other side, either checking to see if I needed anything or maybe with some message from my aunt. Instead, a stranger stood in the hall, which meant that he had to be one of my cousins.

"You look like you don't remember me. Guess I can't blame you," he announced. "Last time we saw each other, you were practically a baby and I was only about ten myself. I'm Blair Shaw, Nathan Shaw's second son."

He really didn't need to tell me he was a Shaw; he had the same dark, brooding looks that I saw in photos of my father and his brother. The Shaw look wasn't exactly handsome, but it was attractive and interesting. A Shaw face had character, and this Shaw got the full measure of it.

Blair Shaw was tall, a little over six feet. His hair was jet-black, cut very short at the sides, left longer on top and combed to the left. His eyes were the only thing about him that didn't scream "Shaw family"; instead of being dark, they were a brown so light they were almost tan. It looked strange with his complexion and hair, but it wasn't unattractive.

Wearing a gray suit and white shirt, tieless and open at the collar, he looked like he stepped out of some clothing store's fall catalogue. Not a big chain, not something with a lot of money behind it, but successful enough to hire models who made their clothing look good.

"I'm Holly," I told him. "Shaw, of course."

"Naturally." He quirked a smile. "I was down on the cliff's

edge, taking in the scenery, when I saw you leaning out of your window a little while ago. Thought I'd come up and reintroduce myself."

"I'm glad you did," I said, meaning it. "I haven't seen anyone but Aunt Lydia and that huge butler of hers."

"Elijah? That guy," he said, answering his own question. "Nobody actually knew you were coming."

Without my asking him to, Blair pushed the door open, stepped into the room, turned, and closed it behind him. Cousin or not, I didn't like the idea of a strange man inviting himself into my room, but he was already in now, standing by the window, admiring the view. I didn't see any point in making a scene.

"I guess Aunt Lydia likes you," he said, his back still to me. Then he turned and added, "All I can see from my room is the driveway and pine trees."

He settled himself on the edge of the bed, took a package of cigarettes from the inside pocket of his jacket, and held it out as if offering me one. I was surprised to learn he smoked; I didn't smell it on him and I was usually pretty sensitive to the scent.

"No, thanks. I don't smoke and I'd appreciate it if you didn't smoke in here."

"I shouldn't at all, really," he said, looking at the pack in his hand. He replaced it in his pocket and got to his feet. While I stood by the door, he took a quick turn around the room, ending up by the foot of the bed, facing me. "Nice room, isn't it? They're pretty much all the same from what I've seen, but there's at least eight of them just on this floor. I think there's a couple bigger ones upstairs." He jerked a thumb upwards. "I guess Aunt Lydia's pretty rich, huh?"

"She mentioned ten million dollars."

"Apiece? For each of us? Or to split?" He didn't wait for an answer. "Did you talk to her long?"

I shrugged. "For a while."

"What did you think?" He flopped onto the edge of the bed;

the casual way he did it, like a big, loose-limbed kid, was at odds with his looks and the way he dressed.

"She's... a strange lady."

"That's one way to put it." Blair leaned forward, elbows on his thighs, fingers laced together, and looked up at me. "Did she tell you anything about what she expects from us? Why we're here, I mean?"

I shook my head. "I don't really know anything that wasn't in the letter. She kind of drove the conversation."

"Same here. I never got a word in."

Blair stood, slipped the cigarettes from his pocket, and moved to the window. He cranked it open as wide as it would go, and then plucked a cigarette from the pack and lit it. He took several puffs, blowing the smoke out of the window each time, then flicked the half-smoked butt through the window and closed it.

Finally, he turned and looked at me, leaning his hips against the windowsill. "You know, I always thought the Shaws were a good-looking bunch, if you'll excuse a little bragging, but you're absolutely the best-looking Shaw I've ever met."

"Thanks, but I'm not technically a Shaw. I was adopted."

"I know," he said.

I didn't know what to say to that, so I just watched as he fiddled with the band of his watch and stared at a point on the floor. After a few moments of silence, I asked, "Do you know why Aunt Lydia invited us all here?"

Blair looked up, simultaneously clapping his palms against his thighs, and stood. "Well, cuz, our dear old Great Aunt Lydia is dying. That's what she claims anyway. She didn't tell anyone exactly *what* she's dying from, but she seemed pretty serious about it when she talked to the rest of us last night, even if it was only for a couple of minutes to welcome us to her humble little house."

He started pacing the room, rubbing his hands together. I got the feeling he wasn't much good at sitting still. "Anyway, Aunt

Lydia should be somewhere in her late seventies or thereabouts, and that's about when most people die." He reached the far end of the room and turned. "Right?" He nodded, answering himself again, and went on. "Now here's what she wants from us. It's weird as hell, but she's rich, so she can afford to be weird."

He went to the big picture window, glanced out and then started walking back towards me. "Great Aunt Lydia raised our parents—my dad, your dad, Aunt Sara. I assume you know that. But she never knew any of us. For some reason I can't figure out, now she wants us around when she dies. She never had children of her own, apparently. She didn't get married till she was in her forties, so I guess that makes sense. But now, because she's got no kids of her own, she wants all of her grandnephews and nieces gathered around the family hearth, even if we are complete strangers."

He paused, took a breath through his nose and looked me squarely in the eye. "And here's the pitch, Cousin Holly: you, me, my brothers, our cousins—any of us and all of us—can get a piece of Lydia Orlov's fortune when she goes. But only under one condition: we have to live here, in Dacha Orlov, with her until she kicks off."

I waited, but he had nothing else to add. I said, "It's like something from an old movie."

"Or a cheapo reality show," Blair countered. "Either way, it's what she told the rest of us last night. Now that you've joined the party, I'm guessing she'll gather us all together sometime later today or tonight and go over it again. In the meantime," he reached past me and opened the door to the hall, "have you seen much of the place? I spent last night and all this morning exploring. Let me give you the grand tour." Without waiting for an answer, he was out in the hallway and moving towards the stairs.

I went and got a pair of comfortable, soft-soled shoes, one of three pairs I stored in the closet. I slipped into them, thinking about Blair Shaw. He was good-looking and likable, but he was also a smooth-talker, and family or not, it was hard for me to trust people with a ready line of chatter. I didn't believe he meant me any harm—we were in a house full of relatives, after all—but I wasn't sure I liked how quickly he decided we were buddies either.

Still, having a friend in the house, someone to talk to and maybe bounce ideas off of, would be welcome. I also didn't want to offend him. Mom was gone and I didn't have much family left on her side. Getting to know the Shaw family could be nice. Besides that, until I heard otherwise from Aunt Lydia, or someone speaking on her behalf, I had nothing to do. A tour was as good a way to pass the time as any.

CHAPTER FIVE

"The place is pretty quiet this morning," Blair told me. "Nobody really seems to want much to do with each other at the moment, so we're all more or less on our own, relaxing, just hanging around." He glanced at me. "Shaws are born freeloaders, you know, and this is like a paid vacation for everyone. I've never been much good at taking it slow, though; I get bored easily. I'm glad you showed up when you did."

The long second-floor hallway was just a series of closed doors. As we passed each one, Blair pointed out which of our relatives was staying in the room. We went down the stairs and around the corner, back into the reception hall I already saw. Just off of it was the dining room; its central feature was a huge table that looked like it was carved from a single piece of some dark, heavy wood. There were at least twenty matching chairs, including an elaborately decorated one at the head of the table.

"Piotr Orlov was the biggest money in this part of the state for years," Blair explained. "He seems to have given some pretty extravagant dinner parties back in the good old days." He pointed at a door on the opposite side of the room. "The kitchens are through there, with servants' quarters on the other side, I'm told.

Besides the giant, Aunt Lydia has a skinny old Eskimo lady named Eleonore to cook for her and an old guy named Ned who shovels snow. I imagine he also handles the lawn and that stuff whenever the snow disappears. They all live here in the house. There's also a girl who comes in to clean, apparently, but she lives in town and I haven't seen her."

"They're called Inuit."

"What?" Blair asked, turning.

"'Eskimo' is offensive. People prefer Inuit—or whatever tribe they're actually a member of. I guess you'd have to ask."

A little color came into Blair's cheeks, but I think it was anger at being corrected rather than embarrassment. "Fine; I'll ask old Elly next time I see her. Moving along…" He brushed past me, back out into the hallway. So much for not offending him.

On the opposite side of the big hall were three rooms.

One was a library. Three walls of floor-to-ceiling shelves contained thousands of books. From what I saw, they were about half in Russian and half in English, and the books in both languages leaned more towards reference, biographies, and histories than fiction, though there were a few novels here and there. I wondered if the books in English were Aunt Lydia's and the ones in Russian her husband's. The room also had a great, battered old oak library table, its top completely bare except for a telephone, and several comfortable-looking, overstuffed leather chairs. There wasn't a speck of dust anywhere that I could see, but nothing in the room looked as if it was used recently, either.

"How long has Piotr Orlov been gone?" I asked, flipping through a book randomly chosen from the nearest shelf. It was a history of railroad expansion across Alaska.

"I'm not sure," Blair answered. "Fifteen, maybe twenty years."

Putting the book away, I said, "Aunt Lydia has been a widow all that time and she's only just now reaching out to everyone." I turned to Blair. "That's really weird."

"Yeah. On with the tour?"

"Lead the way."

The room next door was a TV room or family room—whatever you want to call it. It wasn't that different from the big central hallway, but it was much smaller, the furniture looked more comfortable and it was obviously much more used. There was a stereo system in one corner, with two chairs on either side of it, and nearby, a big, wraparound sectional sofa faced a huge, boxy television on wheels with a screen that must have been at least sixty inches. It was the kind that people who could afford them bought before LCD and plasma TVs were even invented. It was probably as old as I was.

The last room on this side of the great hallway was probably Piotr Orlov's den. It had a definite masculine feel—the walls were paneled in dark wood, and its dominant feature was the biggest pool table I ever saw. There was also a good-sized round table, covered in green felt like the pool table, but with niches just the right size for poker chips. Off in one corner of the room, there was a small bar, and across from it was a cluster of four leather chairs, positioned so that people could talk easily and semi-privately.

All three rooms were spacious, well-furnished, and obviously expensive, but like the library, the family room and den gave me the impression of being abandoned—as if these rooms belonged solely to Piotr Orlov and after his death, they went unused.

Hands on hips, Blair said, "Nice little place Aunt Lydia's got, huh?"

"It's kind of sad..."

"I know what you mean. I wouldn't mind living here, though, except for it being in the middle of nowhere. Even then, with a little modernization, I could make do."

We moved back out into the main hallway. There didn't seem to be anything else in this part of the house I hadn't seen. I walked to the nearest wall and examined a photograph. It was black and white, showing a younger Aunt Lydia, standing at the edge of a cluster of trees, bundled up against the cold; next to her was a man of about sixty or so, with a tangle of wild, white hair and very heavy features: solid lump of nose, thick lips, iron jaw. He was holding a rifle in one hand and an obviously dead fox in the other. Neither of them were smiling, but the man—Piotr Orlov, I guessed—had a look of satisfaction.

"I wonder how Aunt Lydia met Piotr Orlov."

"You'd have to ask her, I guess."

"I think I will." I turned from the photo. "Where to next?"

Blair wasn't quite done with the conversation though. "Why do you ask about Orlov?" He grinned at me; it was crooked, mischievous, like a little boy planning to pull a girl's braids. "Are you looking to meet a millionaire of your own?"

"Why would I be? The way Aunt Lydia seems to have things planned out, I'll be one myself, won't I?"

His smile disappeared. "I wouldn't count my chickens."

It was my turn to smile now. "Aunt Lydia already told me she thinks I'm going to be her favorite niece."

"Well then," Blair spread his hands apart, "I guess you're set for life, aren't you?"

We wandered back to the front area of the house, making small talk, just getting to know each other a little better. Blair was thirty-one, he was an attorney, specializing in mergers and acquisitions, a junior associate at one of those mega-sized law firms. "I'm just a grunt," he told me bitterly, "doing legwork and pushing papers. Four years without even a cost-of-living raise. Getting Aunt Lydia's letter was like manna from heaven."

"Now who's counting their chickens?" I wrinkled my nose at him.

"Oh, shut up," he said, but there was no heat in it.

From the front hallway, we turned left, going into the all-glass wing that was visible from the front of the house, where Rick dropped me off. This hallway was tiled, instead of wood-floored, and I imagined how cold it would be if the heat wasn't cranked up. Before we went too far down it, though, it grew warmer and the air became damp.

"What's down here?" I asked.

Blair smirked and jogged ahead, around a corner. An instant later, a blast of warm, heavy, and very moist air hit me. I turned the corner; Blair held open a glass door with one hand and with the other, gestured like a magician revealing the end of his big trick. "Ta-da!"

"Wow."

Beyond the door was an indoor pool. It wasn't huge, probably thirty feet long, but it was surrounded by gorgeous stone tiling and looked out over a bank of windows only separated from the edge of the cliff the house sat on by a thin strip of walkway and a low stone wall. Even from the doorway, the view was stunning; as beautiful as it was, the one from my room didn't even compare. I looked up; the ceiling, too, was all glass. I was sure that the view at night was incredible. I hoped I'd have a chance to see it.

Scattered around the rim of the pool were deckchairs, and in the near wall was a door that I guessed led to showers and changing areas. A small, gray-haired man came from a doorway in the far wall, carrying a long-handled brush. He noticed us and waved, calling, "Hello, Mr. Shaw! And you must be a Miss Shaw!"

"That's Ned," Blair told me. We both waved back as the older man began pushing the brush along the tiles at the far side of the pool.

"Cleaning it up for us, probably. You a swimmer?" he asked me.

"I love swimming, but I don't have a suit. It never even occurred to me to bring one to Alaska in February."

"I know, right? I'm sure we can find you something though." He gave me an up and down look that I didn't like.

I moved closer to the pool, then turned and pointed at the skylight. "I want to come back here at night," I told him. "I'd love to just lie in one of those chairs and stargaze."

Blair glanced up. "That does sound nice. We'll have to find the time some night."

I wasn't thrilled that Blair just assumed I meant the two of us, but it wasn't worth making a thing of.

"Want to see the patio?" He gestured to a door across from us. "It wraps around most of the building and the view is unreal." Before he finished, he was already moving along the side of the pool.

"Wait, I don't have my coat," I told him.

Without turning, Blair called back, "Just for a minute. You'll be fine."

He opened the door, looking back at me expectantly. I could already feel the creeping cold, mixing with the damp, humid air around the pool; near where Blair stood, wisps of steam swirled and danced their way outside. Hurrying against the chill, I joined him. "Just for a minute."

It wasn't obvious from my room, a trick of perspective or something like that, but the patio was immense—probably half as wide as the house itself. It was paved with multicolored flagstones, half of it shaded by a freestanding wooden awning that matched the design of the house, and half of it open to the sun. There was no furniture now, because of the season, but the area was mostly cleared of snow, and it gave me an idea of what it looked like in the summer. With one of the chaises from the pool and a nice cold drink, this would be a wonderful place to spend a warm afternoon.

Around the rim of the patio was a stone wall about four feet tall, built almost directly on the lip of the cliff—a safety measure to keep people from getting too close. I went right up to the wall, leaned my elbows on it and gazed out. The view was literally breathtaking, and only part of it was the cold. The drop was almost sheer and it must have been the full three thousand feet. At the bottom, blurry from the height, lay a tumble of rocks and some scrubby little trees, all of it covered in a thin powdering of snow. In the distance, mountains even higher than Foster's Peak clawed at the sky, their upper halves lost in a wreath of clouds.

"Always save the best for last."

I was so lost in the sights that Blair's voice startled me. I realized he was only a few inches away, leaning against the wall next to me, so close our hips almost touched. Trying not to be obvious about it, I shuffled a few inches to my left, putting space between us.

"It is incredible," I told him.

"Think old Orlov built this place so he could see the Motherland? That's what Sarah Palin said, right? She could see Russia from her house."

The joke didn't even deserve a response. "Well, thanks for the tour," I told him, "but I'm going in. Brrr." I made a production of hugging myself and briskly rubbing my arms as I turned towards the house.

I could feel Blair's eyes on me as I walked away, but after a moment, he caught up. "The door to the main house is over here." He took my elbow and guided me in the opposite direction from the pool.

Blair opened a door into a little alcove with two other doorways leading deeper into the house. One must have been to the main hall, and I guessed the other probably led to the kitchen, so things could be served out on the patio.

Even after only a few minutes outside, the warmth of the house was heavenly. I could feel muscles loosening as the heat penetrated them. Blair brushed by me to open the nearest doorway. Not all of the tension was from the cold.

When we came downstairs earlier, the main hall was silent

except for our voices and footsteps and the crackling fire in the hearth. Now, there was the sound of muffled conversation and soft music coming from the family room. Blair smirked at me. "They're all together, which means they've been gossiping— probably about you."

Blair was apparently a loner, at least before I arrived, because he clearly didn't consider himself part of the group of his siblings and our cousins.

"Introduce me?" I asked.

The smile disappeared, replaced by a faintly disapproving look. "I'll have to, I guess." He moved across the hallway, opened the door to the family room, and waved me inside. "Let's get it over with."

There was a cluster of people seated on the sectional sofa by the television, two men and two women, deep in conversation. The TV was on, but muted, showing a blurry view of what looked like NASCAR racing. None of them were paying it any attention.

The stereo was on, too, but turned down low, playing a song I recognized as Tony Bennett's, but didn't know the title of. Seated in one of the chairs by the stereo, slumped low and staring at the wall, apparently deep in thought, was a thin, pale young man of about my age. That must have been Jonathan.

Blair clapped his hands and the conversation stopped all at once, like a switch was flicked. "Everybody, Cousin Holly has joined us." Five pairs of eyes turned to Blair then shifted and settled on me. He glanced at me. "Let me make the introductions."

Blair, I knew, was Nathan Shaw's middle son. His older brother was Marcus, who looked like he was somewhere in his middle thirties. His complexion was a little darker than Blair's and he wore his dark hair longer and combed straight back; it shone faintly with the residue of some sort of hair product. I couldn't tell how tall he was, but even sitting, it was clear he was much heavier than his younger brother. His middle was thick, bulging the red polo shirt he wore, and he had the beginnings of middle-aged jowls, covered in a couple of days' worth of beard. His wife, Chelsea, was almost his opposite: she was slim and fair-skinned and had red-brown hair and blue-green eyes. She wore a loose, semi-blazer with ruffled sleeves and a blouse that was open at the throat, showing off her cleavage. She was younger than her husband by several years.

Jonathan was Marcus and Blair's younger brother. He left his seat by the stereo and came over to take my hand, smile, and introduce himself. His hand and his voice were both light and fluttery, but there was also a touch of solemnity when he spoke, as if he was just waiting for some great tragedy to befall him. His hair, too, was dark, worn long and combed over to one side, but his skin was very pale, as if he spent all of his time indoors. The paleness accentuated the softness of his face; that and its smoothness made him seem slightly feminine. After shaking my hand, he smiled and said, "I hope we'll be friends, Holly."

Ryan and Nora Hill were the children of Sara, my dad's older sister and Blair's father's younger sister. Ryan, like Jonathan, stood and offered me his hand. He was tall, at least a couple of inches taller than Blair, but like Marcus, he was inclined to huskiness. He was a big man, with wide shoulders, but his arms and stomach were flabby, and the T-shirt and jeans he wore didn't do much to help. In a good tailored suit, I thought, his height would be a lot more impressive. His hair was dark, but receding, and what was left he kept cut short. He seemed to be about the same age as Marcus, or maybe a little younger. He told me, "I'm glad to meet you, Holly. I was just a kid last time I saw your dad, but I remember Uncle Spencer fondly." I think he really meant it too.

Ryan's sister, Nora, was much younger than him, not quite thirty, I guessed. She showed a remarkable resemblance to Aunt Lydia—at least what I imagined Lydia must have looked like at the same age. Nora was petite, very slender, and no more than five feet tall, with jet-black hair and large, dark eyes set in a narrow face. She was beautiful, if fragile-seeming, and the dress of subdued colors and tights she wore reminded me of ribbons wrapping up a small gift. She didn't speak when Blair introduced us, only smiled shyly and dipped her head.

"I think that's everyone," Blair said. "Don't worry about keeping the names and faces straight, we're all pretty much interchangeable." He laughed, but nobody else did.

Marcus stood from the couch. As big as he seemed, he actually wasn't quite as tall as Blair, surprising me. He gestured and said, "Come on over and grab a seat. I'm glad you finally got here. Maybe now Aunt Lydia will stop dicking around and get down to business."

"What do you mean?" I asked, without moving towards the sofa.

Marcus frowned. "I mean we all got the same letter, right? And it was pretty obvious what it meant, mystery bull about Lydia's death and fortune notwithstanding. I asked her a couple times last night to lay it all out for us, but she said she preferred to wait until everyone was here and nobody knew if you were even coming." He huffed. "Well, at least you're here now. If you didn't show up, I got a feeling this whole trip would have been wasted."

"Aunt Lydia mentioned ten million dollars to Holly," Blair said.

"Did she?" Marcus asked me, his eyes going wide. "What exactly did she tell you?"

"That's all." I shook my head slightly. "She asked me if I was interested in ten million dollars."

"Why the hell didn't she tell me that when I asked her?" Marcus's eyes narrowed and I could practically see the numbers spinning behind his eyes as he made calculations. "Ten million dollars divided between us wouldn't be a fortune, but it's not too shabby either. More than a million-six for each of us." He turned to Chelsea and asked, "How does that sound, sweet pea?"

Of all the people in the room, Chelsea gave me the coolest greeting, but now it was like she completely forgot about me. Her eyes held a brightness that wasn't there before. She said to her husband, "How do you figure that? Six into ten? The letter we got was addressed to Mr. *and* Mrs. Marcus Shaw. A share of it should be mine."

"Oh, come on." Marcus scowled. "Don't start that."

"Chelsea," Blair put in with a crooked little smile. "You aren't really a Shaw."

"Neither is Holly!" she snapped. She looked at me. "You were adopted, weren't you?"

"Yes."

Chelsea looked back at Marcus. "See?"

Marcus smiled like he was indulging a spoiled child. "Okay, you're right. You deserve a share. Whatever money we get will end up with both of us anyway."

While those three talked, Nora somehow appeared next to me unnoticed. She spoke for the first time. "I'm glad you're here, Holly," she said softly, almost whispering. "Maybe we can get this all over with now." She hugged her arms to herself, just as I did outside, and added, "I don't like being in this house."

"What's wrong with the house?" Ryan asked, but she ignored him, and said to me, "Did Blair tell you what he thinks Aunt Lydia has planned?"

"About us living here until she passes on?" I asked.

Nora nodded, her little chin just barely moving. "That's what he *says* she told him, but she didn't tell the rest of us that, so who knows?" She leaned in close and said, "I hope he misunderstood her. It can take a long time for someone to die even if they're sick. I don't want to stay in this house any longer than I have to."

"Why not? It's a beautiful place."

"It gives me a crawly feeling. I don't like being out in the middle of nowhere in a place without any phone signal or even wifi, and I don't like that big guy, Elijah. I don't really like Aunt Lydia, either, just between us."

"But you like money, don't you?" Blair asked, apparently hearing her. Nora just shrugged, gave me another tiny smile and went over to sit by the stereo, in the chair opposite the one Jonathan occupied earlier.

Marcus and Chelsea were off by themselves now, whispering together, leaving me, Blair, Ryan, and Jonathan by the sofa. "Well," Ryan said, "I've been cooped up enough for today. Think I'll take a little walk around and get some fresh air." He said a general goodbye to the group and then left.

Blair maneuvered me off to one side of the room, his back to the others, and asked, "What do you think?"

"I don't know," I admitted. "It's pretty mixed. Jonathan and Nora don't seem to want to be here."

"But they want the money. Can you blame them?" I couldn't. He went on. "People are getting edgy. Except for greeting us yesterday and then dinner later on, Lydia's ignored us. We haven't even seen her at all since last night. Marcus was actually hoping she passed overnight, he told me earlier."

"That's terrible."

Blair looked at me, like he was searching my face for something. "Is it? It's why we're here, after all."

That's when it really hit me for the first time. Here we were, in this beautiful house in the middle of nowhere, a group of strangers with nothing in common but greed and a little family history. We were all invited to share the last days of a relative none of us ever met before, to get a chance to know her before it was too late. But, of course, that wasn't why we came. We came for the money that was hinted at, and now we were all just waiting for her to die.

A little shiver went down my spine that had nothing to do with the temperature.

CHAPTER SIX

Dinner wasn't until eight o'clock that night. I grew up eating around five thirty or six o'clock, and even as an adult I rarely ate dinner after seven so I was pretty hungry by the time Elijah made his rounds, calling us all down to the huge dining room. We ate huddled together at one end of the massive, carved wood table. It was just the cousins; Aunt Lydia was absent. There was a place setting at the head of the table, but it was left empty, because it belonged to Aunt Lydia as the head of the household. Nobody dared to sit there.

Elijah served everything, wheeling plates and platters out from the kitchen on a cloth-draped service cart, like in a hotel. No other servants appeared, even when Elijah had to make more than one trip for a single course. Once, when the door to the kitchen opened, I got a quick glimpse of a tall, spare woman who must have been Eleonore. She seemed to be trying to get a look at all of us, but she disappeared the instant I noticed her.

Elijah was the model of speed and efficiency: he was always there exactly when someone needed something, but otherwise was almost invisible. He never spoke a word that wasn't necessary, and he was always exactingly polite when he did. He could have made a fortune as a waiter at a high-end restaurant. I wondered how long he'd worked for Lydia and how she found him.

Despite his efficiency, Elijah made me uncomfortable, and I knew I wasn't the only one. He didn't do anything threatening or even out of the ordinary, but he was so fast and so quiet, he could appear at your elbow without you even knowing it until he scooped up an empty salad bowl or set down the plate with your next course. It made me a little nervous, never knowing if he was going to pop up in any given instant. Conversation at the table was normal when we first sat down, but by the middle of the meal, it fell off almost entirely.

"He kind of freaks me out," Blair half-whispered, after Elijah disappeared through the kitchen door to fetch after-dinner coffee and sweets. Of course, he took the chair next to me when everyone was seating themselves. He was on my right side, at the end of the table, and Jonathan was on my left, picking at the remains of a steak he barely touched. The youngest Shaw brother must have heard Blair, though, because he leaned over, whispering past me, "Me too."

"He's the perfect waiter though," I said. "And I get the feeling that Aunt Lydia relies on him for pretty much everything."

"He does seem handy," Blair admitted. Elijah came back through the door, pushing the cart, loaded with a silver coffee service this time, cutting short anything else Blair might have said.

Even if the atmosphere wasn't very pleasant, the food was spectacular. Eleonore was either a genius in the kitchen or she had the absolute highest-quality ingredients to work with. Probably both. The vegetable soup we were first served was aromatic with herbs I couldn't identify and spread warmth throughout my entire body after just a couple of spoonfuls, and the salad that came after was probably the best I've ever had. I would have been satisfied with just those two courses, but when they were done, Elijah brought out fist-sized beef medallions that were charred crispy brown on the outside and the most perfect shade of pink inside. For dessert, there was coffee and a strawberry cake. I could almost feel it settling in my thighs, but it was so good I couldn't help myself.

The meal was only the first surprise of the evening.

After we finished the meal, we filed out of the dining room. Elijah, as if on cue, appeared in the archway leading to the front door of the house. Behind him stood a familiar face: Charlie Shelton, the man I met on the plane. His rumpled tweeds were gone and now he wore a navy suit and carried a briefcase. He seemed taller and slimmer than he did on the airplane, but it was probably an effect of the change of clothing.

"Everyone," Elijah said, his deep voice booming through the hall. "This is Mr. Charles Shelton, Mrs. Orlov's attorney. We will all now go up to the missus's room."

It was plain that everyone wanted more information, but we were off-guard, drugged by the good food and the late hour, and nobody spoke up. I suppose that was Aunt Lydia's plan.

Elijah set off for the stairs to the upper floors, Charlie Shelton behind him. Shelton glanced at me as he moved past, but made no sign of recognition.

One by one, we followed Elijah's lead, Marcus and Chelsea practically on Shelton's heels, everyone else spaced a step or two apart to keep from tripping each other up.

The higher we climbed, the greater the sense of tension. Dinner was uncomfortable, but this was something else entirely. I expected, as I'm sure everyone else did, that we were finally going to get some answers. Was Aunt Lydia really dying? Was it possible she was actually already dead? I only saw her for a few minutes when I first arrived and that was hours ago. Was her sudden death the reason she didn't join us for dinner and Shelton —apparently a lawyer, not a salesman, like I guessed—was here now?

No, I decided; that last part didn't make sense. Shelton was on the plane with me that morning and Aunt Lydia was alive when I arrived. His visit here must have been planned long before. He did mention he made frequent trips here though...

I didn't like the way my thoughts were running, but I couldn't help it. I imagined we were a funeral procession, lining up to view a body, not a family going to speak with an elderly, but living, relative. It was ghoulish and for a moment, I hated myself for it.

It was a relief when we reached the third floor and Elijah opened Aunt Lydia's door, motioning us all inside. Aunt Lydia was propped up on her bed in the same position she was when I first met her, and still very much alive. Only a living woman's eyes would glow with amusement the way hers did.

I was relieved, but not all of my cousins shared that feeling. Marcus and Chelsea were openly disappointed. Aunt Lydia was a sharp-eyed lady and I was certain she was taking in all of our reactions, gauging our responses—maybe even assigning us numbers, ranking us. She did tell me she thought I was going to be her favorite niece, after all.

"Nieces and nephews," Lydia said, once we were all gathered around the bed. "This is Charlie Shelton, my attorney."

Shelton moved to stand at Aunt Lydia's right. There was no expression on his face when he looked at us, but I was sure he was judging us just the same. "Hello, everyone." He turned to Lydia. "Would you like to get right to the reading of the will and the codicils, Mrs. Orlov?"

Lydia waved a hand dismissively. "The legalese isn't necessary. Just tell them what they need to know and make sure you put it in terms that they can't fail to understand. If you read them the actual documents, you'd just have to keep stopping to explain it all anyway."

"All right, that makes sense." He set the briefcase down on the bed, then looked out at all of us. He cleared his throat and began,

"Ladies and gentlemen, Mrs. Orlov has been my client for close to ten years now. My office is in Seattle, but I handle many of her business matters and I make regular trips here to discuss various matters." His eyes touched mine for a moment, then moved away again. "A couple of months ago, however, she called me and instructed me to liquefy a great deal of the estate's assets and make some arrangements regarding the funds that were produced. She also asked me to gather information on all of you, learn your current whereabouts and situations, and gave me the task of writing up a new will for her. That will has very specific, and somewhat unusual provisions, though I assure you that they are all ironclad, legally speaking."

From the inside of his coat, he took a sheet of paper, folded in half. He unfolded it and read, "The following are the nieces and nephews of Lydia Anne Shaw Orlov. Marcus, Blair, and Jonathan, sons of Nathan Shaw. Ryan and Nora Hill, son and daughter of Sara Hill, née Shaw. Holly Shaw, daughter of Spencer Shaw."

Blair cast a wicked little smirk of satisfaction at Chelsea; Marcus's wife was not counted as a Shaw. She either didn't see it or chose to ignore it. Her face was carefully blank and she stared attentively at Shelton, the most important person in the room at the moment.

"Mrs. Orlov makes money bequests, both for the family and much smaller ones for the household staff," Shelton went on, "but I'll have to explain the specific provisions she makes for all of you family members, the children of her nephews and niece, whom she raised after the untimely death of her parents." Shelton's head moved slightly as he looked at each of us. "Mrs. Orlov has expressed to me that she regrets having been separated from all of you, and now, in her final days, she requests your presence.

"She realizes," he nodded in Lydia's direction, "that both the trip here and a stay at Dacha Orlov represent a significant disruption in your lives, particularly those of you with careers. However, the terms of her will provide very generous financial remuneration for any such inconveniences. More than I feel is fair, if I can speak frankly."

Lydia's eyes narrowed, but she said nothing.

"At any rate, to put it simply," Shelton said, "you give your aunt the solace of knowing she was able to connect with what remains of her family before she leaves this world, and in return, you'll be rewarded. The caveat is that in order to qualify for a remembrance in your aunt's will, you must remain in residence here in her home until her death."

Someone made a little noise of surprise; I'm not sure who. This was what Blair told me about earlier, when he barged into my room, and what Nora confided in me that she hoped wasn't true. I looked over at Nora; her already large eyes were giant now, and she looked as if she might start crying. Poor girl. Did she really hate being in this house that much?

"This may sound like an unusual condition," Shelton was saying, "but Mrs. Orlov's reasoning, as she explained it to me, is really quite sound. To put it bluntly: she doesn't know any of you and she would like a chance to observe and learn about you. If she were to just hand out the money, she would get nothing but lip-service instead of the meaningful connections that she wants. And please remember that Mrs. Orlov doesn't have to leave anything to any of you—or to anyone else, for that matter. This is a matter of generosity on her part, and she has a right to set any conditions that she likes. If anyone thinks these conditions are unfair or that she is asking too much, they are free to leave at any time. Round-trip plane tickets have already been provided and—"

"That's enough, Charlie," Aunt Lydia cut in. "You've explained everything already and now you're just putting words in my mouth. Get on with the financial part."

Shelton's jaw clenched tightly when Lydia cut him off. Now, he nodded and said, "Of course, Mrs. Orlov." I guess if he worked for her this long, he knew what she was like. I imagined he earned quite a bit of money from her over the years if he was willing to come all the way up here from Seattle just to be treated like another servant.

Shelton opened the briefcase and extracted a sheaf of papers. He cleared his throat again and said, "Mrs. Orlov understands that these provisions may be hard to believe. You don't know her, after all, any more than she knows you. Actually," he paused, a semblance of a smile on his face now, "Mrs. Orlov probably does know quite a bit more about each of you than you know about her. None of you were hard to build dossiers on. But I digress."

I guessed those dossiers didn't include photos since he didn't recognize me on the plane.

Shelton shoved the papers in his hands at Marcus, the person standing nearest to him. "So there are no doubts about the veracity of Mrs. Orlov's financial claims or any question about what each of you will be entitled to, should you fulfill the terms as laid out, I've prepared a brief summary that each of you can have a copy of, if you like."

Marcus accepted the papers and began to read. His eyes grew almost as big as Nora's. "This says that the money's already been deposited with Chase, at their main branch in Seattle. The bank has instructions on disbursement and the money is guaranteed." His hands dropped to his sides, the papers loosely held. His mouth was open and working like a fish. He managed to find his voice, adding, "There's sixty million dollars on deposit, an equal share for each of us. Ten million dollars each."

The silence in the room was evidence of the shock everyone felt. Both Aunt Lydia and Charlie Shelton watched us, clearly enjoying the aftermath of the bomb they dropped. Lydia mentioned ten million dollars when I met her. I never imagined she meant for each of us. She probably knew that. She probably told me about the ten million specifically so that I would tell the others and they could make their own conclusions. That was my entry into her game.

Blair nudged me with his elbow and smiled, but it was

Chelsea who first spoke. "Oh, Aunt Lydia," she said. "That's so generous of you."

"It's too generous," Shelton said. "In a few more years, the assets I had to sell to achieve this kind of liquidity would be—"

"Be quiet!" Lydia snapped. "Those details are between you and me. Now tell them the rest of it. We aren't done yet."

"Of course, Mrs. Orlov," the lawyer said, and this time he couldn't hide his annoyance. He took a moment to compose himself, looked out at all of us, and said, "It's Mrs. Orlov's choice whether to explain her exact ailment to all of you, but she has been told by several different medical experts that she doesn't have long to live. She doesn't know if that means days, weeks, or months, but her passing could come at any time. It is, as they say, in God's hands.

"You'll remember that in order to claim an inheritance from your aunt's will, you'll have to live here, with her, in her home until the moment of her death. Some of you might get bored waiting. Some of you might decide you simply can't be away from the friends and families and jobs you've left behind. As I said before, you can leave this house at any time. If you aren't present when Mrs. Orlov passes, however, for any reason, no matter what it is, you'll forfeit your share of the trust and the sixty million will then be divided equally among those who remain."

Aunt Lydia dismissed first Shelton and then, after a long look at each of us, everyone else. I was tired, but I knew I wouldn't be able to sleep. I didn't want to go back to my room and be left alone with my thoughts. I found myself in the family room, and I wasn't the only one. In ones and twos, all of the cousins, plus Chelsea, ended up clustered on the huge sofa.

Ryan Hill was the first to say what we were all thinking. "How do we know this is all, you know, real? Like, on the level?"

"It looked real to me," Marcus answered. "The money's on deposit with Chase, signed over to us, and it gets disbursed the moment they get official word that Lydia's croaked."

"Don't put it like that!" his wife said, slapping his arm.

Marcus scowled. "Why not? It's the truth."

"It's morbid," Nora put in.

"Whatever," Marcus said. "Whatever you want to call it, it looks legit to me. I want to call my own bank in the morning, though, and see if my guy there can look into it. Just in case. What's the time difference between here and Chicago?" he asked Chelsea.

"How should I know?"

"This is all too weird," Jonathan said, the first time he'd spoken in hours.

Ryan turned to him. "You got that right. It's just... I don't know how to put it. She doesn't want us pretending we like her—I get that. But the way this is set up, it's like she doesn't even care one way or the other. We just hang around, eating her food, sleeping in her house, watching her TV, and then at the end she pays us for it?"

"This crappy TV?" Jonathan asked, with a mocking tone.

"You know what I mean," Ryan shot back.

"What really interests me," Marcus said, "is this deal with people leaving and the numbers getting shuffled around. I mean," he looked around at all of us, "I don't know about the rest of you, I'm staying no matter what, but suppose the old lady's lying about how sick she is or that her doctors are just plain wrong. What if she drags on for a couple of years? Six months down the road, one of us says screw it and takes off. Then it isn't six into sixty million, it's five. The second somebody leaves, it goes from ten million each to twelve, and it jumps up faster each time. Three people leave, it's twenty million each for whoever stays."

"I think you're all missing the real point," Blair announced.

"Oh? Then what's the real point?" Marcus's voice practically dripped sarcasm.

Blair ignored his brother's tone. "It's this: *why* did Aunt Lydia make the arrangements this way? Why do those who remain get the shares of those who left? Why not just say it's ten million each, and if someone leaves, their share goes to her favorite charity?"

"You really think that woman could even name a charity?" Chelsea asked. "She doesn't seem like the type to me."

Marcus, still looking at Blair, shrugged. "More incentive, maybe, in case the days do drag on. I mean, what else is there? What do *you* think the reason is?"

Blair's face grew cold, as if all the human warmth seeped out of it. It was like looking at a mask and it gave me a feeling as crawling as any Elijah inspired. "If someone leaves, why doesn't their share revert to the estate for other uses? Forget charity, okay? That lawyer, Shelton, all but said that the estate isn't as rich as it could be and I seriously doubt it's as rich as it was when Piotr Orlov was running the show. So why divide any excess money up among the heirs? Even if it wasn't set up like that, we'd still hang around. I'd wait just as long for ten million as for twelve, and I don't have to ask to know the rest of you would say the same thing. So I repeat the question: why?"

Everyone was listening as intently to Blair as we did when Charlie Shelton was telling us about the will. I looked around the faces of all these relatives I'd only just met. Dark Shaw eyes and faces that shared an obvious resemblance and each showed different emotions: curiosity, greed, suspicion—even fear in Nora's case.

"Why do you think she did it then, Blair?" Jonathan's soft voice was almost lost in the huge, otherwise silent room.

Blair stood, moved to the big, boxy television set. He placed a hand on it then turned to face the rest of us. "There's something wrong here. Something we're not seeing. First, why is Aunt Lydia suddenly interested in all of us?"

"I don't think that's strange," Chelsea said. "A lot of people want to reconnect with family when they know their time is almost up."

"Right," Blair agreed. "But the key is *reconnect*. Have any of you met Lydia before yesterday?" He already knew the answer, so he didn't wait. "As far as I know, she's never concerned herself with any of our folks—which is strange since she's practically their mother—much less any of us. She never even sent any Christmas cards, which is pretty standard aunt stuff, I think."

"Did anyone ever try reaching out to her?" I asked.

Blair raised a finger. "Excellent question, Holly, but one I can't answer." He scanned our faces. "Does anyone know?" A few heads shook, but nobody had anything to say.

"So why?" Blair went on. "Why invite us all up here? Love? For people she's never met? A sense of familial duty?" He scoffed. "Does that seem like the lady upstairs?"

"Well, who else is she going to give all that money to?" Marcus whined. "She doesn't have any kids of her own."

"Sure," Blair agreed. "But that doesn't mean she has to leave it all to us. She's got at least three people in this house she's probably known for years, and I'm sure she must have some friends somewhere in the world—people she has actual connections to anyway."

"Blood is thicker than water, Blair," Chelsea said.

He laughed. "That's good. Clichés are exactly what we need right now, Chelsea. What have I just been saying? Do you think family actually matters to Lydia? Did you see her? Did you get a look at her face? I was watching her the whole time Shelton was talking and she was having a blast. She's toying with us, dangling us on the string of her money, and making us dance to whatever tune she likes."

"Do you really think that?" Nora put in, her voice small and brittle.

Blair turned to her. "Absolutely. She's playing a game."

"I got the same feeling, when I first met her," I said. I looked at Nora. The other girl met my eyes but quickly looked away. "I even said as much to her, and she didn't deny it."

"What kind of game?" Marcus asked.

Blair looked at his brother, then turned, walked to the nearest corner of the room and came back, as if taking time to gather his thoughts. Finally he said, "Look, the money's in a trust. You saw that for yourself." Marcus nodded. "I'm an attorney myself and I'll tell you, this is *not* how this sort of thing is done. Usually a trust is set up years in advance *in case* something happens so there's no quibbling or to make sure your family is taken care of. People discuss it with a financial planner, make long-term decisions about that kind of money. They don't decide on a whim and just call their attorney up. Especially not if it's everything you've got, like Shelton hinted. That makes even less sense, because as long as the money's in that trust and the conditions for disbursement haven't been met, nobody can touch it. Nobody. Not even Lydia herself."

"So she doesn't need the money," Ryan said.

Blair snapped his fingers in Ryan's direction. "Exactly! Hit the nail on the head. The money doesn't matter to her, it's just the bait for her game. And it's worked so far, it got all of us here. No matter what happens next, the money's never going to be in her hands again, and she might as well forget about it. Shelton knows that, too, and it obviously bothers him. So let's look at the situation this way."

He gestured towards Nora. "Let's say Nora decides she's had enough and hops the first flight back to civilization. What happens? You," he pointed at me, "are two million dollars richer, and so are you and you and you," he added, pointing to everyone else in turn, except Chelsea. I was sure he left her out as another dig.

"Why? What did each of you do to deserve another two million dollars? That's a lot of god-damned money—for absolutely nothing! So *why?*"

Everyone was quiet, but I could practically see the gears working inside their heads. They probably all had ideas, but nobody wanted to be the first to say it.

So I did. "To see what we'll do."

Blair looked me right in the eye. "Bingo." He turned to Chelsea; the mocking little smirk was back. "Got any clichés for that one?"

"I do," I said. "Less is more."

The way everyone looked at me, I immediately regretted saying it.

CHAPTER SEVEN

We were having breakfast. The mood was better than the night before, everyone getting to know or catching up with one another, over mounds of fluffy scrambled eggs, golden toast, crisp bacon, some of the most amazing coffee I've ever had, and what tasted like fresh-squeezed orange juice. Cousins and spouses were chatting, the conversation swirling around the room as topics and partners exchanged. The only pairing that remained static was me and Blair, and I didn't have much to do with that.

Blair had been telling me things from his school days and now was relating a story about a tennis match he played when he was in college. I wasn't really listening, though. I was watching the other members of the family seated around the table, enjoying how they were interacting, how they played off one another and created a unique kind of atmosphere I'd never before been a part of.

As much as I was enjoying myself being surrounded by the family, though, I was a little troubled, too, because we weren't all there. Aunt Lydia was missing, which I expected, but so was Jonathan, and neither Marcus nor Blair seemed to have noticed.

It bothered me and finally, I asked, "Where's Jonathan this morning?"

Blair didn't seem happy I'd interrupted his story, but all he did was shrug. "Probably in bed. It was always impossible to get him up on time when we were kids."

Maybe that was the case, and I was just thinking too much about it, but it seemed odd that out of all the visitors to Lydia's home, Jonathan was the only one who wasn't buzzing with excitement. Even if he didn't care about the money, this was a kind of family reunion, wasn't it? Maybe I just felt differently about the very idea of 'family' than he did.

I was still thinking about the Shaw family, both as people and as a concept when Ned, the groundskeeper, burst into the living room, startling everyone into a kind of stunned silence.

"Elijah!" the old man gasped. His cheeks were reddened from cold and there was moisture in his hair and on the shoulders of his coat. He must have just been outside. "Where's Elijah?"

The huge butler appeared as if from thin air, took the much smaller man by the shoulder and led him out of the room without a word to either Ned or anyone else.

There was an uncomfortable silence for several moments while we waited, expecting one of them to return and provide some sort of explanation. Finally, Marcus asked, "What the hell was that about?"

It wasn't long before we had the answer to that question, and the one I asked Blair. Elijah came into the dining room from the hall door and announced, "Young Mister Shaw has been killed," and informed us that Ned had found Jonathan's body outside, beneath a dusting of fresh snow. He told us that the police had been called and should arrive shortly.

As bad as I felt the night before, when I made that senseless comment about less being more, I felt even worse now. Because it meant, of course, that there were only five cousins left and that the game was finally in full swing.

Mitch Goddard held the rank of sergeant in the Alaska State Police, making him the highest ranked police officer in the region. He was in charge of the state police substation in Foster's Place. The only other officer assigned there was a young trooper named Abbott. We learned all of that not long after they arrived at Dacha Orlov.

An hour or so after Ned came charging into the dining room, the troopers' white and black, blue-streaked Ford SUV pulled into the gravel circle in front of the house. Sergeant Goddard climbed out of the driver's seat, leaned back inside the vehicle to say something to his partner, and then marched up the steps to meet all of us. Nobody said the words out loud, but it was clear that none of us wanted to be on his or her own, so we kept in a group after hearing the terrible news.

Goddard's uniform was all in shades of blue; he wore a protective vest, but no coat. His only concession to the cold was a dark, woollen hat. Abbott, bundled up against the weather and wearing a campaign hat, followed him at a distance. I could feel the younger officer's eyes on us. I gathered his job was to watch Sergeant Goddard's back.

"I'm sorry this had to happen while you're all here visiting, folks," Goddard told us after introductions were made. He was about forty, tall, but not very wide. All of the Shaw men except Jonathan had much broader shoulders than Goddard. He reminded me of a broom and I imagined that if he took off his hat, his hair would puff out to complete the picture. His face was blandly handsome, in a TV commercial actor kind of way, but his eyes were sharp and intelligent.

As a group, we all went through the door and into the main hall. Elijah appeared and gestured for Sergeant Goddard to join him off to one side. A whispered conversation followed and even with Goddard's height, Elijah had to stoop to match the policeman's level.

They spoke for only a few seconds. Then Goddard nodded and did something very strange. Instead of asking to be taken to the body or giving us any kind of instructions, he turned and went through the arch leading to the upper floors.

"Where is he—" Blair began, but Trooper Abbott cut in, saying, "We'll get down to brass tacks soon."

Blair gave the younger man a sullen look, but kept quiet after that.

When Goddard returned, somewhere between five and ten minutes later, his hat in hand—his hair was cut short so it couldn't puff out like I imagined—he went right to Abbott. As with Elijah, there was a whispered conference. The younger trooper looked at all of us, his expression carefully blank, then said, "Yes, sir," and left, heading towards the front of the house. We heard the door open and close a few seconds later.

"Now then," Goddard said to the group in general. "Who found the body and where?"

"I did, sir." As one, we turned to see Ned, standing in the doorway of the dining room. He was half-hidden behind the doorframe, his shoulders slumped. He looked like a small boy waiting for punishment. My heart went out to him.

"C'mon out here. You're Ned Withers, right?"

"Yes, sir," Ned answered, slowly moving away from the door's protection.

Goddard asked about the circumstances of finding Jonathan's body. Ned looked around at all of us, then lowered his eyes and said, "We got a little snow last night. I didn't think it'd amount to much, but I'm always up early and I got to keep busy, you know? So I figured I'd give the walkways and the patio a shoveling before breakfast, in case any of the folks wanted to take a walk or anything like that. I did the front and then I started around the side of the house." His eyes rose to the trooper's, then fell again.

"That's the north side, around where the wing with the pool comes out. Well, I went around to the north wing and there's a walkway there that connects with the patio further on and there he was—poor young Mister Shaw, lying sort of half under some brush alongside the pathway, all covered in snow."

"Show me," Goddard commanded.

Ned nodded and started for the front door, Goddard on his heels. I knew Blair had already been out to see where his brother's body lay—Marcus refused when Blair tried to get him to go, too—but he followed Ned and Goddard anyway. No one said anything to him, so I went along too. I wasn't exactly eager to see the body, but just then, I didn't want to be left alone with the other relatives. Blair wasn't exactly a friend, but the rest of them were practically strangers. Besides, nothing could possibly happen in the company of Goddard.

Goddard and Ned were a little ahead of Blair, and I trailed after him by several feet. Our spread-out little group moved over the light snow and just as I came around the corner, Ned pointed mutely. I knew what to expect, but it still surprised me. I let out a little gasp; both Blair and Goddard turned at the sound. Goddard's brows drew together, but he didn't say anything.

Jonathan lay face down, one arm flung outward and the other beneath his body. His legs were half-hidden under the edge of the shrubbery and a thin layer of snow covered him. There were no obvious signs of violence, but even at a glance it was clear that the body was missing some vital piece, the thing that made a body a human being. I felt tears burning in the corners of my eyes. I didn't know Jonathan well, but I thought he was someone I could be friends with if we got the chance.

Goddard carried his hat out of the house, apparently forgetting about it. Now, he pulled it down over his head and squatted by the bush. Without touching Jonathan's body, he studied it for a few moments, then stood and said, "I don't see a wound. I don't even see any blood."

"Maybe it's in the front," Ned offered.

"It would have to be. I think... Wait—"

Goddard interrupted himself and gently parted some of the bush. "There's blood back here. Not much, but..." Without looking at any of us, he ordered, "Stay here. Nobody move a muscle." Then he stepped gingerly around the side of the bush and disappeared into the thin woods surrounding this part of the property.

I turned to Blair, only because I didn't want to look at Jonathan and wasn't sure where else to look. His eyes glistened, like he was holding back tears. He noticed me watching him and shook his head slightly. Neither of us had anything to say.

After a few minutes, Goddard came back, but from the direction of the north wing, appearing around the side near the exterior door to the pool. "There's not much of a trail, just enough to follow. It goes about fifty feet back there, curving around back towards the house, then there's a spot with quite a bit of blood. The ground around here's been trampled so much, though, that I can't tell if the boy made it here under his own power, trying to get help from the house maybe, or if whoever did this moved him."

Goddard sighed, hitched up his trouser legs, and then lowered himself to the level of the body again. He put one hand under Jonathan's shoulder and very gently lifted, then rolled him over onto his back. The wound was obvious now: low on the chest, just above the belly, there was a ragged hole in Jonathan's shirt, crusted with blood.

"Young guy," Goddard commented. He looked up, turning from Blair to me. "Twenty-two, twenty-three?"

I shook my head. "He was a year or two older than me. I'm twenty-four."

Goddard made a noise in his throat. "It's a shame. What was his name again? Shaw?"

"Jonathan Shaw," Blair said. His voice was tight. Muscles

stood out in his jaw. "He was my younger brother. He was twenty-six."

"I'm sorry for your loss, Mr. Shaw," Goddard said.

I saw and heard enough. I turned away, retracing my steps to the front of the house. Just before I rounded the corner, I heard a car's engine and the grind of gravel under its tires. There was a white van with EMERGENCY painted on the side in black block letters parked on the edge of the circular drive. Two men climbed out of it; neither wore any sort of uniform, just regular winter clothing.

The older of the two walked up to me. "Morning. Mitch around?"

"You mean Sergeant Goddard?" I pointed behind me. "Back there."

"Thanks," he said, nodded at his companion, and trudged towards where I left Blair, Goddard, and Ned. They must have been here for Jonathan, but I didn't want to find out for sure. I couldn't think of the soft-spoken, pale young man riding in a body bag, stuffed into the back of an old van like a rolled-up carpet.

I started crying again as I hurried into the house.

———

I was sitting with Nora in front of the muted television when Blair and Sergeant Goddard came into the entertainment room. Blair's face was hard as stone; Goddard looked like someone put him through the wringer. I wondered what they'd said to each other.

"Your cousin is being taken into town," Goddard told me, without even acknowledging Nora. "Doctor Chapman has cold storage and he operates as kind of semi-official coroner, since we're so far out here."

I looked past Goddard, silently questioning Blair, but he

lowered his eyes to the floor and found a seat in one of the chairs on the far side of the room.

Before anyone said another word, Elijah appeared in the doorway. "I've asked the others to gather, Sergeant."

"Thanks," Goddard told him. The big butler nodded and then disappeared again.

In less than a minute, first Marcus, then Chelsea appeared in the doorway, followed quickly by Ryan. When they were all seated, Goddard moved in front of the TV, positioning himself to speak to the group the same way Blair had the night before. He took a little notepad and a pencil from the pocket of his vest. "Let's start with some background."

I introduced everyone and then explained our family relationships, since nobody else seemed likely to. As I did, Goddard scribbled in his notepad, then began asking questions. He hadn't been here long and it was still early in the day, but he seemed very tired, and when he spoke it was without any sense of urgency.

He asked, "When was the last time any of you folks saw Jonathan alive?"

The previous night, Ryan told him, he saw Jonathan go into his room right before he, Ryan, went into his own.

"What time was that?"

Ryan looked uncertain. He glanced at his sister, but Nora wasn't any help. She seemed barely aware of the rest of us. Ryan said, "It must have been a little before eleven. I'm not really sure. We all had a kind of family meeting in here and then everyone went upstairs to their own rooms."

"Did anyone else notice the time?" Goddard looked at Marcus. "Mr. Shaw? Jonathan was your younger brother, correct?"

"I didn't notice the time. I didn't see him after the group down here broke up." Marcus answered the question as if Goddard asked what he had for breakfast; as if it didn't matter one way or another. That surprised me. Even if he wasn't sobbing and tearing his hair out, Blair was clearly upset by their brother's death, but Marcus acted as if Jonathan was just some stranger he read about in the news. If it was a cousin, maybe I could understand that... but Jonathan was his own brother.

Goddard let out a breath, then finally addressed the key point. "This wasn't an accident. It's not an easy thing to consider, but Jonathan was clearly murdered. Can any of you give me a reason why someone would want to hurt him? Either someone in this house or any other person?"

I think Goddard was trying to be kind, or at least diplomatic, in the way he phrased it, but it had the opposite effect on Blair.

"The murderer must be one of us, don't you think, Sergeant?" Acid dripped from every word. "We've only been here a couple of days. The only people around that any of us know are right in this godforsaken house, and every one of us has a damned good reason for killing Jonathan."

"Blair," Marcus said warningly.

"Who then?" Blair challenged him. "Who outside of this house would have bothered Jonathan? He never hurt anyone and he never even had the chance out here."

"I don't know..." Marcus said. "Maybe some locals came up the mountain to fool around in the woods or whatever. You know how drunken townies can get. Or meth." He sat up straighter. "I read that this state's got a huge meth problem. Right?" He looked at Goddard. The officer looked back at him without expression.

"Jesus Christ, Marcus!" Blair said. "Are you seriously telling me you think Jon went outside, sometime close to midnight, without even a jacket, and then just *happened* to come across a bunch of drugged up crazies who came *all the fucking way up from town* just to have themselves a good time on someone else's property?" He said the last several words slowly, like he was speaking to a not very bright child.

Marcus flushed and his jaw tightened. When Blair clenched

his jaw, the Shaw features looked hard, almost dangerous. When Marcus did it, he looked like he was about to throw a tantrum. "Maybe they thought he had money. Or maybe..."

"Maybe what?"

"Maybe he tried to hit on some of them. That kind of thing doesn't sit well sometimes, you know."

"For God's sake, Marcus." Blair put his hand over his eyes, as if he just couldn't look at his brother anymore. Quietly he asked, "You think someone killed Jon for being gay? Just because you're a bigoted asshole, doesn't mean that everyone else on Earth is."

Marcus opened his mouth for an angry retort, but Goddard's voice ripped through the air like a shot, stunning the brothers into silence. "Enough!" He stared hard at both men and when he was sure he had their attention, he said, "Listen, both of you. I understand how difficult this is. And believe it or not, you could both be right. There are people out there who would kill someone for ten bucks if they thought they could get away with it, and I'm sure there are some who don't look kindly on certain lifestyles."

"But do you really think they'd come all the way up a privately owned mountain to do it?" Blair asked. His voice was strained; I could tell how difficult it was for him to keep himself in check.

"I can't rule it out," Goddard answered. "Right now, I can't rule out anything."

"Okay," Blair said slowly.

He paused and when he spoke again, his tone was different; it was the same tone he used when he'd laid out his thoughts to us the night before. I was beginning to think of it as his Lawyer Voice. He told me he was just a grunt in a big law firm, and I decided that he was wasted outside of a courtroom. "Even if we're willing to stipulate that all of Aunt Lydia's neighbors—the closest being, what? Ten miles away? Something like that. Even if we concede that they're all homophobic cut-throats, perfectly willing to kill at the slightest opportunity, why would Jon be outside in the middle of the night, without his jacket, during a snowstorm, and all by himself where these hypothetical murderous strangers could find him? You don't know this family very well, Sergeant. Since we got here, we don't go very far from our rooms and when we do, we pretty much all stick together in a clump—or at least pair off with a buddy. We're out of our element, surrounded by varying numbers of more or less strangers, and Jon was one of the less bold among us. I know my brother, and the only way he would have gone outside at night was with someone he knew. In other words, one of us."

Goddard looked at Blair for several long moments, without blinking, drawing audible breaths through his nose. Finally he said, "Did you go outside with Jonathan, Mr. Shaw?"

"No."

Goddard's eyes swept across the rest of us. "Did any of you folks go outside with Jonathan?"

No one spoke, but Ryan and Nora both shook their heads.

"You don't really think anyone's going to just admit it, do you?" Blair asked sarcastically.

"You never know, Counselor." He jotted something in his notebook.

That took Blair aback. He was visibly startled for an instant before catching himself. "How did you know I'm an attorney?"

"I've met a few in my time, Mr. Shaw, and you fit nicely into one of the archetypes."

"Whatever." Blair crossed his arms and leaned back in his seat. He looked at Marcus. "Why don't you say something? He was your brother too."

"What do you want me to say, Blair?" Marcus was perched on the edge of the sofa cushion, his shoulders hunched. His mouth, his jowls, his whole body seemed to sag. Somehow, I didn't think it was from grief though. If I had to name it, I'd say Marcus was afraid.

"I want them to find whoever did this just as much as you do," he added, but it sounded half-hearted. I looked hard at the big, shapeless man and decided that maybe it wasn't fear, after all; maybe he was just in shock.

Goddard was scribbling in his notebook again. None of us spoke and it seemed like everyone was doing their best not to look at anyone else. Last night, we talked about some of Aunt Lydia's heirs being eliminated. Blair brought it up first, but I was the one who made the worst implication.

I forced myself to look at my cousins. They were all on edge. I was, too, for that matter. Nora seemed the worst off, though—she looked like she might explode into a panic attack at any moment.

Did one of these people take what I said last night seriously? Was someone in this room a murderer? Not just a killer, either, but someone capable of destroying a member of their own family? We all had a very good motive for doing it and I realized suddenly that no one had brought it up.

"Sergeant Goddard," I began. Goddard stopped writing and looked up, meeting my eyes. "There's something you should know." Out of the corner of my eye, I saw Blair focus on me. Marcus, too, sat up a little straighter, waiting to hear what I said next. "Aunt Lydia has written some unusual conditions into her will. It leaves a total of sixty million dollars to us, but we can only collect if we're living in this house when she passes away. Whoever is here when Lydia dies will receive an equal share of the money. Last night, when she told us about it, it was a six-way divide…"

"And now it's five." Goddard finished my thought.

I expected him to jump on the information as the fragment that would make everything clear, put all the other pieces into some sort of recognizable shape and order. Instead, he just looked at me as if I'd told him something very obvious, like his pants were blue. "I already know that, Miss Shaw, but thank you."

The trooper's calm indifference was more than Blair could take. He jumped from his seat and stood in front of Goddard, his face a mask of fury. "Then why the hell did you go on about the townies killing for a buck or because someone screws differently than they do? Will you tell me that, *officer?*" He said the last word like it was something filthy.

"Back off, Mr. Shaw." Goddard spoke quietly, but there was an undeniable threat in his tone.

Blair hesitated, his lips pressed into a thin line and his eyes narrowed as if he was trying to see through the policeman. But he did take several steps back. He didn't sit down again though. More composed, he said, "I don't understand why you bothered with all of that when you already knew everyone here has the best possible motive for murder."

"What do you want me to do?" Goddard asked. "Do you want me to take all you back to town and stick you in my two-cell jail? I don't have any evidence against you or anyone else in this room. A motive is something, but it's just one piece. As an attorney, you should know that. Besides..." He paused. "Mrs. Orlov has explained to me that you are both guests and valued family members. She's a very important person in this area, and she understands the seriousness of the situation, but she's asked me the favor of handling this as quietly and as discreetly as possible. I would do that anyway, so agreeing wasn't an issue for me."

"A genteel murder investigation," Blair muttered, just loud enough for everyone to hear.

"Call it whatever you like, so long as you don't interfere with how I do my job," Goddard countered.

"But you haven't done anything yet." We all turned to the source of the voice, surprise on every face but Goddard's. It was the first time Nora had said anything at all.

"It might look that way to you, Miss Hill, but I assure you, I'm doing everything I can at the moment. Out here, you have to make do sometimes, and between the two of us, Abbott and I will have things covered as best we can. In fact, he's already cataloguing the scene as we speak. Now, if you'll all excuse me." He started towards the door.

"Wait, you're leaving?" I asked.

Goddard stopped and looked back at me. "Right now, it's not your business how I handle my investigation, but if it'll put your mind at ease, I'm going to speak with Ned Withers again—in private—and then I plan to speak with the butler and any of the other staff who might be around."

I don't know what I looked like to him then, but he must have felt the need to add, "Maybe I don't look it, but I've been a cop for twenty years and I have certain methods. Until those methods fail me, I'll stick with what I know to do." He looked past me to the rest of the people in the room. "Don't anyone go too far from this house, if you'd be so kind."

He nodded curtly and disappeared through the doorway, closing the door behind him.

CHAPTER EIGHT

Just after lunch, Nora fell apart.

I was in my room, trying to read, when something thumped against the other side of the wall. My heart jumped into my throat and I jolted into a sitting position on the bed. I was only vaguely aware that the book fell out of my hands, bouncing off the edge of the bed to the floor. Heart fluttering, breathing rapidly, I waited; only a moment later the sound came again, and this time, I heard muffled cries, like someone begging for help without words. Nora's room was next to mine.

I rushed into the hallway, turned and tried Nora's door. It wasn't locked. As I opened it, Chelsea appeared from across the hallway, wearing a short bathrobe, her hair wrapped in a towel-turban. Our eyes met, but neither of us spoke. I went into Nora's room. Chelsea followed.

We found Nora slumped against the wall our rooms shared, half undressed, her knees pulled up to her chest. Her breath came in ragged gasps and I could actually see her pulse pounding in her temple. She stared straight ahead, tears running down her cheeks, mouth working silently, her head thumping rhythmically against the wall over and over again. I knew she wasn't seeing anything, and I doubted she felt any physical pain.

"She's having a panic attack." Chelsea took one of the woman's arms and without looking ordered, "Help me!"

Nora was tiny and between the two of us, there wasn't any trouble getting her up and onto the bed. We laid her down, and Chelsea took charge, rubbing the girl's inner arms, manually clenching Nora's hands into fists, talking softly to her all the while. The tears stopped quickly, but sweat glistened on Nora's forehead and her face was so pale it scared me.

It took several minutes, Chelsea gently working Nora's muscles, stroking her, speaking quietly and calmly to her, but finally, Nora's breathing slowed, and the vein in her temple stopped fluttering.

I knew she was actually conscious of her surroundings when she grasped Chelsea's hand. It was another moment before Nora's eyes focused, and when they did, her huge, dark pupils met Chelsea's blue-green ones. Nora started crying again. It was different now, though, softer and more of a release than a sign of distress.

Chelsea squeezed Nora's hand. "You're okay, sweetheart. We're here. It's okay. You're safe." Without being obvious, she motioned to me and I took Nora's other hand. Nora flinched when I touched her, but then she realized who I was and looked a little embarrassed.

"Stay right here, honey," Chelsea told the girl, releasing her hand. She went into the bathroom. Water ran and then she returned with a damp washcloth. Chelsea washed the girl's face, cleaning away the sweat and the tears, speaking soothingly while she did.

When she was done, she set the cloth on the nightstand. "Are you okay now?"

Nora's face was still pinched and pale, but she nodded. "I'm sorry," she whispered.

"Don't be," Chelsea told her. "We're all stressed." She glanced at me.

"It's okay, Nora." She turned to me. I smiled, trying to make it as warm and gentle as possible. "We're family. We're here for each other."

Nora's face crumpled and tears gathered in her eyes again.

"Sshh, sshh, sshh, honey. Shhh, it's okay," Chelsea said quickly, taking up the cloth and dabbing at Nora's face again. "You're okay. We're here. Nobody can hurt you."

Chelsea leaned forward, whispered something in Nora's ear. Then, to me, she said, "Stay with her a minute." She left the room. Nora's eyes tracked her as she went, and when Chelsea disappeared through the door, I could almost feel the panic surge through her.

Chelsea was back in less than a minute, one hand loosely clenched and the other holding a glass of water. "Here, sweetie." She motioned to me and I helped Nora sit up. "Open wide," she told the other woman. Nora obeyed like a docile child and Chelsea popped whatever was in her hand into Nora's mouth, then held up the glass and tilted it as she drank.

"You'll sleep for a while now, honey, and when you wake up, you'll feel better, okay?" Chelsea set the glass aside and then shifted Nora until she was lying flat on the bed, piled pillows beneath her head. Chelsea brushed the hair away from Nora's forehead and made soothing sounds. Soon, Nora's eyes began to droop then closed entirely. After another few moments, her breathing was slow and steady. She was asleep.

"Let's go," Chelsea whispered to me. I nodded and went out into the hallway. Chelsea followed, slowly and softly closing the door behind her. She moved to the doorway of her own room, then looked back. "That poor kid's scared shitless."

I was amazed. When I first met Chelsea, I got the impression that she was aloof, maybe even uncaring. I chalked it up to most of us being strangers. When she went toe to toe with Blair, arguing about the money, I felt like she was maybe even a little crass. Seeing her with Nora, though, the way she handled her and the panic attack so expertly, my opinion was changing. I guess everyone has hidden depths.

"You can't blame her," Chelsea went on, pulling the towel from her hair. She looked at it as if she'd never seen it before, wasn't sure how it got onto her head. She clenched both hands around the damp towel and sighed. "I never really knew Jonathan —he was pretty young when Marcus and I got married, still in middle-school—but he didn't deserve what happened to him."

"No one does."

Chelsea nodded. "Yeah."

"How did you—"

"Know what to do?" Chelsea smiled in a way that was somehow self-deprecating.

"I'm sorry," I said quickly. "I didn't mean to pry, it's just... you were really good with her. I was kind of amazed."

Chelsea swung the towel back and forth slowly, like a pendulum; she watched it instead of me. "I had my share of panic attacks when I was younger." She looked up but didn't meet my eyes. "I take a couple different meds for that. Don't worry, though —I just gave Nora an Ambien. She'll sleep for five or six hours. Hopefully it'll do her some good."

"Hopefully."

An uncomfortable, embarrassed silence fell over us. Chelsea put up a tough front and I learned something about her she probably didn't want anyone to know. I wasn't sure if it would bring us closer or push us apart.

"I'm gonna hop back in the shower," she said after a minute.

"Okay. I think I'm going to go see if I can talk to Aunt Lydia."

Something flashed in Chelsea's eyes. "Why?"

"I'm going to tell her about Nora. We both know why she's scared: she's afraid someone's going to kill her, just like Jonathan.

I'd be lying if I said I wasn't scared too. Under the circumstances, I don't think we can stay in this house. I mean... do you?"

Chelsea looked me straight in the eye. I could feel the wall coming up between us again. "If you want to ignore what that cop said, and if you don't care about the money, go. Feel free, like the man said. Marcus and I aren't going anywhere, though."

"But..." I felt my teeth scraping against my lower lip, a nervous gesture from childhood I thought I'd outgrown. "Aren't you scared?"

"I didn't say that." There was tension in the way she pressed her lips together. It made the tiny lines around her mouth deepen, giving her a harder look. There was determination and maybe even defiance in her eyes though. "I didn't say Marcus and I aren't scared. Jon was his baby brother..." She said the last part very softly, before finishing, "But we're not leaving."

"Okay," I told her. "I guess you're braver than I am. I'm going to talk to Aunt Lydia and when I do, I'll tell her Nora and I want to leave."

"Do you really want to, Holly?"

The question surprised me. Until she asked, I thought I did. Images of Nora, tears streaming down her face, mouth moving silently as she knocked her head against the wall, raced past my mind's eye. I shook them off. I didn't find fault with Nora and I didn't look down on her for her feelings, but no matter what happened, I wasn't going to end up like that.

"I do and I don't," I said. "I could certainly use the money."

Chelsea quirked a little smile of satisfaction. As she closed the door, she said, "Couldn't we all."

CHAPTER NINE

As I walked down the long hallway towards the stairs, all of the doors were closed, just as they were when I arrived the day before. The house was a little emptier now, though, and I could feel it, even if nothing obvious was changed.

I knew Nora and Chelsea were in their rooms, but I didn't know about any of the other cousins. Except Blair. He wasn't at all satisfied with the way Sergeant Goddard conducted his investigation and he all but told me he'd be investigating on his own. My mom liked Perry Mason novels, so a lawyer playing detective wasn't exactly an unfamiliar concept, but I didn't know how well that worked in the real world. I could never tell Blair that though. Whether he said it out loud or not, I knew Jonathan's death hurt him deeply. He probably felt like he just needed to be doing something and I wasn't going to tell him differently.

After Goddard left the family room that morning, there wasn't much discussion. Someone, I don't remember who, brought up the fact that Goddard mentioned a coroner performing an autopsy, but after that was finished, Jonathan would need to be transported back home. Without any hesitation, Marcus announced that he was going to call down to Foster's Place and see what he could do about arrangements for Jonathan's body. I think it was Marcus's way of showing that he, too, was upset by his brother's murder, even if it was very different from Blair's way.

I was deep in thought, remembering the way Marcus looked, and the expression on his face, before I realized I was halfway down the third-floor hallway, heading towards Aunt Lydia's door. It was then that I noticed Elijah.

As big as the man was, he was light on his feet and somehow able to make his presence simply disappear, something we all noticed at dinner the night before. Now, he squatted in the recessed doorway of Aunt Lydia's room, sitting on his heels, compressing his huge body into what seemed like an incredibly small space. When I noticed him, his eyes were already boring into me. I had to fight to keep from looking away.

Elijah unfolded himself as I approached, rising straight up until he filled the doorway. I wondered if the man was Aunt Lydia's only caregiver. Aside from Ned and a very brief glimpse of Eleonore, I hadn't seen anyone else.

Lydia seemed vital enough, especially for a woman who claimed to be dying, but she was elderly and there were all sorts of things that could happen to an older person with or without warning. I would expect someone as wealthy as her to have a professional around—a live-in nurse, something like that. There was a doctor in Foster's Place, I already knew that, but I doubted Lydia was his patient. She wasn't the type to accept some country doctor's services.

There was also the question of what Elijah was doing now, camped out in front of Lydia's room. He must have had household duties, and neglecting them seemed out of character. Was he here on Lydia's instructions? Or did he simply elect himself her protector after the morning's terrible discovery?

I stopped a few steps from the butler. "Hello. I came to talk to Aunt Lydia."

The man looked down his thick, blunt nose at me and shook his head. "The missus is resting," he said quietly.

"Well, I'm sorry if I have to wake her up, but something happened that I really need to talk to her about and it just can't wait."

As I said it, I stepped forward, reaching past Elijah to the doorknob. Before I could turn it, his fingers latched onto my wrist, and he yanked, pulling me away from the door like I weighed nothing at all. My feet actually left the floor for an instant.

My heart pounded and I knew my face was flushed; I could feel the heat. I looked up at Elijah, angry words on the tip of my tongue, but unable to get them out.

For a long moment, neither of us moved. I was breathing heavily, but Elijah was as calm and silent as ever. I glanced at his hand, still on my wrist. His fingers were very long and as hard as steel. It was what I imagined being handcuffed felt like. This close to Elijah, he seemed taller, wider, more massive. The top of my head didn't reach the middle of his chest and I had the feeling again of being a child. I tried to pull my hand away, but I couldn't even budge Elijah's arm, much less free myself. It was like he had his own gravitational pull and I was trapped in it.

I wasn't afraid when he first touched me, only surprised and angry. The longer he held me, though, the worse it got. Fear crawled out of my belly and up my spine, replacing the anger. It was well over a minute since he first grabbed me, and still he said nothing, made no move except to lift me away from the door. How long would he keep me prisoner and what did he plan to do to me?

"Please let go." I tried to make it a command, an order, the way Aunt Lydia would. I was a member of the Shaw family, and her guest. It came out trembling and weak. I almost didn't recognize my own voice.

"Mrs. Orlov is resting," Elijah said.

"Okay. You've made your point. Let go of me, please."

He didn't.

Ice dumped into my bloodstream and raced through my body. My pulse grew faster. I was beginning to feel the same fear that Nora must have.

"Please..." I said again. Elijah just looked down at me, expressionless, his eyes dark and deep, the scars and pits on his face redder than I remembered. I didn't want to keep looking at him, but I was afraid to look away too. He might have been a statue some artist created to express a nightmare.

I wanted to scream, but I had enough anger left that I wouldn't give him the satisfaction. He was a servant, an employee of my aunt, who was just on the other side of the door, and this house was filled with members of my family. No matter what Elijah wanted to do, no matter what was going through his mind now, he wouldn't dare hurt me.

The realization washed away some of the fear, letting the anger rise again. I took a deep breath, then let it out in a snarl. "Let me go." I put as much force in it as anything I've ever said, and to punctuate the command, I stamped the heel of my shoe down hard on the end of his foot. It wasn't one of the soft-soled shoes I wore when Blair gave me the tour; I put on a pair of pumps with chunky, wooden heels that morning and slipped into them again when I left my room for Nora's.

Elijah's eyes widened and he pulled away, so his back bumped up against the door. He released my wrist at the same time. There was real surprise on his face. With his size and his looks, I doubted many people ever fought back against him. A person like me doing it rattled him.

Something soared inside me. I confronted the monster and won. Maybe the smart thing to do then was to retreat, go back to the safety of my room and calm down, or find one of the men—Blair or maybe Ryan—and tell them what Elijah did. But I didn't like the idea of running scared to anyone, male or female, so I let the feeling of triumph push me another step forward. I turned the knob of Aunt Lydia's door, pushed it open, and marched inside, closing it behind me.

Aunt Lydia wasn't asleep and she didn't look at all surprised by my bursting in uninvited and unannounced. She was propped up in her bed, the only way I'd ever seen her, awake and alert, just as if she was expecting someone. Maybe not me, but a visitor anyway. Part of me hoped to catch her off-guard in coming here like this, but I would have to live with the disappointment.

"Well, come right in, Holly," the old woman said.

Behind me, I heard the door click shut and whirled on my heel. I know I closed it and I never heard it reopen. Elijah must have meant to follow me, maybe drag me back out into the hall, but instead, seeing that Aunt Lydia accepted me into her room, just quietly went away.

"Don't mind Elijah."

I turned. "Does he always guard your door like that?" I stepped closer to the bed, stopping at the foot and looking down the length of it at my great aunt. The bed was so big and she was so small, it seemed like she might sink into it, becoming lost in its depths at any moment.

There was a hint of a smile on her face as she answered. "Not always. He has many duties around the house."

"So why today? Why, with a house full of nieces and nephews, is he standing guard outside your door? And aren't you curious how I got past him?"

"'Why today', she asks." Lydia let out a bitter laugh, then sighed. "Oh, my dear girl." She briefly lifted a hand before letting it fall back into her lap. "You should be able to guess that all of you nieces and nephews are the reason Elijah feels the need to protect me."

"Us?" I couldn't hide the surprise in my voice.

Lydia nodded. "Despite his domestic skills, Elijah is a rather uncultured man in many ways. He wasn't born to his position and the life he led before wasn't one that instilled any trust in strangers." Her eyes found mine. "He's been in this house a long time and after what happened to poor Jonathan, he's probably feeling very protective of me. You may not believe that members of this family could hurt one another, but Elijah is under no such delusions. And neither am I."

The morning was gray and overcast and still, a remnant of the snow that came in the night, but now, in the afternoon, the clouds were churning, moving quickly south. For a moment, they parted enough that a beam of sunlight stabbed through the window, hitting Aunt Lydia like a spotlight. It etched the fine lines in her face a little deeper and made her perfectly styled white hair seem to glow with an inner light. It reminded me of a Renaissance painting I saw once. And then the clouds came together again, swallowing the light and ending the moment.

"Now, as for your other question, you seem eager to tell me about how you made your way past Elijah, so go right ahead."

"It wasn't easy," I began, watching her watch me. I saw what Blair meant before—no matter what else was happening, Aunt Lydia was enjoying herself. "He told me I couldn't see you and when I tried anyway, he grabbed me and wouldn't let go. I had to give him a stomp." I gestured to my shoes, though Lydia couldn't see them from where she lay.

She smiled again, more obvious about it this time. "You must have been awful anxious to see your poor old aunt, dear. People are usually afraid of Elijah. When he says something, people generally do as he tells them." She paused. "I'm learning new things about you, Miss Holly Shaw."

"Like what?"

"You don't scare easily."

That wasn't true. I was terrified when Elijah took hold of me.

I couldn't just give in, do nothing to help myself though. I told Chelsea she was braver than me, but maybe I was stronger than I realized.

"Anyway..." I changed the subject. "Elijah said you were resting. I assumed you were napping. I know barging in was rude, but—"

"Resting does not necessarily mean sleeping," Lydia said. "Resting can mean just relaxing... contemplating..." Her tone was dreamy and a faraway look came into her eyes, but disappeared almost instantly. It was strange, almost scary, to see her like that, so out of character from the Lydia Orlov I thought I was coming to know.

She snapped back to herself and focused on me. "You should know that, dear. I realize you have a career, but I hope you take the time to relax now and then."

"How can you relax when Jonathan was killed in your own house?"

I didn't mean to put it like that; it just sort of burst out of my mouth.

"Believe me, I am not unbothered by it. If you think I'm cold or cruel, so be it, but I promise you it's been weighing on my mind. I've thought of little else since Elijah told me this morning."

"Well..." I wasn't sure how to go on. "What do you think?" I finished lamely.

"What am I supposed to think, Holly dear?"

Anger seized me. "Don't you feel bad? Don't you feel any *guilt*?"

"Why should I?" she countered, shifting slightly, settling herself more deeply among the pillows. "I didn't particularly want Jonathan dead, but I don't mourn him either. I didn't even know him. Why should I feel guilt over a stranger's death?"

"It's obvious!" I shouted. My hands were clenched at my sides and I wanted to hit something very badly. I almost wished Elijah was in the room; he would make a good target. "Jonathan is dead because of *you*, because of the way you worded your will."

Lydia was silent for a long time. All expression left her face and she just stared at me, as if trying to see inside me. I imagined that I could actually feel the weight of her gaze on me.

Finally, after what was probably only a minute but seemed like an hour, she said, "Are you accusing one of your cousins of murdering Jonathan?"

I hesitated. The question was on my mind all day. Nobody dared say it, but I was sure everyone was thinking it. And as logical as the money might seem as a motive for murder, we couldn't be sure of anything, so no one wanted to make any accusations. As long as it wasn't brought out into the light, though, we would never have any answers either.

Slowly, I said, "One of my cousins... very possibly did kill Jonathan."

"Or you yourself did."

I wasn't surprised and I didn't get angry. Lydia was probably looking for one of those responses; I knew her that well, at least. "Yes, you're right, Aunt Lydia. I should be included on the list of suspects. I have as much to gain as anyone. That's not the point though," I went on. "It's *your* will, *your* little game that caused this. It matters who did it, yes, but the why is just as important. Someone in this house might just be greedy enough to kill a relative." I thought of Blair; Jonathan's death seemed to hit him very hard, and I didn't think it was an act. "Maybe not a close relative, like a brother, but cousins hardly count as family as far as some people are concerned. Otherwise, I don't think I'd just be meeting all of these people for the first time."

"You sound like you're making a case against yourself, Holly."

"Maybe it does sound like that, but I know I didn't kill Jonathan. I can't say that with certainty about anyone else any more than they can be sure about me. But my point is that this whole situation started when you and Mr. Shelton told us about the conditions of your will. I'm pretty sure I know why you did this, and now you have your answer, so you'll just have to let this be the end of it. You have to call Mr. Shelton and have him void your will or rewrite it or something."

Lydia's face grew very cold and hard. She no longer looked like a tiny little lady supposedly dying of some mysterious illness. She was a woman of iron will who could step out of that bed and conquer any challenge set before her. "Are you trying to give *me* an order?"

The way she looked at me, I wanted to back down, but I'd stood up to Elijah. Aunt Lydia wasn't any scarier than the huge butler. "I'm just saying..." I swallowed. "You saw how this affected everyone and you can't let it go on. You don't want anyone else to be hurt, do you?"

Lydia's face was like stone and she was so still, I wasn't sure she was even breathing. If anyone else walked in and saw her, they might think she passed away there was so little life in her expression or body.

Finally, with a voice like polished metal, she said, "Let me tell you a story, Holly dear. It's about my relationship with the Shaw family. When I'm done, maybe you'll understand why I wanted my will structured the way it is."

"I don't—"

"Be quiet!" she barked.

I shuddered. There was no humanity or softness in her at all now, only a cold rage. I wanted to run from the room, find a phone and call Rick to come pick me up, take me back to Foster's Place. The airplane to Fairbanks wouldn't be back for days, but I thought I even wouldn't mind waiting in the tiny airport if that's what it took to get away from Lydia the way she was in that moment.

I knew it was impossible though. Lydia wouldn't let me leave the room. She would make Elijah stop me. I may have surprised him once, but it would never happen again. He was too huge, too powerful, and now he'd be wary of me.

"Sit down," Lydia commanded. I didn't argue. I couldn't. I pulled the chair away from the wall and set it a couple of feet from the bed. When I sat, I felt strain in muscles I didn't even know I was clenching. I sat rigidly in the hard, uncomfortable chair, knowing I wouldn't be able to relax while I was in that room.

Lydia looked at me, her face still expressionless. When she spoke, the anger remained, but it was more muted. "I don't know if you've ever heard about my generation of the Shaw family. My parents, your great-grandparents, were Nathan and Emily. Your uncle is named after my father, his grandfather. I was their younger child, by several years. My older brother, your own grandfather, was James—Jimmy, I called him—and his wife was Charlotte. They had three children of their own: Nathan, Sara, and Spencer, in order of birth."

I didn't know the names of my great-grandparents, but I knew the rest.

"I loved my brother very much," Lydia continued. "He was handsome and clever, and he could be very generous and kind, if it suited him. He could also be cruel and vindictive and petty, but he always treated me well, so it was easy to overlook those parts of him. His wife, Charlotte, I knew much less well. She was pretty, dark-haired, and fair-skinned. A good match for my brother in looks and temperament. She loved him deeply – I know that much. And he hurt her more profoundly and more often than anyone should be expected to endure."

She inhaled loudly through her nose, as if she had to brace herself with extra oxygen to endure the memories. When she spoke again, she was quieter. "Jimmy was clever and handsome, but he had no real skills or the desire to learn any. I recognized that long ago, but not until it was too late. Mother and Father passed in an accident when I was a teenager and Jimmy was barely twenty. He inherited everything, except for a small stipend that I wouldn't come into until I was twenty-one. Without anyone to tell him different, our family's money flowed through Jimmy's hands like it was water. Spending money was the only talent he ever had aside from deceiving women —myself among them. He never wanted from me what he did from others, of course, but I was taken in just the same. I thought my brother was a wonderful person, and Charlotte loved him very much. I believe he loved her as much as he was able, but ultimately, she was just someone to help him carry on the family name while he continued to sow his oats, if you understand my meaning."

I didn't say anything, but I didn't need to. Lydia wasn't paying any attention to me as she spoke. I thought she'd decided to make me her confidante, whether I wanted to be or not, but now I wasn't sure that my presence even mattered. She might well have continued to tell her story regardless of whether I was in the room.

"Jimmy spent his life searching for something. I don't know what it was and I doubt he did either. He traveled a great deal, leaving Charlotte at home with Nathan and later Sara. I heard from him rarely, saw him even less, and I think he communicated with me more often than with his own wife.

"I was in college when the money ran out. I was twenty years old, in the middle of my junior year at Bryn Mawr, still undecided as to a major, and not worrying too much about it. College was the first time I was away from home. It was less than twenty miles from home, true, but I was on my own and enjoying my new life as an adult. I learned of the money when I was called to the college's business office and told that my tuition payments were two semesters behind. I had thirty days to square my accounts.

"I was frantic; I couldn't understand what happened. Sometimes a monthly check for spending money came late, but it always showed up, and in the three years I was away from home,

Jimmy always made sure the school bills were paid. When I couldn't reach anyone by phone, I skipped my classes for the day and used all of the cash I had to take a taxi home.

"When I arrived, the house was quiet and no one greeted me at the door. I found Jimmy in his den, the shades drawn. He wasn't surprised to see me and he didn't lie to me when I asked what was going on. The Shaw family was broke, completely. I didn't believe it, but he showed me the mountains of past-due bills, the bank ledgers with empty balances. It was his fault—he freely admitted that. Unlike our father, who was a hard-driven man, Jimmy never worked a day in his life, but he spent money as if someone—as if Father—was still earning it by the fistful. Now, there was nothing left."

Lydia's eyelids fluttered and she looked at me, actually seeing me for the first time in many minutes. "I won't bore you with the details. I had to leave school, of course, and I went to work. The house was paid for, but there were still taxes and other expenses that I couldn't possibly hope to meet by myself. Jimmy had no skills, no experience, but he promised that he would find a way to make money too. He couldn't hide the situation from Charlotte, either, so he didn't try. She accepted it better than I would have in her shoes; she genuinely loved that foolish, selfish man.

"I worked a variety of meaningless jobs, trying to keep body and soul together not just for myself, but for my brother, his wife, and their children. Eventually, the small trust left to me matured and that made things a little easier, but we couldn't live in anything like the style we were accustomed to and it hurt Jimmy, even if it was his own damned fault.

"Jimmy was clever, as I said. Maybe not truly intelligent, but he had wiles, and our family still had connections. Jimmy used those connections to try rebuilding the Shaw fortune. He swindled and he deceived and I believe he outright stole when he could get away with it. He wasn't honest, not by any stretch, but he worked harder in those years than he ever had in his life.

"And he was successful to a degree. The Shaws would never be rich again, but his income became comfortable. Jimmy no longer played around and his relationship with Charlotte grew warmer. They had another child—your father, Spencer.

"With life stabilized for my brother's family, I started thinking about finding my own way again, perhaps working my way through the rest of college. I was twenty-six then, still young.

"The accident eliminated any chance of that."

I waited, but Lydia went silent. I couldn't imagine what she was seeing in her mind's eye and I was afraid to interrupt.

She continued. "They were at some sort of event—a business dinner or something; I don't know—and it must have gone well. Jimmy drank very little in those years, simply because we couldn't afford the alcohol he preferred and he hated to lower himself to anything lesser. He must have been raging drunk that night though; a policeman later told me that the amount of alcohol in his blood was more than three times the legal limit. Whatever came before, Jimmy and Charlotte were killed instantly when his car hit the side of a tractor-trailer truck that had the right of way."

She leaned back among the pillows, her eyes on the ceiling. I had the feeling there was something in them she didn't want me to see. "They were killed, and in the same second, I became parent to three young children. Spencer was barely six months old at the time. I was glad when Charlotte asked me to be her children's godmother. It made me feel that much closer to them. I never thought anything would come of it."

Lydia shifted again, her eyes searching for and finding mine. "Understand this, though: I never shirked my duty. There was no one else for those children and I'd been part of their lives for more than five years. I also still had the self-sacrificing idealism of youth; the same impulse that made me work to support my brother's family drove me to do my best as their foster mother. I gave of myself as much as any birth mother could and made a voluntary sacrifice of the best years of my life to those children. When the last of them, your father, Spencer, turned eighteen, I was forty-four years old, an old maid. A spinster. A woman who lived her life entirely for other people."

Lydia paused again, but now her face was pale and her breath seemed to be coming hard. The strain of talking about all of this, of telling me, was too much. "Aunt Lydia, you don't—"

"I'm not through!" she snapped, then continued as if I hadn't spoken at all. "I thought then that maybe I could finally have a chance at a life of my own. I still wanted to be part of the children's lives, but they were adults and could find their own way.

"The story doesn't end there though. Oh, no.

"There was a sealed codicil to Jimmy's will that I never knew anything about until an attorney phoned, just a week or so after Spencer's eighteenth birthday. When we gathered in this lawyer's office, I learned that when Jimmy died he was very well off. Not rich exactly, but far wealthier than I ever guessed. The will I knew of mostly detailed arrangements for raising the children, to be left in my care, of course. The codicil, not to be opened until the youngest Shaw child came of legal age, dealt with the money. And as I sat there, listening to the lawyer read from the documents, I thought now, perhaps, my brother would finally show his appreciation for everything I gave up for him and his family."

Lydia's eyes narrowed. "Can you imagine how I felt when I heard that Nathan, Sara, and Spencer were to divide the assets equally, including the house and the grounds it stood on, except for five-thousand dollars left to me 'to be used to defray the costs of living until such time as Lydia can support herself'. The children—*my* children, far more than Jimmy's at that point— were given a tremendous head-start on building their lives while I was treated as an afterthought."

"Please, Aunt Lydia…"

She ignored me. It was like she couldn't hear anything but her own voice she was so lost in her own story.

"All three had the Shaw good looks. Nathan already talked about starting his own business before any of us knew about the money and now he had his seed money. Spencer was to begin college in the fall and he could pay for it without need of loans or scholarships. And Sara—she wasn't a party girl, not exactly, but she was never without a boyfriend or two. I was sure she would be married before long, with her father's money a nice dowry, if that term isn't too old-fashioned to make sense to you.

"Suddenly, after years of our just scraping by, the children had the whole world in the palms of their hands. With money in their pockets, they could do anything, go anywhere. None of them wanted to stay in the family home, of course. They wanted to go out into the great, wide world and decided to sell it. Even without getting all the upkeep it needed over the years, the house and the land were still worth a million dollars or more. 'But where will Aunt Lydia live?' No one asked that question, not even me, until it was far too late. I came home from work a few days later and the children were finishing some paperwork with a realtor. I was stunned. I didn't think they'd really go through with it. I underestimated their greed.

"They hoped to hide it from me for a while longer, but they had the decency left to be embarrassed, at least. That didn't stop them selling my home—the only one I ever knew, aside from three years in a Bryn Mawr dorm. 'Where will I go?' I asked. 'I've spent my life on you children.' I could go anywhere I wanted to, Nathan told me. As he said it, there was an edge in his voice that reminded me of Jimmy. My brother never spoke to me like that, but I saw how he treated others when we were young. I ignored it then, made up excuses. Being the target of that... disdain, I understood how badly I misunderstood my brother. Now, his son stood in front of me, a young man I spent more years raising than my brother ever did, and I saw Jimmy in Nathan's face and the way he spoke. I knew that somehow, even without his father in his life, Nathan learned more from Jimmy than he ever did from me."

Lydia let out a shuddering breath. She brushed away a stray lock of hair, her hand trembling.

"Less than two weeks later, the house was sold and I was on the street. Forty-four years old and homeless. I had some money and I had a job, so I wouldn't starve, but I just didn't care."

Lydia looked at me for the first time in quite a while and it was like she was just realizing I was still there. Her voice was a hoarse whisper as she said, "I loved those children and they betrayed me. *That* is the inheritance all four of us received from my brother, James Patrick Shaw." Her voice was so low, I had to learn forward to hear her.

I sat back in the chair as Lydia collapsed against her pillows. The room was silent except for the wheezing of her breath. Trying not to be obvious, I studied her and saw, for the first time, a woman who seemed to be dying. Her complexion had lost all color, leaving her pale and waxy-looking; even her hair no longer had any luster. Her thin chest rose and fell with labored breathing and I could actually see the sweat forming on her brow. I was never worried for her until that exact moment.

"I'm going to find a phone. You need a doctor." I stood.

"Sit down," Lydia ordered. Our eyes met and I saw the fierceness raging inside her. She was regaining control of herself, pushing aside Lydia Shaw, the lonely, hurt woman, and again becoming Lydia Orlov, the wealthy widow.

"Sit down," she repeated.

I didn't want to upset her more than she was, so I sat. I was afraid any resistance might push her over the edge, past any point she could return from. *Your cousins would love that*, I thought. Just for a second, I hated both myself and them.

Somewhere, Lydia found the strength—or maybe the sheer stubbornness—to keep going. "I got an apartment and spent a couple of months wallowing in self-pity. I hated what my life had become and I hated who I was becoming. I woke up one morning, dreading going to work, standing behind a counter, repeating empty promises about makeup and perfumes to women looking for miracles. I was a middle-aged woman who never accomplished anything or did a single thing for herself. Finally, I allowed myself to be angry." Lydia's voice grew stronger. "I was so angry that it burned up all the sadness and despair and self-pity. I never before did anything for myself, but that didn't mean I couldn't start. I got out the phone book, picked up the phone, and before I had a chance to talk myself out of it, I called the first travel agent listed and booked myself a cruise. I would take a vacation, the first in my entire life, on the money my brother left me. When I came back, if I ever did, then I would worry about everything else.

"And off I went, the very next day, flying to San Francisco. I took a beautiful ship up the coast, enjoying the sea and the sunshine, eating food like I hadn't since before Mother and Father died, visiting cities I never dreamt I'd see—Seattle, Vancouver.

"It was as we left Vancouver that I met him: Piotr Orlov. He was a very rich and very lonely man. He called himself a widower, but I learned later that wasn't true—or possibly wasn't, we never knew for certain. He left his wife behind in the Soviet Union when it first began to collapse, choosing to save his assets instead of her. At the time, though, I didn't know and maybe I wouldn't have cared if I did. I was also very lonely, and my soul was sorely battered. Piotr was older than me by almost twenty years, gruff and not very handsome, but he was the first man to seriously pay attention to me since I was a girl and for that, I thought I loved him.

"We had nothing in common but our loneliness, but it brought us together. He was a wealthy, well-read man who could speak on many subjects. I was a woman from a good family and still attractive when I made the effort. Before the end of that trip, Piotr proposed and I accepted without a thought, except that I would never have to go back to that small, lonely apartment in Philadelphia again."

Lydia's gaze captured mine. "As for Nathan, Sara, and Spencer, well…" She shrugged. "You children know what became of them."

I shifted uncomfortably in the chair. Except for that moment when I wanted to call a doctor, I had been sitting on the hard wood for a long time. My rear end was numb and still somehow sore. I ignored it. Lydia spent close to two hours building up to something, and she was about to reach the end. "I guess they wasted all that money."

She nodded. "They did. One by one, I received phone calls and letters from them, asking for help. First, Nathan—he opened a car lot apparently without knowing anything about the business. He was broke inside two years. Sara wanted money to help clear her husband's debts. After her first letter, I never opened another. At least Nathan was *trying* to build something. Spencer sent cards—birthdays, holidays—and pretended he was simply keeping in touch, but inevitably, each note got around to the subject of money.

"And you know, Holly, I never realized until I started getting those cards how bitter I really was. I loved those children, I really truly did, and they just threw me away. But even so, to not help one's children when you're able to do so… I never thought I was that kind of person. They were the ones who did that to me."

She made a sound that was half sigh and half groan. "Piotr and I had several homes when we were first married—Anchorage, Seattle, San Francisco, Los Angeles. Somehow, letters found their way to each of them for years. I never responded and eventually they just stopped. I learned why later."

"They all died."

Lydia nodded. "Nathan had a heart attack. He was a big,

strong boy, and I gather he became a husky man and then a very fat one. With Sara, it was breast cancer."

"And my dad had an accident." He died in a car crash, like his own father. "I was four."

Lydia's head bobbed again. "Yes, I know. All three of the Shaw children, gone too soon, and each of them leaving behind children of their own, none of whom ever had a taste of the life their father and I were raised in and I found my way back to."

The old woman went quiet again. She had regained some of her color and she was quickly becoming the Aunt Lydia I knew. For just a second, though, I thought I saw hesitation on her face. "I suppose I haven't really explained myself, have I?"

"I'm... not sure," I admitted. She'd certainly told me a lot of things I would never have known otherwise. Some people might have doubted her—Blair certainly would have taken everything she said with a grain of salt—but I believed her. No matter what she said, I didn't put lying past Lydia Orlov, but not about this. Her pain was too obvious and too real.

"Well, I'll be brief then. I've worn myself out." She locked eyes with me. "I've never told another person about all of these things —not even Piotr, from whom I otherwise had no secrets."

I didn't say anything. She continued. "The past is past and here we are, with a new generation of Shaws. There are six of you—no, I'm sorry. Five now, with Jonathan gone." I winced at how easily she seemed to forget him. "Five of you, each the son or daughter of one of the children I raised and then put out of my life, just as they put me out of the life I built for all four of us. All of you are here, hoping for a share of the fortune Piotr Orlov left me. Can you guess why I would do such a thing when I never gave a penny of it to your parents?"

"Maybe you feel guilty about not helping them. Or..."

Lydia smiled—a small, grim smile without any humor. "Or...?"

"Maybe you want to reconnect with what's left of your family before it's too late."

Lydia's smile shifted just slightly, and though I couldn't say how, it took on something sinister. A shiver went down my spine. "I'm sure you all would like to believe that, dear, but it's far from the truth."

Then what is the truth? I wanted to ask, but couldn't bring myself to. I didn't want to know. I wanted to stand up, leave the room, and forget about all of this. I wanted my share of the money as much as anyone, but I never wanted to know all of her secrets and motivations. It was my fault for coming in here to begin with though. I thought I'd be confronting Aunt Lydia and instead, she'd turned it right around.

"I've never felt an ounce of guilt over what happened to all of your parents, Holly. They hurt me as badly as any person can hurt another, but I never lashed out, I never tried to take any sort of revenge. I simply ignored them. I didn't owe them anything and I don't owe any of you, either. But still, I was curious and my time is short."

"Curious about what?"

Lydia clasped her hands in her lap and her face took on the look of a very satisfied cat. "I was curious how much of your parents and your grandfather you children have in you. Jimmy would do anything for money, I learned, once we no longer had any of our own, and his children were quite willing to put their foster mother out on the street for a little bit more than he left them. So what, I wondered, would you and your cousins do for money? For ten million dollars? For twelve million dollars? For fifteen…?

"Does the math sound familiar, dear?" She began laughing, dry and wheezing, like the cackling of a storybook witch. "I had a theory about the Shaw family, and so far, it's proven true. It didn't even take very long!"

She began laughing again and didn't seem to notice when I

left my chair and moved to the door. I opened it, thinking only of getting away from the laughing woman, forgetting all about Elijah until I saw him standing in the doorway. As scared of him as I was, it was nothing to how I felt about Lydia Orlov. I paid him no attention, just hurried down the hallway, practically running. I didn't stop until I was back in my own room with the door locked and a chair beneath the knob, just to be sure.

CHAPTER TEN

Sergeant Goddard returned to Dacha Orlov in the early evening.

I was sitting in one of the chaises by the pool, watching Blair swim laps, his arms and legs moving so slowly it looked lazy. Through the skylight overhead, I could see nothing but a heavy grayness. The sun hadn't actually set yet, but shortly after we arrived at the pool, dark clouds gathered overhead, closing off the sky. It looked like there would be no chance to see the stars, like Blair and I talked about when he first showed me the pool, but it was the least of my concerns.

Blair continued around the pool, following the outer rim, never seeming to tire. I'm sure he could have put on more speed if he wanted, but he seemed content this way. As he passed, I noticed again that his body was more tanned and toned than I would expect from a man who claimed to live a sedentary, work-oriented life.

As I watched Blair, Elijah appeared from the door to the house. We were on the far side of the pool when he entered, but rather than walk around to speak to us, he kept his distance, remaining standing inside the doorway. The distance forced him to shout as he announced that Sergeant Goddard would like everyone to gather in the family room.

Earlier, I was alone in my room, sitting on the bed, just staring out of the window and thinking about everything Lydia told me, when there was a knock on the door. For an instant, I thought about ignoring it, just pretending I wasn't there. Whoever it was might try the door if I didn't answer though, and when they found it wouldn't open, that would only cause more problems.

"Who is it?" I called.

"Blair. I've got a surprise." Despite his brother's death, still so recent, I thought I heard a hint of laughter in his voice.

I pulled the chair from under the doorknob, put it aside, and opened the door. Blair held something behind his back. He whipped his hands around with a "Ta-da!" and showed me two swimsuits: a pair of men's trunks and a one-piece women's suit. "Look what I found. Want to take a dip?"

I did, actually; I hadn't been swimming in ages, but I always enjoyed it. There was something else more important on my mind though. "Come in," I told him, throwing the door wide. "And close it behind you."

I went to the window as Blair came in, shut the door, and stepped further into the room. He tossed the two suits on the foot of the bed. "What's on your mind?"

I gave him the gist of Aunt Lydia's story about the Shaw family, and her part in it, about how our parents supposedly treated her, and why she brought all of us here. Blair listened and never said a word until I was done, but I could tell he was digesting it, analyzing, thinking about what it all meant.

Lydia's telling took about two hours; my condensed version took about fifteen minutes. When I was through, Blair picked up the swim-trunks and said, "I'm going to go change. Do you want to meet me or go down there together?"

I was confused. "About what Lydia told me—"

"Later," he cut in. "I think better in the water."

That was forty minutes before and if Blair had any thoughts by the time Elijah came to fetch us he hadn't shared them.

Now, the members of the Shaw family, except Lydia, were gathered in the family room. The big, boxy television was rolled to one side and chairs were in its place. Marcus, Chelsea, Ryan, and Nora were all seated on the sofa, Marcus and Chelsea on one end and Ryan and Nora on the other. Nora must have been woken up to join the group, as her hair was mussed and her eyes were puffy from sleep.

Sergeant Goddard nodded to us as we came in. I spread our towels on the middle part of the sofa and Blair and I sat.

That morning, Goddard was confident in his position and, if not exactly energetic, ready to move forward in whatever way was necessary. Now, he seemed very tired and almost reluctant. He stood in the space between the two chairs across from the sofa, scanned all of our faces, and then nodded almost imperceptibly, as if to himself. "Thanks for gathering so quickly."

Before he could continue, Elijah appeared, wheeling a cart with coffee service and a huge, chrome coffee urn. Without a word, he offered each of us a cup. Marcus and Ryan both accepted, but Chelsea and Nora turned him down. So did Blair and I. The swimming relaxed me a little, but I had a feeling that coffee, combined with whatever Sergeant Goddard wanted to tell us, would just make me anxious again.

When Elijah offered Goddard a cup, he refused, then changed his mind. I thought I saw some strange glimmer of amusement flash in Elijah's eyes, but it might have been my imagination.

The trooper took a sip of his coffee, sat down on the arm of one of the chairs, and faced us again. "Let me get right down to it, since there's no pleasant way to talk about a death. I wouldn't normally discuss an ongoing investigation at all, but as a favor to Mrs. Orlov, and considering the victim, I promised to keep the family informed."

He slurped from his cup and let out a small sigh of satisfaction before continuing. "Now, Doctor Chapman, down in town, isn't a medical examiner by trade, but he does a pretty credible job when it's necessary, and he's told me a few things. I don't need to go into specifics, but he's convinced me that whoever attacked Jonathan knew exactly what they were doing. They likely either had medical experience or at least knowledge. Anatomical knowledge, at any rate."

"What does that mean?" Chelsea asked.

"It means," Goddard began, but sighed. "It means, Mrs. Shaw, that your brother-in-law was killed with a single stab wound, under the ribcage and directly into the heart. I've seen a lot of knife wounds and they're mostly stabbings in random places or surface slashes. I've never seen so accurate an attack before. That takes skill."

"Or luck," Blair said.

"It's possible," Goddard admitted. "There's another thing, too, that's important: this kind of wound, I'm told, doesn't produce a lot of external bleeding."

That didn't make sense to me. "But there was all that blood…"

"Correct." Goddard nodded. "Doctor Chapman tells me that the heart would have stopped almost instantly, and what little blood there was would have pooled inside the chest cavity with very little of it escaping from the initial wound."

"I saw Jon." Blair's voice was tight.

I stole a glance and saw that Blair's anger was building again. Maybe it's terrible to say, but it made me feel a little better—Blair couldn't have been the killer when just talking about it made him this upset.

"Look, I saw where Jon was found," Blair said. "There was *a lot* of blood. But your guy is saying—what? That someone purposely opened up the wound and spread it around?"

"It looks that way, yes. There's another thing." Goddard finished the coffee in his cup, set it down on the chair next to him and stood. "Jonathan wouldn't have been able to drag himself through the bushes. Death would have been within seconds."

"So someone carried him..." Marcus said.

"And left him for us to find?" Ryan finished. The big man's color was visibly draining. "That's... shit, it's like a horror movie."

Nora gasped and hid her face against her brother's shoulder. Nobody else made a sound for a few moments.

Goddard nodded again. "Yes, and that tells us a few things. Jonathan wasn't as big a man as you, Mr. Hill, or his brothers, but he wasn't exactly small either. He weighed a good one-sixty-five, too much for most people to lift or even comfortably drag."

"By themselves, you mean," Blair said.

"That's true," Goddard agreed. "It would take a strong person or two working in concert to move the body."

Fear gripped me. That was something I never even thought of; all this time, I was worrying about which one of my cousins might be a killer when it was entirely possible that two—or even more—were working together.

I looked first at one side of the sofa then the other. I already decided Blair couldn't be the killer, but there were two obvious pairs: a husband and wife and a brother and sister.

I didn't think Nora was capable of something like this, not with the terror I saw in her earlier. That just couldn't be faked, not by the best actress in the world. But it was possible that the cause of her fear wasn't what Chelsea and I assumed. Could Ryan have somehow coerced her into helping him? Maybe Nora's fear wasn't of an unknown killer, but rather because she knew exactly who the killer was.

What about Marcus and Chelsea? Could a woman commit a murder, or help her husband kill his own brother, and then act as tenderly towards a suffering woman as Chelsea did Nora? I didn't know.

The room was quiet, everyone as lost in their thoughts as I was.

Blair broke the silence. "Do you have a suspect?" he asked.

Goddard put his hands on his hips. "No."

"Bull," Blair said, but without any heat. He met and held Goddard's eyes. "You have six of them sitting right in front of you."

Goddard shook his head. "I'm not going into that again, Mr. Shaw. I understand your frustration and your anger, but—"

"But this way, you don't upset the great Mrs. Lydia Orlov by arresting any of us and spoiling her little game. How much did that favor cost?"

"Mr. Shaw!" Goddard put command into his voice, his face flushed with anger.

Blair looked to his left then his right, trying to take all of us in. "Has Holly told any of you what Lydia told her about why we're here? No? Then we'll need to have a pow-wow after this."

"Shaw!" Goddard barked. When Blair turned to him, he said more softly, "Calm down, will you? I understand how you feel, but have you ever heard that old line about justice and how it moves?"

"Grinding slowly, but exceedingly fine?" Blair sneered, but it was half-hearted. "I've heard it."

"Like I said before," Goddard dug his wool hat from the back pocket of his trousers, "I have my own methods and whether you believe it or not, I do know what I'm about. I'm here right now in an informational capacity. I've only just started the real work."

We all just sort of sat in place, trying not to look at one another, no one speaking, as if each of us was embarrassed by whatever she or he was thinking.

Then Sergeant Goddard pulled the hat down over his head, thanked us for our time, and wished us all a good night, as if there was any chance of having one until the killer, or killers, was caught.

CHAPTER ELEVEN

I didn't feel like talking, but I told the others the condensed version of Lydia's story, going through the parts I considered most important even more quickly, and in less detail, than when I talked to Blair. I don't know how much family history the rest of the cousins knew, but no one seemed overly surprised or angry. I decided later, in my room, that it was more due to a growing numbness than anything else. So much happened to all of us in so short a time that I suppose it was inevitable.

We split up after that. I went back to my room, accompanied by Blair as far as the door. He seemed like he didn't want to be alone, but I was just the opposite: I wanted time to think over what I knew and saw for myself and compare it to the information Aunt Lydia and Sergeant Goddard gave us.

"I'll see you at dinner," I told Blair and closed the door. I locked it, but didn't bother with the chair under the knob this time.

I took a shower, then rinsed out the swimsuit and hung it from the shower head to dry. I wondered where Blair found it; I doubted either Chelsea or Nora brought a suit, and it didn't seem likely to belong to Aunt Lydia or Eleonore. It was a little too small for me, pinching around my thighs and rear, but the fit wasn't too bad overall. If I remembered, I'd ask Blair. For the moment, it was just another one of the house's mysteries.

I slipped into a robe and tried to relax, but without much success. I wasn't tired enough for a nap before dinner and when I tried to read, I found that I went through several pages without absorbing a word. I put the book aside and went to the window.

Down on the patio, Ryan leaned against the low wall that blocked off the edge of the cliff. It wasn't the first time I noticed him down there. I guess he liked the view. Lifting a bottle to his lips, he tilted his head back as if draining it. His arm swung back then forward and the bottle went whipping into the open air, catching a fragment of the weak sunlight for just an instant before disappearing. I turned from the window, feeling like a voyeur. We were all dealing with Jonathan's death in our own way.

I went back to the bed and lay down, staring at the ceiling. I tried not to think about anything, wishing my mind would just sort of drift away and leave me with at least a few moments of peace, but it was useless. I couldn't stop sorting through the events of the last couple days, trying to make sense of it all.

Time passed slowly, but eventually, there was a knock at the door—Blair calling me for dinner. I put on the outfit I wore before we swam and joined him. I wasn't surprised to see the others milling around the hallway, as if waiting for me. We went down to the dining room as a group.

When we were all seated at the massive table, the door to the hallway opened and we had our first surprise of the evening. Aunt Lydia, seated in a wheelchair, rolled into the room, greeted us all cheerfully, and found her way to the head of the table.

"How are you, Aunt Lydia?" Marcus, seated to her left, asked.

The old woman smiled and it wasn't like any of the smiles she wore before. This one was almost warm, and in my mind, a clear image of what she must have looked like as a young woman formed. "I'm doing well enough, Marcus," she told him. "Thank you for asking."

Elijah appeared with the first course. Marcus, probably just trying to make conversation, brought up how dark it was outside the dining-room windows.

Lydia said, "It's something you grow used to in this part of the world during the winter, especially up here on the mountain. Sometimes, the clouds are so thick we don't see the sun at all for three or four days. Either they don't clear or by the time they do, the sun has already set. It doesn't bother me though; I've come to treasure the long nights. There are so many things one can do at night that you'd never think to do in daylight." She smiled at all of us and began eating.

Nobody wanted to comment on what Aunt Lydia said, but Marcus, still trying to draw her out, asked, "These clouds... think we'll get a storm?"

"Quite possibly." Lydia nodded. "We're about due."

That was an ordinary thing to say, but I couldn't get what she said about *things one can do at night* out of my mind. Glancing around the table, it was clear I wasn't the only one.

Our other meals were quiet, almost somber, but that night's dinner was practically festive. Aunt Lydia talked quite a lot and in a way I never heard before. She was lively and chatty, first telling Marcus about other storms Dacha Orlov weathered and then moving on to the climate in the area before talking about its history. We learned the oil refinery that employed most of Foster's Place wasn't founded by Piotr Orlov, but rather he purchased it from its original owner, who operated it at a level that was just barely profitable. Orlov expanded it, creating jobs and tremendous wealth, earning a commendation from the state's governor back in the nineties.

Looking at me over her raised fork, Lydia said, "That was before you were even born, of course, Holly." I nodded and pretended I was very interested in my salad.

Lydia talked on and on. Marcus and Chelsea hung on every word. There wasn't anyone in the room who didn't realize it was only her money they were interested in.

Ryan was quiet and seemed more focused on his own thoughts than the food or what anyone was talking about. His sister, Nora, was so lifeless that if her eyes weren't open and she didn't occasionally lift her fork or glass, I'd have thought she was still asleep. Chelsea's hope, that Nora would feel better when she woke up, seemed misplaced.

And though Blair and I sat next to each other, as was becoming usual, he paid attention only to whatever food was placed in front of him. I was sure his brain was still churning, though, even if he was keeping his thoughts private.

I ate the dinner Elijah served us, and it was good, but I was too distracted by the big, silent man to really enjoy it. I was very aware that the dynamic between us had shifted and certain he was too.

It started when I forced my way past the butler into Aunt Lydia's room. At the time, Elijah wasn't a concern except as an obstacle. He was so good at being unobtrusive as he went about his work that I never considered him as someone with thoughts and feelings. I know how horrible that sounds, but most of the time, he acted like a silent, efficient machine, and it was easy to think of him that way.

Now, though, as he served our food and cleared empty dishes, there were several strange moments that I can't describe or even really give a name to beyond an *awareness* that wasn't there before. He did his work as well as ever, and mostly he still wore the same professionally blank expression, but at times, when he looked at me, it was altered, just a little, as if he was intentionally letting me see something of how he really felt.

I couldn't grasp enough of what he showed me to recognize it. Was it resentment? Hatred? Maybe he even wanted revenge on me for defying him and forcing my way into Aunt Lydia's room. I didn't know, and I thought I should be afraid. The man was a giant and I knew firsthand how powerful and terrifying he could be.

I wasn't afraid though. Not of Elijah—not as long as we weren't alone, at least. With Aunt Lydia around, I was sure that he would keep whatever personal feelings he had in check and only do the things she asked of him. Whatever he felt about me, I was safe enough. Besides, it might all be in my head and there was already something I could be sure I needed to fear.

Something Lydia said jerked me out of my thoughts. I looked down the table at her and asked, "I'm sorry, what did you say, Aunt Lydia?"

A trace of irritation crossed her face. "I said that I suppose Holly told all of you about our conversation earlier this afternoon."

The room was very still. Everyone was watching Lydia, waiting for whatever came next. "Well," she said finally. "It's all true. I raised your parents as if they were my own children and for my efforts, they tossed me aside like garbage as soon as there was a little money to be made. They're all gone now, so all of you are left to take the brunt of my anger and hatred."

Marcus looked at Chelsea and something unspoken passed between them. Then, to Lydia, he said, "Now, you don't really mean that, Aunt Lydia. I mean—"

"What? What exactly do *you* 'mean', Marcus?" Her eyes met the big man's and there was no question as to whose will was stronger. He looked away immediately. Lydia sipped from her water glass, then gently replaced it on the table. Calmly and quietly she said to all of us as a group, "Why shouldn't I mean what I said? I have no reason to feel kindly or charitably towards any of the Shaw family." She turned on Marcus again. "Can *you* think of why I should?"

"Um, well..." Marcus looked like a little boy caught misbehaving. "We're family," he finished weakly.

Lydia tilted her head and looked down her nose at him. "And I suppose you believe that alone is worth sixty million dollars."

"I don't think money means much to you at all," Chelsea put in.

Slowly, Lydia's gaze shifted to the younger woman, and just as slowly, a smile spread across her face. "You're right, Chelsea dear. The money doesn't mean a thing to me. There's nothing it can buy me that I want or need and I don't have much time left anyway."

Blair looked up from his plate and spoke for the first time since we entered the dining room. "Let's talk about that, as long as we're being so blunt."

"The money?"

"Your health," Blair countered. "You told us you're dying, but you seem pretty healthy to me."

That afternoon I was certain Lydia was going to pass out or even die right there in front of me. I left that part out when I told everyone about the conversation. I wanted to say something to Blair, but it wasn't the time or place.

"Are you really even sick?" Blair asked.

Lydia's smile remained fixed in place. "Doctors have used the expression 'borrowed time.'"

"Does it come and go? Yesterday, you were bedridden, today you're wheeling yourself around just fine."

"Who said I was bedridden?" Lydia asked. "I never did. If you made an assumption, that's no fault of mine."

"Then... you really are dying?" Chelsea asked.

Without turning to her, Lydia said, "You can only hope."

Blair was getting angry again. Color crept into his face. It was slight, but I'd spent enough time with him to recognize it. "Aunt Lydia, you all but told Holly that you want to watch us kill each other off."

Lydia lifted her napkin and dabbed her lips. When she set it down again, the smile was gone. "Did I say that?" She looked up, and though she was no longer smiling, her eyes blazed with delight. Blair was right about Lydia enjoying herself. There was no way to doubt that now. "Are you afraid, Blair?"

"Should I be?"

Aunt Lydia breathed deeply through her nose, eyes locked on Blair. "If you are,"—her gaze swept across the table—"you are perfectly free to leave. I can have Elijah call that boy Rick right now, if you like. There will be no flight to Fairbanks for several days, but there's a motel in town. Of course, I'm sure it's not as comfortable as your rooms here."

"If I decide to leave this house before you die, it'll only be to spoil your fun."

"At last," Lydia said, drawing the words out. The smile returned. "It's all out in the open, isn't it? Our mutual hatred."

Blair shook his head. "I don't hate you. I don't understand you well enough to feel strongly about you one way or the other."

Lydia seemed surprised. "At least you're honest."

"I try to be, despite what people think of lawyers."

Marcus tried to laugh at the joke, but it sounded more sick than amused. Everyone ignored him.

"How do you want this to end, Aunt Lydia?" Blair asked. "Do you really want us all dead, except for whichever one can live with the consequences and the guilt?"

"I don't care, as you put it, one way or the other. I have a great deal of money and none of you have very much at all. Money is power and as long as you're here, in my home, you're all in my power. All I want is to see what comes of it. If you choose to simply wait out the remainder of my life, so be it. If more of you go the way of poor little Jonathan…"

She didn't finish the thought. Next to me, I could feel waves of tension pouring off of Blair's body. Marcus broke in, saying, "Sergeant Goddard thinks some locals killed him."

"No, he doesn't, you goddamned moron! Grow up!" Blair exploded. Marcus's head whirled around and the look he gave his younger brother was a mixture of anger and hurt. Blair jabbed a finger towards Lydia. "*She* told him to lay off us so her little game can play out and he's either on the payroll or so damned scared of her, he's going along with it."

"An investigator must consider all possibilities." Lydia's voice was very cool, very patrician now. "As an attorney, you know that, Blair. Besides, I would never dream of interfering in a police matter. I'm sure Sergeant Goddard is doing his best, even as we speak, to find the murderer. If the guilty party turns out to be one of you, I won't shelter you from him or any other authority. Sergeant Goddard doesn't have an easy job, way out here, away from the most modern methods and from most of his brother officers. Far be it from me to make his work any harder." She lifted her glass and sipped from it, as if to say she was finished with the whole line of discussion.

"You're the murderer."

It was said so quietly, I almost thought I imagined it. But Ryan, sitting next to his sister, definitely heard. He shushed Nora. She ignored him, pushed back from the table, and stood. Without taking her eyes from the plate in front of her, she said, much louder, "You're the murderer. Jonathan died because of you."

Lydia scoffed. "Ridiculous. I've never harmed a hair on anyone's head in my life. All I've done is invite my nieces and nephews into my home and made you the heirs to a great deal of money. If harm comes to any of you, it will be your own doing."

Nora was visibly trembling, her chest rising and falling rapidly with short, shallow breaths. I started to get up, to go to her, but she turned and ran out of the dining room. We heard quick steps crossing the hallway. The sound disappeared when she must have reached the thickly carpeted stairs.

"Are you happy?" Blair asked.

Lydia smiled. It reminded me of a huge snake I saw once, in the zoo, right after feeding time. "Of course I am. I have my dear nieces and nephews with me."

"Then you'll be disappointed when we stop playing your game and check into that motel you mentioned."

The old woman laughed. "You won't do it. It's an option, but you won't go through with it. None of you can afford to." She wagged a finger at Blair. "How much debt do you carry from law school, Blair? How much do you make a year pushing papers and doing the work of the men whose names appear on the briefs you prepare? Do you know how many years it'll take you to pay off those student loans? I do."

Lydia turned her finger on Marcus. "Marcus sells computer software, but he's very bad at it. It's a wonder his wife has stayed with him this long." She pointed at Ryan. "Your cousin, Ryan, is a salesman too. Shall I list all the jobs he's been fired from? Car sales, insurance, even shoes!" She laughed again.

Finally, she looked at me. "And Holly, the best of all of you, I think. I'm not entirely clear on what she does. She's some sort of office girl, but I know how much money she makes and it's barely enough to keep up on the rent and the car payments, and to pay the minimum on all those credit cards she has."

She sneered. "None of you will walk away because none of you will ever have another chance like this. Now..." She clapped her hands and Elijah appeared, as if summoned by magic. Lydia waved a hand. "Clear this away, please. I don't believe any of us has any appetite left."

CHAPTER TWELVE

"She's insane."

"I don't think so."

Blair and I were sitting in lounge chairs by the pool, leaning back, staring up at the blank, black sky.

After Lydia ended dinner, we all went upstairs as a group, collectively worried about Nora. She locked herself in her room again, and no amount of coaxing or pleading would get her to open the door. Ryan wanted to break the door down, but Chelsea suggested we just leave her alone for a while. After some arguing, we all went our separate ways.

I went into my own room, but as soon as I closed the door, Blair knocked and invited me for a walk. It was too cold and too dark to go outside, I pointed out, so he suggested a walk around the pool. I was sure he wanted an excuse to talk about what happened. I had a few things on my mind, too, so I agreed.

Out in the hallway, there was more arguing coming from the room across the hall. Marcus and Chelsea were fighting. I glanced at Blair, but he pretended not to hear so I did the same. On the way down the stairs, we passed Ryan coming up. He clutched a bottle of whiskey to his chest like something precious.

We were all dealing with the situation in different ways and none of them seemed healthy.

Without a moon or any stars, the huge, steamy-damp room we sat in was lit only by the lights on the bottom of the pool, giving the space a shimmery look that I loved. I wished I could enjoy it.

In the half-light, Blair shifted in his chair until he was propped up on his hip, facing me. "You don't think this is crazy? C'mon..."

"I don't think *she's* crazy. Maybe what she's doing is. I don't know. I think she really does hate us though. I didn't get a sense of it until tonight, but I think that's what's bothered me right from the start."

"Yeah, but..." Blair shook his head and fumbled inside his jacket. He extracted a cigarette from a pack, and stuck it in his mouth, but didn't light it. It was the first time I saw him with one since he came into my room right after I arrived.

Without looking at me, he said, "So the kids she sacrificed herself to raise were ungrateful. Horribly, miserably ungrateful. They were little bastards and she has a right to be angry, but I'm sure the same thing happens in thousands of families. How many of those parents try to kill the kids?"

"She didn't," I corrected. "She just ignored them."

"Don't play semantics with me," he snapped, plucking the cigarette from his mouth and angrily flicking it into the darkness. He sighed. "Sorry. You're right, it's just—she's angry at the worst kind of ingrates, and she has a right to be, but none of them are even alive anymore. Shouldn't that end it? Why does it have to come to murder?"

"We're doing the killing, Blair. One of us, anyway. And not for revenge, for money. Sixty million dollars is a good motive." I looked up at the sky, wishing there were stars to see.

Blair was quiet for a couple minutes. I could feel him staring at me through the murky, shifting light. He moved slightly and shadow fell across his eyes, hiding the upper half of his face, like a mask. I realized I could never really be sure of what Blair was thinking, even if he was the closest ally I had. The thought was creepy. I tried to push it away.

"Holly," he said, his voice seeming faraway and hollow, like listening to a bad cellphone connection. "Do you really think one of us killed Jon?"

Sometimes Blair's mind took strange twists. He told Goddard that one of us killing Jonathan was the only way his death made any sense. I didn't know why he was asking me what I thought about it now. His intelligence was sharp, though, and he was constantly trying to work out whatever came next, so he must have had a reason.

"You said it yourself: that's what must have happened."

"I know." He turned to face the clear, blue water of the pool. Alternating bands of light and shadow danced across his face now. "Maybe part of me wants it to not be true just because it's what Lydia seems to want so badly. In theory, it's the only thing that makes sense. Maybe if the money was distributed differently or if we were different people or if this house wasn't in the middle of nowhere... But I've been doing the math all day, over and over, and all the elements put together just don't add up to anything else."

"You're wondering who," I said. It wasn't a question.

Blair nodded. "We all benefit from Jon's death, but who's the one that actually did it? That's where I get stuck. Every option seems impossible." He glanced at me, then looked away again. "You and Nora I wouldn't even consider for a second. Ryan is a big guy, but he's a creampuff. Chelsea is a greedy bitch and I'm sure she can be bloodthirsty, but is she actually capable of killing someone? I don't think she could manage it by herself; the stabbing, yes, but moving Jon's body around?"

"What about Marcus?"

Blair shook his head. "He'd have to help her and I want to

believe that no matter what was on the line, no matter who was asking him to do it, he'd never go that far. At least not to our little brother. Not to Jonathan."

"That leaves everyone out except you."

He nodded again, slowly this time. "That's the same conclusion I came to, except I know I didn't do it."

It felt like we were going around in circles. "Then who did?"

"Aunt Lydia herself."

I let out a huff of annoyance. "You don't believe that. Even if she isn't really bedridden, she doesn't have the strength to do any of that."

"No, but Elijah does. I think we both know he'd do anything she told him to do."

I did have that feeling, and remembering the man's incredible strength when he gripped my arm, I knew he was capable of it and that he probably would do most anything Lydia asked him to. But murder? That was a pretty big step. I said so.

"Maybe, but you have to admit it's possible."

"Okay, it's possible."

I climbed from the lounge chair and moved to the huge window that overlooked the sheer side of Foster's Peak. Weak light, reflected from the shimmering waters of the pool, made spots of snow on the thin band of stone-paved pathway circling the house glow dimly. Beyond that, there was nothing but darkness. It was like we were all alone, floating in space, just this big house filled with people who couldn't trust each other—and maybe one who already killed and was planning to do it again. I shuddered at the thought.

Suddenly, strong hands were around my upper arms. Before I could really register the surprise, Blair turned me, pulled me close, and said, voice low and husky, "Do you want to leave, Holly?"

This close, there seemed to be some inner light behind his pupils, and there were tension lines around both his eyes and his mouth. The wet heat from the pool made the room a little warmer than was comfortable and I could see tiny beads of sweat on Blair's forehead.

"I don't know." I tried to pull away. His hands kept me firmly in place. I was reminded again of Elijah's hands and the way he held me—and the look in his eye at dinner. Blair was starting to scare me. "Let go," I told him.

As if he didn't hear me, he said, "We can beat Lydia at her own game, Holly, and whoever killed Jon too. We stick together, watch out for each other, and we'll both go home rich."

Looking into Blair's eyes, I was afraid of one of my cousins for the first time. I realized how deep the fear I felt since Jonathan's body was found really ran. It was heightened by Elijah and again when Lydia told me her story. Her admitting at dinner that she didn't care if we lived or died just added fuel to the fire. I realized, too, that while Blair was my friend, or at least on the way to becoming one, he was also a rival for Aunt Lydia's money.

Blair's hands began to move, kneading the flesh of my arms, caressing me even as he kept me trapped.

"Please don't. Let go," I said again, afraid and confused. His own rationalizations said he was the one most likely to have killed Jonathan and here I was, alone with him, in a room where any number of accidental-seeming deaths could happen easily.

He didn't let go though. Instead, he pulled me closer, and then his mouth was on mine. His lips parted and I felt his tongue against my lips and then my teeth. I kept them clamped tightly shut and squeezed my eyes closed as hard as I could.

Then it was over. Blair pulled back, but still he didn't release his hold. At least Elijah didn't try to kiss me.

"It's not incest, if that's what you're worried about. We're not related by blood."

Finally, he let go and I stumbled away, opening my eyes and moving to the closest chair. I sank down onto it, feeling weak and helpless. So much happened in the short period since I first boarded the plane back in Ohio, but this wasn't anything I could have expected.

I sat for a long time, breathing deeply, trying to calm myself. I should have gotten up and left, gone back to my room, and secured it the way I did after leaving Lydia's room that afternoon. But I didn't. I couldn't. As much as I wanted to get away from Blair at that moment, part of me kept saying that I could use this —Blair wanted to be my ally and I needed someone I knew I could trust.

"Let's go for a swim."

I looked up to see Blair stepping out of his slacks. He'd already removed his jacket and shirt and placed them, neatly folded, on another chair.

"I don't have my suit," I told him.

Blair folded his slacks and set them with his other clothing. Then he came to me, lifted me gently from the chair and began to undress me down to my underwear. He didn't exactly force me, and I even helped him, but it was like I had no say in the matter. The sense of helplessness was overpowering.

Then we were slipping into the water together. I came back to myself enough that it was a dive and not just falling into the pool.

My body knifed smoothly into the sparkling blue water. I dove deeply. Even though the only lights in the room were on the bottom of the pool, somehow it seemed darker in its depths than it did up on the surface. Sharp pangs of fear sliced through me. I suddenly wanted to be out of the water very badly. I flipped over and kicked towards the light and air far above me.

The deepest end of the pool was the side farthest from the door into the house, and when I broke through the surface of the water, I realized it was also the darkest part of the room. After the heat of the water, even the warm, damp air above felt cool as it swept across my face and shoulders. It was a strange sensation that I wasn't sure I'd ever felt before, and if I wasn't distracted by that feeling, and the thoughts swirling inside my head, I might have had a better idea of what happened next.

All I know for certain is that one of Blair's hands was on my shoulder and the other gripped my wrist. His hands groped upwards, sliding across slick, wet skin, and then without warning, the water was over my head.

Blair's hands disappeared from my body. I thrashed in the water, losing all sense of direction. I almost screamed, but caught myself, knowing instinctively that I'd just be filling my lungs with water. I tried to orient myself, but somehow every direction seemed darker and blacker than the last. I had no idea which was up and which was down, which way would lead me back to the air and which one would kill me if I moved towards it.

I can never go swimming with Blair again, I thought, feeling sad about it, even as I was aware that I might be drowning, never to go swimming again at all.

I kicked at the water, arms flailing like I'd forgotten how to swim. The water churned violently around me and I knew it was my doing. Panic was setting in. The helplessness was back full force.

Then strong fingers were around my wrist, clamping down like iron. Elijah's face sprang to mind. I was lifted from the pool, spewing water like a dolphin blowing, unaware of how much I swallowed until it started pouring out of me.

I fell to my hands and knees on the flagstones surrounding the pool. Through dim and burning eyes, I saw Elijah towering over me. It wasn't my imagination then. I didn't care. All I cared about was that I could breathe again. Air filled my aching lungs even as I was choking up pool water.

The giant butler quickly backed away several steps, giving me room and putting distance between himself and the water, looking at the pool as if he was wary of it. I stayed on hands and knees, gasping and choking. After a minute or two, I was strong enough to get to my feet. My entire body burned with the kind of muscle-ache I only experienced once before, when I tried a spin class and decided I didn't need to be *that* fit. The whole time I was on my knees, weakened, struggling for breath and coughing up water, I felt Elijah's eyes on me. Now he wasn't a monster though—he was my hero. It wouldn't last long, I knew that, but I was grateful that he saved me from whatever happened in the pool.

I met his eyes and said, "Thank you," then turned, gathered up my clothing and padded barefoot back into the house. There was no sign of Blair anywhere along the way.

CHAPTER THIRTEEN

Locked in my room, the chair under the doorknob again, I began to wonder how much of what I experienced was real and how much my fear, and the craziness of everything that happened since arriving in Lydia's house, was making me see things in the worst possible way. I felt sorry for Nora, cracking and giving in to panic, and of course I wanted to help her, but I realized that some little part of me felt superior to her. That part believed I was tougher, braver than my fragile cousin. Now, I didn't know.

I also didn't know what exactly happened in the pool. Blair kissed me, and he undressed me, and then we were in the water. I felt a sudden surge of absolute terror and then...

Then what? Did I really believe Blair tried to drown me? And even if I did, could I swear that's what happened? Could I call Sergeant Goddard and tell him, "My cousin tried to murder me," and be absolutely sure it was true? I didn't want to believe it. I was starting to think of Blair as a friend, at least, if not family.

There was that kiss, too, and what he said afterwards. *It's not incest...*

A chill went through me.

I sat in the darkness, the bed's comforter wrapped tightly around me, trying to remember, to reconstruct everything that happened at the pool. I tried to dredge up details I might have noticed but wasn't aware of in the moment. Every time I went through the sequence, though, it ended the same way. Blair pulling me into the pool with him, his hands on my body, the water suddenly over my head.

And just as suddenly there was Elijah, his strong grip lifting me from the water one-handed, as if I was a small child. I was amazed—almost stunned, really—when I realized who my savior was. I never thought I'd be glad to see the man, but I was. If I was alone and he appeared like that in any other context, I'd at least be uncomfortable, Aunt Lydia's control over him or not.

I wondered how long Elijah watched us, how much he saw and how much he heard. Was it just a coincidence he was there or was he following us? And if he was, did he intend to spy on us or did he somehow feel I was in danger, like he did Lydia?

I just didn't know anything I could be absolutely sure of. I couldn't know what was in Elijah's mind and I couldn't say what Blair was actually trying to do. And where did he go? When I left the pool, he was nowhere to be found.

I let out a breath and squeezed my eyes tightly against the darkness. All I had were pieces of a puzzle and how I felt about each of them. And even then, I wasn't entirely sure of my own feelings.

Knocking on the door brought me out of my thoughts. It was quickly followed by Blair's voice whispering, "Hey, Holly! Are you in there?" The doorknob rattled. "Can I talk to you? Please open the door. I know you're in there."

My heart thumped hard in my chest and for an instant, it felt like water was closing over my head again. I took a deep breath and let it out slowly. I didn't really want to talk to Blair, not until I had things sorted out better in my own mind. I pulled the comforter closer. I was safe, Blair couldn't get in here. Nobody could get in unless I opened the door for them.

"Holly?"

A couple of minutes passed, but Blair was still outside the door. "Holly..." he said. "If this is about that kiss, about what I said, I'm sorry. I was out of line."

If Blair really did try to drown me, maybe this was part of it—framing it as a misunderstanding. *"I kissed her, yes, but of course I never tried to drown her,"* he could say. *"She just got scared and overreacted."*

His voice came again. "Holly!" It sounded more urgent this time. I still didn't answer.

I slid from the bed, the comforter draped over my shoulders, and stood by the door, listening. If Blair knew I was there, he didn't give any sign. He didn't say another word and after another minute or so, I heard his footsteps moving down the hall, then a door open and close.

I let out a breath that I didn't realize I was holding, and felt every muscle in my body unclench. Now, I really was safe. Whatever Blair was, murderer or just too aggressive, I didn't think he'd try anything again that night.

I unwrapped myself from the comforter, tossed it onto the bed, and went into the bathroom. I took a long hot shower, then put on the warmest pajamas I had with me, and climbed into bed.

I tried not to think about anything while I was in the bathroom, but now, alone again in the darkness, it was impossible to shut my brain off.

Was Blair a murderer? Could he have killed his own brother? The pain and anger he felt was real, I was sure of that, but I didn't think he could have hurt Jonathan. But that didn't mean he wasn't capable of hurting someone else. It wasn't impossible for two people to have the same idea, especially when it was so obvious.

I didn't want to believe it, so I chose not to. Blair wasn't a murderer, he was just someone I rejected. I decided that's how I would have to treat him from now on.

I finally fell asleep with that thought lodged in my resolve.

In the morning, I woke up exhausted. I know I slept, because I remembered having dreamt, though I couldn't remember what those dreams were about—only that they were weird and I wanted to wake up from them. I got my wish, but first thing in the morning, the situation didn't seem much better.

I made the bed—I still hadn't seen the maid—stripped off my pajamas and got into the shower. The hot water felt so nice that I didn't want to get out. After I dressed, I removed the chair from under the doorknob and went out into the hallway. All the other doors were closed. I didn't listen at any of the doors, but I got the feeling that there was no one behind any of them.

There was no one in the main hallway on the first floor either. I went into the dining room, but it, too, was empty. There was the sound of distant voices behind the door to the kitchen, but I was hesitant to just walk in there and ask for breakfast. I never met Eleonore, had only seen her the one time, and I didn't want to seem demanding.

I went back out into the hallway, wondering what to do with myself. I was so lost in my thoughts for a moment, already comfortable with the idea that I was more or less alone, that the voice startled me. "Miss Shaw?"

I turned and saw Rick, the gypsy cab driver who brought me to the big house on the mountain, standing in the big archway to the front entrance. He was wearing the same leather jacket as when I first met him, but he'd added a baseball cap with a Seattle Seahawks logo. He was still very handsome. His dark eyes sparkled and he grinned sheepishly at me. "I'm always scaring you. I'm sorry."

"No, it's..." He startled me more than anything else, but it wasn't really his fault. I didn't want to explain though. He probably already knew about Jonathan's death, so I was sure he could guess.

"What are you doing here?" I asked, changing the subject.

"Oh, I ran up some mail."

"Mail?" Was he a postman too?

"Yeah," he nodded, "Mrs. Orlov's got a P.O. box, but these folks don't get into town very much, so I bring it up once a week."

Now that Rick mentioned it, I realized I hadn't seen any sort of vehicle here. There wasn't even a place to put a car or truck—no garage, or even a carport—that I was aware of. That seemed more than just odd.

"Plus," Rick added, "I wanted to see the spot where... you know." He seemed a little embarrassed by the admission.

"Where my cousin died, you mean?"

The young man winced. "Well, when you put it like that it makes me sound like a ghoul or something. I'm kind of a true-crime buff, though, and we don't really get much crime around here." He shrugged.

Rick was an outsider, someone without any stake in anything that happened here. I knew him even less than I knew my cousins, but he was friendly and despite my initial impression of him, I decided he was harmless enough. He might make a good sounding board. I had to take a chance and trust someone.

I sat in one of the chairs lining the hallway and invited Rick to do the same. He hesitated a moment, then joined me. I looked at him for the space of several breaths as he looked right back. A grin split his face, showing me straight, very white teeth. "So...?" he asked.

"So you know a lot about crime and stuff?"

He shrugged. "As much as anyone who watches Investigation Discovery, I guess."

"Did you talk to anyone… about what happened?"

Rick nodded. *"Everyone's* talking about it. Everyone around here knows Mrs. Orlov, and everybody knows everybody else's business, so, yeah, people are talking."

"Well," I paused, all of a sudden unsure. Did I really want to give him fuel for the rumor mill? I decided it couldn't be helped. "What do you think?"

Rick lifted his shoulders again. It was very expressive. He added, "I think Sergeant Goddard will do his best to sort it all out."

"Do you think it was someone inside this house or someone from town?" I didn't mean to go that far, but it just sort of came out.

"From town?" Rick looked a little surprised. "I mean… Anything's possible. There's some rough dudes around here, you know. Especially up at the refinery. That kind of work doesn't attract the most civilized guys."

I looked at my shoes; they were the same soft-soled shoes I wore the first day I was in the house. "I guess I wouldn't know. I barely even got a look at the town," I told him.

"That's right," Rick said, as if just realizing it for himself. "I was in a pretty big hurry to get you out here, but it was orders from Mrs. Orlov—if you showed up, I mean."

We were quiet for a moment. I didn't have anything more to say, and I supposed Rick didn't either.

"Hey, listen."

I looked up. Rick was watching me, his eyes bright again. "You wanna see it? Foster's Place."

I looked past him, through the arch to the front door. My eyes roamed around the room, taking in the expensive furniture, the artwork, the framed photographs. It was a beautiful room, but it was empty and cold, despite the roaring of the heating system and the small fire in the hearth. The rest of the house was the same: everything was beautifully constructed and very valuable, but had no soul. This was a house, but it wasn't a home. It certainly wasn't mine or my cousins' and I wasn't even sure it was Aunt Lydia's. Just then, the thought of staying in it, living here, until Lydia passed away was too much to even consider.

I stood up. "You don't mind?"

He grinned. "Mind? I'd be thrilled. I don't have much going on today, so you'd be doing me a favor, keeping me busy."

"I'll change my shoes and get my coat."

Rick's old Ford barreled down the mountain going even faster and more recklessly along the steep, winding road than when he brought me up. We raced across the plains separating Foster's Peak from Foster's Place, and then we were on the same passingly familiar street I saw when he drove me from the tiny airport. I saw the same little stores and houses lining the street, and what were probably the same cars and trucks jammed up against the curb, that I saw two days earlier. Now, though, they didn't look shabby or old. They looked real and comforting.

The Explorer turned down a side street that was much narrower than the main road. There were fewer buildings along this street, but they were larger. Most of them looked like warehouses, although I did spot an auto-body shop.

"Where are we going?" I asked.

Eyes on the road, Rick answered, "You haven't eaten yet, have you?" He glanced over. "It's early, but this place'll open for me."

"For you?"

Rick turned from the road long enough to throw me a wink. He spun the wheel, applied the brakes, and came to a sliding stop in the gravel parking lot of a small, two-story building with a wood-shingled awning and a sign that read CITY CAFÉ. The building looked like it started life as a house, and from the curtains in the upper windows, I guessed there was still an apartment up there.

"C'mon." Rick waved me after him; he was already out of the truck and heading around the side of the building.

We went through a door marked PRIVATE – EMPLOYEES ONLY and directly into the restaurant's kitchen. There were three people working, getting ready for the start of the business day. A middle-aged woman with thick black hair pulled into a messy bun at the base of her neck stood in a doorway off to one side, holding a sheet of paper in one hand and the handset of a cordless phone in the other.

"Hey, Mimi!" Rick smiled as he flapped his hand in greeting and made his way across the kitchen like he owned the place.

The woman looked up, frowned slightly, but then must have seen who it was because her expression lightened. She said a hurried goodbye to whoever she was talking to on the phone and returned Rick's greeting. Taking Rick's hand lightly, she looked at me over his shoulder. "Is this your new girlfriend?"

He laughed. "You're my girl, you know that. No, this is Holly Shaw. She's visiting." He looked to me, gestured in my direction then at the woman, and added, "Holly, this is Mimi Foxe, she makes the best damned eggs Benedict you ever had."

The woman, Mimi, frowned. "For Sunday brunch only. You know that."

"Come on, I promised!"

Rick's back was to me, so I couldn't see his expression, but whatever it was, it worked. Mimi's face softened and her expression turned to good-natured resignation. "All right, okay. Just this once," she warned, waggling a finger.

"You're the best, Mimi. Two, please, and coffee." Grinning, Rick led me to the dining area.

The room was cozy, with maybe a dozen tables, all covered in white cloth, and a breakfast bar in one corner that could seat another six people. The walls had both framed, color photos of wildlife scenes and black-and-white photographs of what must have been the refinery. It seemed strange to decorate with those, but I supposed all the businesses in the area owed it their livelihoods.

At a table near the kitchen doorway, Rick pulled out a chair for me, then sat opposite.

"Is she really your girlfriend?" I asked.

The young man chuckled. "I have a lot of girlfriends, but I'm not that lucky. No, Mimi's a friend of my mom's. I've known her since I was a kid."

"Oh," I said. "She seems nice."

"She's the best," Rick agreed.

We made small talk while waiting for the food. The refinery was the only big employer in the area, as I guessed. Most people either worked there or in small places of their own, like this café. There was some tourism, but not much. Mostly hunters and some fishermen. "I know all the best fishing spots," he bragged. "Every summer, I pick up some cash taking groups from the lower forty-eight around to them."

"That must be nice. Do you hunt too? Or just fish."

"Just fish." Something passed across his face. "I don't really like guns. I know how to dress a deer or a moose, though, if I have to for a client. Sometimes they come out here and just want to do the shooting without the stuff that comes after, and I'll get messy if the price is right."

"Oh."

"Surprised that not all Alaskans are gun-happy rednecks?" He was smiling, but there was an edge in his voice.

"Not at all."

The food came, brought out by Mimi herself. Eggs Benedict in hollandaise, but instead of ham or bacon, the meat was crab cakes. It was delicious. We ate and talked. I tried to keep it light. I was feeling better, being away from Dacha Orlov, and the people currently living in it. Rick was a pleasant breakfast companion and I didn't want to think about anything of importance—about what might happen later that day or tomorrow or any other day. Not then.

While we ate, I saw Mimi Foxe peeking through a crack in the kitchen doorway. She seemed very interested in us, though I was sure it was mostly me, if she knew Rick most of his life. It reminded me of what he said before, that it was a small town and everyone knew everything that happened.

When we were done eating Rick shouted his thanks and left through the front door without making any attempt to pay for our food. I wasn't sure about the arrangements he had, but at the very least, I wanted to show my appreciation, so I dug into my coat pocket, took a twenty from my wallet, and slipped it beneath my plate. Then I shrugged my coat on and followed Rick out to the street.

We climbed back into his Explorer and he drove, more slowly this time, back towards the main road. He parked by a tiny storefront bank. As we got out of the car, wind raced down the street, making me shiver. Being cold and in the open air still felt better than being closed up in that house on the mountain though.

"Let's take a walk," Rick suggested.

We walked around, but there wasn't much to see. A clothing store; a general store that was like an unbranded Dollar General or a miniature Walmart; a small grocery store; a pizza place, still not open for the day; the post office; three different restaurant-bars all along the same strip of road. The trip took us down one side of the street and then up the other. It took less than half an hour, even with Rick giving commentary, to see it all.

"Sorry, I guess that's about it," he said as we stood by his truck.

"Don't be sorry." I smiled. "It was good just getting out of that house."

"I can imagine." He looked unsure as he added, "So, do you want to go back or…?"

"Is there anywhere else to go?"

"We could just drive around. You might not get another chance to see the area."

I opened the door of his car. "Let's go then." Anything was better than going right back to Lydia's house. There was still too much there I didn't want to face.

Rick drove out of town, taking the highway towards the mountain. At the fork he showed me that first morning, he turned. The area on my right, as we headed north, was mostly flat, with long grasses poking up through the snow, but here and there were clusters of scrawny trees and bushes. On my left, towards the mountain, the land was steeper, turning into hills in the near distance. Rick was right. There wasn't much to see. But it was pleasant being in the car, feeling the hum of the engine and the vibration of the tires against the asphalt. I started to relax.

I was more relaxed than I realized because I woke up suddenly, scared, not knowing where I was.

"Whoa, whoa," Rick said. I turned and saw him sitting behind the wheel, his hands raised in front of his chest as if he was surrendering. "You're okay. You just fell asleep. You looked so peaceful I didn't have the heart to wake you."

"What time is it?" I asked, trying to push the cobwebs from my brain. My mouth tasted terrible. I must have been asleep for a while.

"Almost three o'clock."

I slept for more than five hours? In the car of an almost total stranger? Heat rose to my cheeks. I felt stupid, careless, and very embarrassed. "I'm sorry."

"Don't be." Rick grinned. "You needed the nap. Like I said before, I had nothing better to do. Taking care of a beautiful girl isn't exactly a bad time, you know?"

A flash of anger mixed with the shame and embarrassment. I gave him a sharp look.

"Sorry, sorry," he said. "Too far again? I got a big mouth." He turned the engine over. I looked through the windshield and saw we were parked in the City Café lot. There were no lights on inside the building. I slept through their entire operating hours, I guess.

"You ready to go home?" Rick asked.

Home. I knew if I said the word out loud, it would leave another bad taste. I didn't want to think of Lydia's house that way, but if I wanted any of the money, I supposed I would have to for the time being.

"Not yet," I said. Looking at Rick, I asked, "Is there any place else at all we could go?"

"Wanna get a drink?"

I said I did.

He took us to one of the bars on the main road. It was a big, dimly lit room that we entered by going down a flight of steps from the sidewalk. It must have been the basement of the building originally, and aside from adding a bar, tables, chairs and a lot of neon beer signs, not much else was done to it. Even though it was still fairly early, there were a number of customers at the tables, and some at the bar. An old-fashioned jukebox stood in a corner, pumping a Johnny Cash song into the air. It was as far from the cold, sterile elegance of Dacha Orlov as I could imagine. I liked it very much.

While I found a table, Rick went to the bar. He returned with two foaming glasses of beer. It was strong, and dark, and hoppy, with enough carbonation that it tickled my nose. I sneezed. Rick laughed. "Local brew—Black Gold Brewing Company. Guy I know started it up a couple years ago, after he had to retire from the refinery. He busted his leg up pretty bad, but that just gave him plenty of time to sit around and drink, thinking this stuff up." He sipped from his glass then made a satisfied sound.

"You know a lot of people."

"It's a—"

"I know," I broke in with a smile. "A small town."

The Cash song ended and was replaced by something I didn't recognize—some sort of hard-driving rock song that reminded me of the 1970s, or at least what I knew of it. It was much louder than the first song and I had to raise my voice to tell Rick, "I like this place!"

"I'm glad!" he shouted back.

A girl appeared alongside the table, wearing a black T-shirt, tight skinny jeans and a white apron tied around a tiny waist. She was petite and dark and pretty. She could have been Rick's sister, but I knew she wasn't from the way she looked at him, and the glare she threw at me. She bent down and whispered something into Rick's ear, but he waved her away.

"One of your girlfriends?" I shouted over the music.

Rick nodded. "Sometimes!"

"She's beautiful."

"Not as beautiful as you, Holly." He grinned like a little boy, then sipped beer. When he lowered the glass, there was foam on his upper lip and he was still smiling.

I didn't know if he was joking or serious. I could never tell because everything he said came with a laugh or a grin. He was handsome and charming, but maybe that was just how he got through life. It still bothered me that I couldn't tell if he meant his flirting or not though. First Blair and now Rick...

"I mean it," Rick said, leaning across the table so I could hear him better. "I wanna get to know you." His hand snaked out towards mine. I moved my hand into my lap to avoid it.

"Your watch," I said.

"What?" He held a hand to his ear, as if he didn't hear me.

"Your watch! It's gone!" I said, louder and pointing at his bare left wrist. The gold watch he wore when I first met him was missing, leaving a slightly paler band on his skin.

"Oh, damn!" he said, then scowled and rubbed his wrist where the watch was, as if maybe it had just turned invisible.

I started to ask him when he knew he last had it, glad for a chance to switch the subject away from his feelings, but I looked up and spotted someone I never could have pictured in this warm, lively place. Elijah, wearing a shiny black parka big enough to keep a small family warm, stood in the doorway across the room.

CHAPTER FOURTEEN

Rick looked over his shoulder, then turned back to me, standing in the same motion. Grabbing my arm, he tugged me across the room, aiming for a curtained door near the end of the bar.

He pulled me along, moving fast. I had trouble following as he weaved around tables and other customers. I almost tripped more than once, but I didn't mind. My only thought was the hope that I spotted Elijah before he saw us.

Ducking beneath the curtains, we went through a storage room, then up a steep, narrow flight of stairs that opened onto an alley behind the bar. I was surprised that it was dark outside; I forgot for a while exactly where we were and how far north Foster's Place was. My breath was coming hard, steaming in the air. Rick pulled me to the mouth of the alley, where I leaned against the building, trying to catch my breath. I thought I was in decent shape, but surprise and running were a bad combination for anyone who didn't run regularly.

"What does he want?" Rick said, close to my ear.

I shook my head, panting, "I don't know. Maybe Aunt Lydia sent him." The pressure in my lungs was starting to fade. I straightened my upper body, my hips still against the wall. "How did he find me though?"

"If you weren't at the house, he must have figured you'd be in town, and he must have guessed you'd be with me because there's no way you could walk. All he had to do was find my truck and then check the places I might be."

Rick looked around the corner. "It's clear." He turned. "What do you want to do? I could take you back to Mrs. Orlov's or I could bring you to the motel, if you want. He'd probably find you again, but it'd give you some breathing room."

What did I want? That was a big question. I wanted to run away from that strange, sterile house on the mountain, away from the cold, grinning old woman who all but told me and my cousins that she wanted us to die.

I also wanted the money though. I never really thought much about money, besides the kind of dreams everyone has about being rich. Things like college loans, rent, car payments, and the twenty-thousand-odd dollars in credit card debt a very stupid, eighteen-year-old me racked up the minute I left home all came to mind. I thought of the crappy office job I would be going back to, making thirty-one thousand dollars a year before taxes. How long would it take me to pay off college and those credit cards?

I wanted to run, to forget about my weird, creepy aunt and just go back to my life—but did I really want all the things that would mean? Not just for right now, but for the future. Lydia said I'd never have another chance like this and it was true. Running away now would mean giving up the only opportunity I'd ever have to be truly free.

In the dim light of the alley, Rick watched me intently, his dark eyes searching my face. "Take me back," I told him.

"If that's what you want. C'mon." He grabbed my hand and pulled me out of the alley.

The Ford was parked around the corner, a short distance down from the bar. Rick led the way, still holding my hand.

Another time, I'd be angry or at least surprised, but now it was comforting, knowing it wasn't just me versus Elijah. I'd been down that road and I didn't want to take it again.

Rick stopped in the shadowed doorway of a closed beauty salon, staring ahead of us, making sure Elijah hadn't somehow beaten us back to the truck. The Explorer sat in a place where lights from the street and one of the buildings converged to shine almost directly on it. There was nobody on the sidewalk, nobody in the street, and unless they were crouching down on the other side of the truck, nobody by the SUV, either. I let out a sigh of relief.

Rick tugged lightly at my hand, giving me a signal. We ran for the truck. My foot hit a patch of slush and almost went out from under me, but Rick pulled harder and kept me upright; I managed to find my balance and stumble along after him.

Then we were inside the Ford and Rick had the key in the ignition. The engine turned over once, coughed, sputtered, and then died. "Are you fucking kidding me?" His voice low and harsh.

Rick tried again, but the result was the same. A huge shadow fell over him. I saw it first and if life was like a horror movie, I would have screamed, warning Rick. I didn't though. I couldn't. The shock was paralyzing. I had sense of being a small child caught in a nightmare and Elijah was the boogeyman. I tried to say something but then the driver's side door was opening, fistfuls of Rick's jacket were in Elijah's hands, and the giant man was dragging the smaller one out of the vehicle.

I finally found a scream. It burst out of me as I scrambled over the console to the driver's side, trying to grab hold of Rick, to pull him back into the vehicle, but I couldn't even get a good grip before Elijah swung him around and tossed him into the piled-up snow at the edge of the sidewalk.

Rick was back on his feet almost instantly, driving forward, his fists darting out. The bigger man took a punch on his chest, then another, but seemed not to even feel them. Elijah swung a single, massive fist that Rick ducked beneath, then stepped back, giving himself room to watch Rick's next move. Neither of them said anything and there were no sounds but feet shuffling in slush and snow, and Rick's heavy breathing.

Rick feinted, then leapt back out of Elijah's long reach, before lunging forward again, his hands flashing. Elijah took the first punch on his chest again, but before Rick could retract his fist, Elijah grabbed his arm, shifting until he held the smaller man's wrist, exactly as he did mine. He swung Rick around, wrapping his other arm around Rick's throat to keep him in place, and then, his back to me, made a short, swift jerking motion. I could actually hear the sound of bone snapping; Rick's scream was only an instant behind it. I thought I was going to be sick.

Elijah wasn't through. He pivoted towards the Ford, swinging Rick around and pinning him against the side of the truck, his forearm against the younger man's throat. Rick thrashed, his arms and legs jerking like he was having some sort of spasm.

I shrieked, "Let him go! Let him go!" hoping someone would hear and come help. No one did. The streets were as deserted now as we thought they were when we ran to the car.

Elijah let go of Rick. The slim, handsome man's body slid down the side of the Ford and into the snow. Then the butler turned. I scrambled backwards to the passenger seat. The panic brought on by the violence I witnessed was overpowering. Somehow, Elijah managed to wedge his monstrous frame into the driver's seat. He closed the door and turned the key. When he did, the engine coughed then caught, as if it was just waiting for him instead of its rightful owner.

My heart thumped in my chest and I couldn't take my eyes off of Elijah as he backed the car into the street and turned in the direction of Foster's Peak. The feeling of victory I had when I outsmarted him in front of Lydia's room was so distant it might as well have happened to someone else. I was much braver in a house full of relatives than I was alone with the man in a stolen car.

Elijah's driving was jerky at first, as if he wasn't sure about the correct pressure to use on the gas pedal and brakes, but by the time we were outside of town and racing through the darkened, snow-covered prairie, he worked it out and the ride was as swift and smooth as when Rick drove.

That didn't make me feel any safer.

Rick's scream and the sound of his arm breaking echoed in my ears. The memory of him lying helpless in the street was lodged inside my brain. And all the while, I sat staring straight ahead into the night, silent, not daring to make a sound or even to look at my kidnapper.

With only the Ford's headlights leading the way, I felt suspended in the black mass of the night, trapped with a monster from my imagination. Elijah was very real though. He never said a word, but I heard him breathing heavily and rasping, and as he drove, occasionally he grunted, as if surprised by some part of the vehicle's operation.

The trip to Dacha Orlov seemed to take forever. The way Elijah drove, it was probably only twenty minutes, but everything was unreal. The only thing I knew for sure was that I was completely in Elijah's power, but for now, at least, I probably wasn't in any danger. I couldn't bring myself to imagine what would happen when we reached the house. All I could do was try to ride out the present and hope.

We climbed the mountain, winding up along the narrow road, and then there was the crunch of gravel under the truck's tires. The SUV slowed and rolled to a stop, right at the bottom of the stairs to the wide porch that wrapped around the front of the house. Through the windshield, Dacha Orlov loomed like a shadow darker than the night. Only a light over the porch pushed back the darkness, and it seemed more like a lure, designed to trick the unwary into entering, than an invitation to warmth and safety.

Elijah opened his door, came around the front of the Ford, and opened mine. "We're home," he announced. There was a weird undertone in his voice that I hadn't heard before. I couldn't look at him. I was more afraid than ever of what I might see.

"Will you please step down, Miss Shaw?" he asked.

I couldn't ignore him forever, but I was too scared to do anything, even something so simple. Elijah hesitated, too, as if unsure of what came next. He took a deep breath, and then I was in his arms, one hand beneath my knees and the other around my shoulders in a princess carry. Light exploded inside my memory and I remembered, very vaguely, my father carrying me to bed like this when I was a toddler. It should have been a warm, happy memory, but it was like a bolt of lightning through my chest.

Elijah carried me to the porch, through the front door, and into the main hallway. There was nobody around to see what must have been a shameful scene. In fact, the entire house felt silent and empty, even more than it did that morning. I didn't know what time it was, but I doubted they were all in bed. It didn't matter. Nobody could have stopped Elijah except maybe Aunt Lydia and for all I knew, he was only acting on her orders.

Elijah carried me up the stairs. I thought maybe he'd take me to Lydia's room, but on the second-floor landing, he turned down the hallway and went to my door. The other doors were all closed. No one could know what was happening, and there was no one to stand in Elijah's way. Even if they knew, would they? Marcus, Blair, or Ryan were all bigger men than Rick, but I doubted they could stand up to Elijah any better than he did.

Elijah opened my door, stepped inside, and deposited me on the bed. I'd been in a half-hypnotized state, but back in more familiar surroundings, I found some of my will again. I scrabbled across the double bed, slipped over the far side and put the mattress between us. Looking at Elijah now, I knew that Lydia didn't order him to bring me back to the house.

Elijah rolled his shoulders, as if working out a kink, though my weight must have been nothing for him. Then he rose to his full height, lit from the side by the light from the doorway. I thought of old, black-and-white horror movies. Those monsters weren't real though.

The man's lips were moving, but at first, I couldn't hear any words. Slowly, his voice got louder. "Miss Shaw... Holly. You shouldn't go off alone like that. There are dangerous people around, and nobody wants to see you hurt."

My breath caught in my throat when I tried to speak, but I managed to force the words out. "No one here's as dangerous as you."

"Holly... you'll be rich soon, if you can survive." He lowered his gaze to the bedspread. "Your cousin is dead, and maybe more people will die, but I can protect you, like I've protected Mrs. Orlov all these years."

He wasn't wrong when he said that someone among us was dangerous, but it was hard to take him seriously. I didn't find any of this funny though. It was terrifying in a vivid and devastatingly personal way.

The man—this man who might be a murderer; I hadn't forgotten about Rick—wanted me to answer him, I knew that, but the only response I had wasn't what he wanted to hear. After what he did to Rick, I couldn't possibly say it out loud. I'm sure he knew though. His face was turned away, but I could imagine his expression.

Elijah started towards the hall. In the doorway, he stopped and, without turning, said, "Just remember who your friend in this house is."

Then he closed the door and was gone.

CHAPTER FIFTEEN

In the morning, there were two fewer people in the house.

I was in the dining room, having breakfast with Marcus and Blair. After what happened the night before, I didn't want to be by myself again, not unless I was safely locked in my own room. Maybe not even locked doors would stop Elijah, but I was sure he wouldn't try anything as long as some of Aunt Lydia's other guests were around me.

All night long, I lay awake, thinking about Rick, wondering if he was okay—if he was even alive. I wanted to call the police, tell Sergeant Goddard or his partner what happened, but there was no cellphone service up on the mountain and I didn't even know if 911 would work here. Once, sometime in the early morning hours, I lifted the receiver of the phone on my dresser to see if I could get an outside line. Elijah's voice immediately said, "Yes?" I slammed the phone back down then returned to bed. It was hopeless. All I could do was say a prayer for Rick, a prayer that someone found and helped him.

Marcus was saying, "I got through to my guy at the bank first thing this morning."

Blair ignored him, focusing on his scrambled eggs.

"He says it's all kosher," Marcus went on. "He checked on everything, said the money is definitely on deposit at Chase, listed under all our names, and that his buddy there says the conditions for disbursement are exactly what Shelton told us they were."

"Well, now you can relax and start planning how to spend it all," Blair said bitterly. "Maybe we can all go in on a nice mausoleum for Jon."

"Don't be like that, Blair." Marcus sounded hurt. "I'm just as upset as you are, but he's gone and we're still here and there's a lot to think about for the future. For all of our futures."

Blair put his fork down and looked at his brother. "Like what?"

"Like what about your job, back home? You gonna keep working for Seaver and Howe?"

"Screw Seaver and Howe." There was no anger; Blair just sounded tired.

"You're right," Marcus agreed, nodding. "The hell with working. I'm gonna retire and finally start enjoying my life."

Blair said, "Now all you have to do is make sure you survive so you get a chance to." He lifted his coffee cup and slurped loudly.

Blair was in a particularly foul mood this morning. I couldn't blame him, but I wanted to talk to him, to straighten out what happened between us and tell him what Elijah did. When I greeted him on entering the dining room, though, he ignored me. I wanted to patch things up. I couldn't lose my only ally in that house.

"All I have to do," Marcus said slowly, "is outlast Aunt Lydia. I think I can do that. It should be simple. If we stick together, we all can."

"Where are Chelsea, Ryan, and Nora?" I asked, joining the conversation.

Marcus turned to me. "Chelsea went to go see about the other two." He lifted a forkful of fried potatoes and continued. "Ryan was really trying one on yesterday. Middle of the day, he stumbled out of his room and banged on our door, thinking it was a bathroom for some reason. Scared the hell out of me. I had to help him back to the can in his room then put him to bed." He popped the potatoes into his mouth.

"What about Nora?" It sounded like Ryan was cracking under the strain, but I was more worried about his sister. The memory of her full-body panic attack was as fresh in my mind as my own fear from the night before.

Marcus shrugged. "Still holed up in her room last I knew. She didn't come to dinner last night and Ryan was still too zonked, I guess." He gestured towards me with his fork. "For that matter, where were you?"

I was saved from having to answer by Chelsea marching into the room, announcing, "Nora's gone. Ryan too."

Blair and I turned to Chelsea. Her husband took on the expression of a dog trying to figure out a magic trick. Marcus asked, "What do you mean?"

"Exactly what I said, dear." She put a nasty little emphasis on the last word. "This whole time, since last night, we've just assumed Nora was up in her room. After that attack she had, I was getting pretty worried, but when I knocked on the door yesterday afternoon, she said she was fine, she just wanted to be left alone. Now, the door's unlocked, her things are gone, and I found this." She waved a slip of paper.

"Let me see." Blair thrust out his hand. Chelsea passed the paper to him and he read aloud, "'I can't stand it anymore. The money doesn't matter to me. I'm going home.'" He glanced at me, then his brother. "It's signed Nora Hill."

"So she's gone then." Marcus tried to hide his glee that the money would now only be split four ways, but he wasn't doing a very good job of it.

"How?" Blair asked. "Did that kid, Rick, come to pick her up? It must have been the middle of the night."

"No." I shook my head. "He couldn't have, he—"

Elijah entered the room, coming from the kitchen. He was carrying a fresh pot of coffee and a plate of cinnamon buns. They smelled incredible, but suddenly, I wasn't hungry at all. The butler didn't say a word as he set the coffee and buns on the table, but I knew he was watching me. I could feel the weight of his gaze. I didn't quite manage to suppress my revulsion.

When Elijah was gone, Blair asked, "Why couldn't he? And if he didn't, how did Nora and Ryan leave?"

"I think I know, but I'll tell you later." I never believed in psychic powers, but I was trying hard to send Blair a telepathic message, willing him with all my might to understand that I didn't want to say anything where Elijah might hear us. Somehow, he seemed to get it, muttering, "Later then."

"So, Ryan went with Nora?" Marcus asked through a mouthful of eggs.

Chelsea cocked one hip and put her hand on it, twirling one finger of the other in the air. "That's the screwy thing. Nora's stuff is all gone, but Ryan's is still in his room."

Marcus seemed to have difficulty swallowing. His eyes swung from me to Blair. He asked Chelsea, "Did you look anywhere else?"

She shook her head.

As a group, we went upstairs and into Ryan's room. The bed had been slept in recently; the sheets were wrinkled and the pillow had an indentation from his head. All of his toiletries were still in his bathroom: toothbrush, toothpaste, electric shaver, deodorant spray. A white, vomit-stained T-shirt and a pair of plaid boxer shorts hung from the shower rod.

"His suitcases are still in here," Blair called from the doorway of the closet. "And there's still clothes on the hangers."

"Same here." Chelsea was at the dresser, one hand still rifling through an open drawer. She turned and added, "His wallet and phone are both still in here. If he did leave, he didn't take a thing but the clothes on his back."

A tiny finger of ice poked around inside my belly. "If he even had that."

"What?" she asked.

"Look in the bathroom. There's a shirt and underwear hanging. They're stained all over." I looked at Marcus. "What was he wearing when you helped him?"

"A T-shirt and boxers."

"That's what's in there. Go look."

I stepped out of the bathroom and went to stand by the bed. All three of them converged, poking their heads inside to confirm for themselves. "I think that's them," Marcus said quietly. He moved away from the door. "He must have puked after I put him to bed and tried to clean himself up."

"So what happened?" Chelsea demanded. "Did Nora drag him away buck naked?"

"Look," Marcus began. "Let's not ask for trouble, okay? All we know for sure is that the two of them are gone and now the split is four ways instead of six." He said it slowly, as if he knew he was treading on thin ice. "We know Nora's gone—she left us that note. It's reasonable to assume she took her brother, isn't it?"

Anger flared in Blair's eyes. "You selfish son of a bitch." He turned and stomped out of the room. Chelsea looked at her husband; she was obviously disgusted with him too. She followed Blair.

I joined them in the hallway. "We'll have to look. I don't really want to wander around by myself, though..." I looked to Blair, but he wouldn't meet my eyes.

Marcus came out into the hallway, saying, "Listen, you guys, all I meant was—"

"Oh, shut up!" Chelsea grabbed his arm and practically

dragged him towards the stairs. "Just come with me and keep your fat mouth closed."

"I guess that leaves the two of us," Blair said without any enthusiasm. "Let's go." He started down the stairs without waiting to see if I followed.

In the huge first-floor hallway, we split into pairs. Chelsea and Marcus went towards the pool while Blair and I planned to search the rooms off the main part of the house. I was a little nervous being alone with Blair after what happened between us, but I was also glad for a chance to talk.

We searched the family room, then the library, without finding any sign anyone was recently in either. In both rooms, I tried to talk to Blair, but he put me off with single-word answers or by changing the subject. He was suddenly very interested in the mechanisms of the old television and the grain of the library's leather chairs.

In Piotr Orlov's den, he surprised me by walking directly to the pool table, picking up a stick from a rack on the wall and asking, "How about a game, Holly?"

I moved deeper into the room, noticing that a shiny, black triangle filled with balls already sat in the middle of the table, as if it was in regular use. I told him, "I don't know how to play. Besides, we're supposed to be looking for Ryan."

"I'll teach you," Blair said, as if he only heard the first thing I said.

"I really don't want to..."

Blair set the stick on the corner of the table. He was smiling, but it looked brittle and fragile. There was nothing at all in his eyes.

"Listen, we need to look for Ryan, but while we're here..."

"Yes?" Blair removed the triangle from around the balls, picked up the stick, and took aim.

"I want to talk about what happened at the pool."

Blair struck out with the stick, scattering balls across the green felt. He walked around the side of the table, lining up his next shot. Without looking at me, he said, "Oh, that. Well, let's talk about it, if you want." He shot and a ball with a blue stripe went into a side pocket.

He straightened and moved to make his next shot. "I can think of two explanations for what happened: one, you think I'm some sort of sick pervert for kissing someone who is legally, if not genetically, a cousin." He sent a green-and-white ball into a far corner pocket, then glanced at me. "Maybe it's not even that— maybe it's just that you don't like me for who I am, forget about all the debatable family connections. That would explain why, when I touched you in the water, you went nuts and started all that thrashing."

He moved so his back was to me, bent over the table, and took another shot. The orange-striped ball bounced off a purple-striped one. Neither went into a hole. "The second explanation is the one I've been trying not to think about. I guess I can't get away from it anymore, though, if you really want to talk about it." He turned and looked at me finally. "You thought I was trying to drown you."

My heart did a little *tha-thump* in my chest, but it wasn't because I was afraid of him. I didn't quite trust him anymore, but the look in his eyes when he met mine wouldn't let me fear him. Blair was hurt. I don't think he would ever say it, but he wasn't hiding it anymore.

"Then what were you trying to do?"

Blair took a step closer to me, then thought better and stepped back. He set the stick across the top of the table and leaned his hips back against the edge. "I'm not really sure myself now. I don't know how far I might have taken it, but—and this is the God's honest truth, Holly—I think I've fallen in love with you."

I've been hearing similar confessions from boys and men since I was about thirteen. Sometimes, I was sure they didn't mean it, and just wanted to see what it would get them. Others I knew were sincere. Whether they were being honest about their feelings or not, though, I thought it taught me how to be a good judge of people's truthfulness, at least when it came to things like this—but now I wasn't sure. There was something about Blair that made me feel like I was just a little less mature than I should be.

"You've only known me for a couple of days," I told him.

Blair sighed. "Pretty full days, you have to admit. We've had more excitement since arriving in this beautiful hellhole than most people get their whole lives." He smiled and it wasn't fake this time. It seemed a little sad though. "Plenty of relationships are built on shared, traumatic experiences."

"I don't think that's a very good basis for a relationship."

Blair's grin turned sly. "We could always base it on sex. We aren't blood relatives, after all."

"Stop it! Don't talk to me like that!" I retreated to a corner of the room, by the built-in bar.

"Okay," Blair said to my back. "I'm sorry. It was just a joke."

I felt him come closer. I thought he was going to touch me, put a hand on my back, or my hip, but when I turned, he was still a few feet away. When he looked at me now, his face was more open than I ever saw it before. It was like he was a different person, without the constant calculating gleam in his eye or the small, self-satisfied smirk. "Holly, I'm sorry. Believe whatever you want, but I really do care for you and even if that wasn't the case, I thought we were friends. Or at least becoming friends." He paused and when he spoke again, his voice was lower and solemn, almost grave. "And you can't really think I killed my own brother, can you?"

"We're all suspects," I told him, but my heart wasn't in it. Over and over, I saw the hurt and the bitterness in Blair's eyes and in his voice when he talked about Jonathan or when someone else did. No, I didn't think he could kill his brother. I told him so.

"Well, that makes me feel a little better anyway." He took the pack of cigarettes from his pocket, clamped one between his lips, then turned, walked back to the pool table and resumed playing.

For several minutes, the only sound in the room was the muted *fwump* of the stick hitting the pool balls and the *clack* when they bounced off of one another. I walked over and watched, wondering if he was good at this or not. I didn't even know enough about the game to make a guess.

When the last ball, the white one he used to push around the others, went into a pocket at the far end of the table, he set the stick back in the rack on the wall and let out another sigh—this one very deep. He turned to me, took the unlit cigarette from his mouth, and said, "If I were after the whole sixty million dollars, I'd probably do it just the way it's been done so far. Jonathan was my brother, and I loved him, but I have to admit that he was the easiest target among us. Not because he was gay or any stupid reason like that," he added quickly. "But because he was weaker than most of us. I don't know much about his personal life these days, but the Jon I grew up with was a mess. Anyway, he would be my first target. I doubt whoever is responsible has ever killed before, so they'd want some practice. Nora would be next, but she took herself out of the equation."

"If we make it through this, I want to give her something," I said. I hadn't consciously thought about it before then, but the moment it left my mouth, I realized it was what I wanted.

"Sure," Blair agreed. "I'll toss something into the pot too. I couldn't live in luxury, knowing part of it was rightfully hers, without feeling guilty. I haven't been a lawyer long enough to lose all empathy. Anyway," he went on. "After Nora, Ryan would be next. He seems like a decent guy, but he reminds me of a big, dopey dog, and what happened with Jon really shook him. He's been drinking a lot, though God knows where he keeps finding it. I haven't seen a liquor cabinet anywhere."

I thought of the scene outside my window—Ryan draining a

bottle and then getting rid of the evidence over the side of the cliff.

"Marcus would be next. If I was doing the killings, I think he's the only one I might actually enjoy getting rid of."

"Blair!" I was shocked. "He's your *brother*."

He nodded, plucked the cigarette from his mouth and crumpled it between two fingers, letting the paper and tobacco flutter to the floor. "And Jon was *his* brother as much as mine, but you've seen how he reacted. Forget all the crap an undersized, sensitive kid like Jon had to deal with at school and wherever, when we were growing up, Marcus was the bully who lived in our own house. I was his target until Jon came along and as soon as our little brother was old enough to understand what was happening, Marcus switched to him. He did everything every asshole big brother has ever thought of to torture a sibling to both of us, but Jon took the brunt of it. I could only protect him so much and for so long." The bitterness was back.

He set the plastic triangle in the middle of the table, then leaned down and began gathering the balls from the place where they collected in a basket hanging beneath it. "Anyway, that would be that, and then it would just be you and me."

"What then?"

Blair smiled over his shoulder. "You don't want to hear it, but I'd try to get the rest of the money through marriage instead of violence." He began putting the balls inside the triangle.

I crossed my arms, feeling self-conscious. "Well, that's not going to happen."

"So I gathered." He finished with the balls, then looked over to me. "The offer will remain on the table, though, up to and including the time our little group is reduced to two members."

"You've either got a sick sense of humor or you really are the killer."

Blair shrugged. "I haven't killed anyone, so I guess I plead guilty to the first charge."

"You didn't try to drown me that night in the pool?" We already talked about it, but I felt like I needed a straight answer, one with no room for interpretation.

"That's a silly question," he countered. "I've never believed that BS about men killing the things they love."

"Stop it. Just answer me."

"Okay, okay." He held up his hands in surrender. "I, Blair Anthony Shaw, definitely did not try to drown you. The only thing I'm guilty of is bad judgment, or maybe bad timing. I should have been more careful not to scare you the way I did. I'm sorry.

"I wasn't entirely sure what happened in the pool myself, but I didn't want you kicking or slapping me while you were thrashing around, so I swam off a ways and when I climbed out, I saw you with Elijah. You seemed fine, and maybe I was a little embarrassed, so I just went back to my room. Forgive me?" He stepped towards me, lifted his arms as if to hold me, but I sidestepped and slipped away.

"Fine," he said. "Be like that, if you want." His tone was playful now and the usual grin was back. It fell suddenly, and he said, "By the way: why couldn't our favorite unlicensed cabby have picked up Nora last night or first thing this morning?"

Shame surged through me. For a little while, I forgot all about Rick. As quickly as I could, I told Blair what happened yesterday afternoon and last night, spending time with Rick and then Elijah discovering us, hurting Rick, bringing me back, leaving Rick's Explorer in the driveway.

"That son of a bitch," Blair said, punching his palm. "I'd like to—"

"Don't," I said. "You didn't see him with Rick. It was like the poor guy was fighting a brick wall. I really hope he's okay."

"Yeah." Blair nodded. "He seemed like a good kid." Changing subjects, he asked, "So Nora and Ryan took Rick's car, you think?"

"They'd have to, if they left on their own. I think Nora probably did anyway. I'm not so sure about Ryan."

Blair glanced at his watch. "Speaking of Ryan, Chelsea and brother dearest are probably about finished, so we better get back to the search ourselves."

CHAPTER SIXTEEN

We couldn't find Ryan, not even a sign of him, and neither could Chelsea and Marcus. Between the four of us, we searched everywhere we could think to, including the kitchen area and the hallway with the servants' quarters. If we asked Lydia, she probably would have given us permission to search the employees' rooms, but none of us wanted to go that far.

We got our first good look at Eleonore when we burst into her kitchen. Seeing her close up, I thought there was something familiar about her, but I didn't have time to dwell on it. The woman clearly wasn't happy to see us, but she kept silent, only shaking her head when we asked if she had seen Ryan and then we quickly moved on.

During the search, Blair and I also found the answer to a question I had almost since arriving at Dacha Orlov. The servants' quarters were off a hallway beyond the kitchen, accessed by a short set of stairs leading down. At the end of that hallway was a door and through it were concrete steps, leading to another, concrete-floored hallway to the garage. There was room for two cars, but it held only an old, cream-colored Volvo station wagon and various odds and ends you could expect to find in anybody's garage.

Blair, as curious as I was, opened the garage door. We were surprised to see how far we were from the house now: it was visible if you looked up through the trees, but we were at least eighty feet down the sloping driveway, recessed in a natural rise that was nearly hidden by the densely-packed brush that grew all around the house. It wasn't exactly invisible, but if you didn't know where to look for it, it could easily be missed just driving up to the house.

The house's garage was interesting, surprising, and even strange, but it was only a distraction. Exploring it didn't help us find Ryan.

On the way back to the house, Ned, the groundskeeper, was standing in the long concrete corridor. It was the first time I'd seen him since Jonathan's body was discovered. He gave us a questioning look, but said nothing as Blair brushed past him without a word. I said, "Hi," but the old man only nodded and continued on in the direction we came from. I guess he didn't like us snooping around in what he probably considered a private area.

After we gave up the search, the four of us reluctantly found Elijah and asked for the state police sub-station's phone number. Blair made the call from the phone in the library. As calmly and concisely as he could, he explained to Trooper Abbott that our cousins, Nora and Ryan Hill, were gone from the house and that Nora left a note, but Ryan seemed to have disappeared into thin air. I wanted Blair to ask about Rick, too, but he shushed me and gave me a look that said *one thing at a time.*

An hour and a half later, Elijah ushered Sergeant Goddard into the main hallway. Instead of using the family room, we all went into the dining room, where Elijah already had coffee ready. Sergeant Goddard looked at Aunt Lydia's chair, at the head of the immense table, then chose the one to its left. He accepted coffee from Elijah, and after we were all seated he started talking. "I found one of your cousins pretty easily. Miss Hill has taken a room at the Bird Creek Motel."

"How is she?" I asked.

Goddard met my eyes only for a second before sweeping his gaze across everyone assembled. "She seems fine to me. Tired, maybe, but not bad. She's already made reservations on the weekly flight to Fairbanks and she plans to stay in town till then."

"Oh, thank God." I breathed a sigh of relief.

"Ryan wasn't with her?" Blair asked.

The trooper shook his head. "No. I asked her about Mr. Hill and she said she assumed he was still here. I told her what you told Abbott. It worried her, but she didn't have any ideas. She said she hopes we find him okay, but she doesn't plan to leave the motel until she can leave Foster's Place entirely."

"That's it?" Blair was disgusted. "Her brother's missing and—"

"How did she get into town anyway?" Chelsea asked, a look of concern on her face. Remembering how she acted back in Nora's room, when the younger girl had her attack, I was sure it was genuine. I was pretty sure I knew the answer to her question, too, of course. I wanted to talk to Goddard about it, but not here, not in front of everyone and with every chance of Elijah listening behind closed doors.

Goddard tilted back in his chair. "Now *that's* an interesting story. I found Miss Hill because Rick Kolit's truck was parked at the Bird Creek. Rick had some sort of run-in last night. He's been at Dr. Chapman's place since about six o'clock last evening, so I knew he couldn't have driven her. When I asked about it, Miss Hill was a little embarrassed to admit that she drove herself. She said she found the truck parked in front of this house, with the keys in it, and decided to borrow it. So my question becomes, how did Rick's vehicle end up here with Rick still in town?"

"Um, about that..." I began, but Blair gave me a sharp look.

Goddard caught it and seemed to understand there was

something I didn't want everyone to know. "Well, we can talk about that later. As for Mr. Hill, when his sister said she didn't know anything, I called around." He sipped coffee before saying, "I confirmed Miss Hill's reservation with Pete, over at the airfield, but not only has Mr. Hill not made one, Miss Hill is one of only two non-locals Pete's talked to about the flight all week, and the other is Charlie Shelton, who's up here pretty regularly. He's also at the Bird Creek, by the by."

Marcus darted a look at Chelsea, but she ignored him. I was sure I knew what Marcus was thinking. Another cousin out of the split. I hated him a little bit right then.

Marcus asked, "So where does that leave us?"

Goddard didn't respond directly. Instead, he asked us questions, as he did when we all first met him.

Who was the last to see Ryan? None of us were certain. We discussed when each of us last saw him: me through the window, down by the cliff; Marcus helping him to the bathroom and then to bed. Chelsea only saw him for a moment when he banged on the door of her and Marcus's room. Blair didn't think he'd seen Ryan since two nights before, when he rushed past us on the stairs, clutching a bottle of whiskey.

"Was he drinking heavily?" Goddard asked.

We looked at each other and almost in unison, the four of us nodded. We all agreed that Ryan was drinking a lot.

"Nora took Jonathan's death pretty hard," Chelsea said quietly. "But I don't think any of us realized how bad it was for Ryan either."

"I see." Goddard pushed back from the table and stood. "I'm sure I'll have more questions for all of you later on, but right now, I think I'll take a look around the house and the grounds."

Before anyone could respond, the door to the dining room opened. I half-hoped Ryan would walk in with some explanation for his disappearance. Instead, Aunt Lydia wheeled herself through the doorway. It was only the second time I'd seen her out of bed.

"Hello, Sergeant Goddard." She crossed the space from the door to where Goddard stood and held out her hand. He took it gingerly, as if being careful not to break something fragile, and quickly released it. From his expression, he was as surprised as the rest of us.

"Visiting us on business again, I see," Lydia said, her voice stronger and richer than I ever before heard it. "I understand the children are concerned about their cousin Ryan this time."

"That's right."

Lydia's eyes took all of us in. She smiled then turned back to the sergeant. "They say he's missing, but don't you believe it. Before this is all done with, you'll find the poor boy has been killed, just like Jonathan was."

Chelsea made a sound of surprise and I could practically hear Blair grinding his teeth in fury. Even Goddard seemed uncomfortable as he said, "Let's not jump to conclusions, Mrs. Orlov." He glanced at the rest of us, then said to Aunt Lydia, "If you don't mind, I'm going to do some looking around now."

"By all means." Lydia was the picture of graciousness.

Goddard turned to go, but I stood and called his name. When he looked back, I asked, "Can I talk to you? In private?"

Lydia's smile was positively reptilian when she looked at me. I think, somehow, she already knew what I wanted to talk to the trooper about. Did Elijah tell her what he did? What, exactly, was their relationship?

"Go right ahead and use the library," Lydia told us. "No one will disturb you."

Goddard thanked her, then motioned to me with his head. He held the dining-room door open for me; we crossed the hall to the library and I returned the favor, holding its door open for him.

Goddard glanced around, taking the room in. Then he looked to me and said, "I don't have a lot of time, Miss Shaw. What's up?"

As quickly as possible, I told him about yesterday afternoon and evening: going into town with Rick, and Elijah somehow finding us; the one-sided fight in which Rick was hurt.

While I talked, Goddard was quiet, only nodding occasionally. When I was through, he said, "I haven't talked directly to Rick yet, but I figured something like that happened. I never guessed the girl would be one of you folks or that the other guy was Elijah." He whistled. "The kid doesn't make things easy on himself, does he?"

"Is he okay?" I asked.

"His wrist is broken pretty bad, but Dr. Chapman says he'll be fine in about six weeks. Might need a little physical therapy, but he'll be okay."

I let out a sound of relief. "I'm so glad."

"Well, if that's it—"

"Could you take me to see him? Rick, I mean."

Goddard hesitated a moment, then nodded. "I want to look around first, like I said, but I guess I could take you over when I see Rick. I'll have to find out if he wants to press charges anyway."

The office of Foster's Place's only doctor was a rambling, low-slung, one-story building. The original building was small, but it spread out in three directions with a series of additions built at different times, in different styles, from different materials. The effect was like a picture assembled from pieces of several different jigsaw puzzles. On the way into town, Goddard radioed his partner, Abbott, to call ahead, so we were expected when we arrived. A husky, middle-aged nurse in Winnie the Pooh-patterned scrubs led us to the recovery room. There were four hospital beds, two on each side of the room, but only one was occupied.

"He's probably drowsy from the painkillers, but you can have ten minutes with him," the nurse told us before leaving. Goddard put a hand on my arm and said, "You take the first five, Miss Shaw," then he, too, left.

As I approached the bed, Rick opened his eyes and gave me a lopsided smile. "Hey, Miss Shaw. How you doin'?" A plaster cast covered his right arm from his hand up to his elbow, but he held out his good hand in greeting.

"I'm so sorry." I took his hand and on impulse I kissed the back of it.

Rick's smile grew broader. "If I knew you'd do that, I'd have let that big ape break both arms."

"Don't say that."

"Sorry, sorry." His smile faded. "You're okay?"

I told him everything that had happened after Elijah took his truck. Rick listened, frowning, then finally shaking his head slowly in a mixture of amazement and anger. "That bastard."

He pulled his hand from my grasp and looked towards the window, even though it was curtained. "I wasn't much help, was I?"

"You did your best. Nobody could have fought Elijah off. He's a monster. I'm so sorry," I told him again.

Rick shrugged, then lifted his right arm as he turned his head back to me. "This is no big deal. It'll heal. I'm just sorry our evening ended so bad. It could have been beautiful." He smiled again, but it was weak. "I'm glad you're okay. Just hang on a while longer and you can go home rich. That's the deal, right?"

I felt a moist burning in the corner of my eyes. It was sadness and gratitude and embarrassment all jumbled up together. What was I supposed to say to that? It wasn't wrong, but it didn't feel right either. I didn't know how Rick really felt, and I didn't have any more affection for him than I did anyone else in this awful town, but how do you say that? It was true that I would be rich if I survived however much longer Aunt Lydia had to live. It was also true that I would go home afterwards. I would go home, on to whatever the next stage in my life was, and Rick would probably stay right here in Foster's Place, driving his unlicensed cab, running errands for people, and guiding fishing and hunting groups.

From behind me, Sergeant Goddard cleared his throat. My five minutes were up.

I took Rick's hand, squeezed it, and thanked him again, both for what he did last night and the day he gave me before it all went wrong. Then I went quickly out into the hallway.

Before long, Sergeant Goddard joined me, shaking his head.

"What's wrong?" I asked.

"Mr. Kolit doesn't want to press charges. 'Just one of those things,' he says." He shook his head again. "I can't force him, so I guess that's the end of that. C'mon." He started down the hall, saying over his shoulder, "I'll give you a lift back. I want to have another look around the place anyway."

I followed and as we passed through the waiting room at the front of the building, Eleonore was standing by the reception desk. She glanced in our direction as we went by, but turned away without a word. I never yet heard her speak, so it wasn't surprising. Still, I wondered what brought her here now, of all times.

Then I was in the passenger seat of Sergeant Goddard's SUV as he backed out of the parking lot and pointed the truck west. It was much newer than Rick's, cleaner and with softer seats, but for some reason, I wasn't very comfortable as we rode back to Dacha Orlov.

CHAPTER SEVENTEEN

I hadn't even taken my jacket off when Elijah appeared in the front hallway. I was stamping snow from my shoes, and when I looked up, he was standing there. I was startled, but he ignored it. "Mrs. Orlov wants to speak with you." He turned and walked away as if there was no doubt that I would obey and follow.

For a second, I thought about just going back to my room. My mom would have called that buying trouble and I didn't need any more of that. I didn't hurry to catch up to Elijah though; let Lydia wait if she wanted to talk to me. Her money didn't mean she owned me.

When I reached the third-floor hallway, Elijah was stood outside the door. There was a look in his eye that wasn't exactly hostile, but I knew it annoyed him to have to wait for me. No matter what he said about being a friend, I needed to remember how dangerous he was.

The butler knocked lightly on the door, paused a moment, and then opened it. I didn't wait for an invitation to walk through.

Lydia was back in bed, the wheelchair nowhere in sight, in the exact place and position I saw her when I first arrived. She was wearing a white dressing gown and on the huge bed, propped up among so many pillows, she looked like a doll belonging to a little girl with unusual tastes.

"Took your time," Lydia began. "Not concerned that I might have been dying? Perhaps that I wanted to leave you some final words of wisdom? I remember how much you enjoy my advice." She smiled, but it was just a lifting of the corners of her mouth. There was venom in her voice and her eyes practically glowed with malicious amusement. *If she really is dying*, I thought, *it's because she's eating herself up on the inside.*

I walked around to the side of the bed, forcing her to turn her head to keep her eyes on me. "I came right up. See?" I swept my open hand down my front. "I didn't even take my coat off."

"Or those wet shoes," she said, making a sour face as she looked pointedly at the little puddles I tracked across her floor.

"Elijah said you wanted me, so I came. What did you need?"

Lydia looked at me for a long moment, her eyes narrowed. Then one small, frail-seeming hand appeared from beneath the covers and made a motion like she was brushing away an annoying fly. "I understand Nora has left us."

"She has," I agreed.

Lydia sneered. "Calling me a murderer and then running away. The little coward…"

"She has a right to be scared. We all do."

The old woman tried to pin me with her eyes. I didn't look away, but I didn't wither under her glare the way she probably hoped either. "You're not afraid. You haven't left."

"I am scared and I've considered leaving. I'm still thinking about it," I told her.

"But you won't, because the money is here."

"Not literally, but you're right. The money is here and if I leave, I'll go away with nothing. I guess I'm just greedier than Nora."

Aunt Lydia's voice went tight as she scoffed, "I doubt it. You're braver, though, and you're bold in the way you speak to me today."

I shrugged. "You said we had to stay here. You didn't say we had to be polite."

Lydia's face relaxed and when she smiled this time, it was much more human. She looked more like the Aunt Lydia I met the day I arrived. "That's true. I never stipulated that, did I?" She closed her eyes and leaned back among the pillows. "I hate all of you, Holly. I won't pretend I don't. You're all tainted fruit from poisonous trees. Still, I almost wish you and I could be friends. You really are my favorite among the lot."

I didn't say anything. I didn't care any longer what she thought of me and I had no intention of being friends.

"So, did Ryan go with his sister?" Lydia asked without opening her eyes.

If she meant to surprise me, to take me off-guard, she must have been disappointed. "No. Nora's staying in town, but she says she hasn't seen him. You must have heard that. You talked to Mr. Goddard."

Lydia opened one eye and grinned. "Of course. And what did I tell Goddard? Mark my words, you'll find the boy has been killed."

She was beginning to disgust me and now that I was warming up, my damp shoes were becoming uncomfortable. Suddenly, I was very tired. I just wanted to crawl into bed for a while. "Was there anything else, Aunt Lydia?"

"I heard you took a little trip into town yesterday."

I stiffened. What exactly did Elijah tell her? Did he mention what he did to Rick? Or to me? I doubted it. I didn't think she'd care about Rick, but she wouldn't want her servant mishandling a niece. That would spoil her game.

"Did you see all the sights?" Lydia asked.

"There's not much to see," I answered. "If you've lived here so long, you should know that."

She opened the other eye and leaned forward, still grinning. "What is it about you, Holly? What do you have that the others don't? I can't find a single word for it. When I was a girl, we would have said you have spunk, but that's not quite it. I've tried a dozen words and none of them fit. What it really comes down to is this: I hate all of you and I've told you so and what I hope will happen and you're simply bound and determined to see that I don't get my wish."

"If there's nothing else," I told her, "then I'm going back to my room."

Without looking to see how she responded, I went to the door, opened it, and stepped through, practically bumping into Elijah's giant form, filling the doorway. His hand flashed out, latched onto my arm, pulled me into the hallway, and pushed me up against the wall outside of Lydia's room.

I didn't scream. Later, I was proud of myself for that, at least. I looked up into Elijah's pitted, scarred face, and directly into his eyes. "Let go, Elijah." It was the first time I ever addressed him by name.

The big man stared right back at me without responding or doing as I asked, but from the corner of my eye, I saw movement. His free hand, huge and rough, brushed my cheek. His thin lips opened and one word, "Soft," tumbled out. Then: "I'll protect you, Holly. Don't worry. As long as I'm around, you'll be safe."

I wasn't wearing the hard-heeled shoes from when I stomped his foot before, but I raised my leg anyway. Before I could bring it down, Elijah released his grip, turned, and started towards the stairs as if none of it ever happened.

I watched until I was sure he was gone, then leaned against the wall, fighting to catch my breath. My heart was pounding and my lungs wouldn't fill. It was a few more minutes before I felt that I could make the long trip back to my room. When I did, I made sure to secure the door. Elijah said he wanted to protect me from whoever or whatever killed Jonathan and now, maybe Ryan, too. Maybe I should have been grateful, but I just couldn't believe it because somehow, it didn't make sense. Why would he care what happened to me more than any other member of the family? And even if I was wrong, even if Elijah was sincere, still all I could think was, *"But who will protect me from you?"*

CHAPTER EIGHTEEN

That night, dinner was especially bleak. With Jonathan gone, Nora fled to town, unlikely to return, and Ryan missing, we were half the family we began with, and only a few days had passed since we all arrived.

I sat next to Blair, near the middle of the huge table. Marcus and Chelsea sat across from us. I didn't want to be there, I didn't want to see anyone, but I was afraid to ask to eat in my room. Poison was an easier way to get rid of someone than stabbing or spiriting them away.

Before I came downstairs, I knocked on Blair's door. Neither of us said anything, but I think we understood each other—at least about this. We came down to the dining room and found Marcus and Chelsea already seated. There was no sign that anything, even water, had been served. Chelsea told us that we were waiting for Aunt Lydia, and that Elijah went to help her downstairs.

The door opened then and Lydia was wheeled into the room, Elijah following behind like her shadow. Lydia greeted us all, then found her place at the head of the table, putting her several seats away from the rest of us. She didn't seem to mind.

She turned to Elijah. "You may serve." He bowed slightly, then disappeared through the kitchen door.

The food was served and conversation began. It was almost entirely one-sided, though, conducted by Aunt Lydia. She didn't seem to mind if no one responded, and she didn't say much of anything that mattered. When one of us did respond, it was usually Marcus. He was still trying to play up to Lydia, as if it mattered. I wasn't sure he really understood the situation we were in.

I focused on my food, trying to tune out Lydia's voice. I found myself noticing Elijah more than usual. Since the first incident outside of Aunt Lydia's room, I was much more aware of him, but during that meal, it was almost as if my eyes were drawn to him magnetically each time he entered the room. He didn't do anything out of the ordinary: he moved silently around the table, serving, clearing dishes, refilling our water glasses when they were empty. He didn't stray from or relax in his work for even a moment, but as he went about his duties with the absolute perfection Lydia expected from him, I was sure that his eyes rarely left me, even if I couldn't catch him at it.

I tried to tell myself that it was my imagination, that he wasn't lingering an extra second or two when he served me, that the time his arm brushed my shoulder when he reached for my glass was just an accident. He didn't treat me any differently than he did anyone else seated at the table, but somehow, he still made me feel like I was getting special attention. Attention that I didn't want.

The moment he grabbed me outside of Lydia's room earlier kept forcing itself into my brain. *Force* was a good word for it. Elijah, with his strength and size, was a force of nature in a black suit. I was child-sized in comparison. I may have outsmarted him once, that first time, but I knew it wouldn't happen again.

The helplessness that made me feel was worse than anything else I ever experienced. The only thing that even came close was when my mother was lying in a hospice ward, slowly dying, but still trying to cheer *me* up. Remembering that, how she looked in those crisp, white sheets, a colorful scarf around her head to hide the hair loss, but still smiling, I choked on a sip of water.

Blair's hand was on my back, gently rubbing. His touch was comforting, not like before. My eyes watering, my face flushed, I tried to give him a little smile, but I don't think it came off the way I meant it. The look he gave me in return seemed genuinely concerned. Despite everything else between us, I was sure that he would help me if he could.

When dinner was finished, Lydia wheeled away from the table, wishing us all a good night. Elijah hurried after her, as quietly as ever. There was no way Lydia could get that wheelchair up the stairs, so I supposed she needed the butler to carry her.

Marcus and Chelsea lingered at the table, talking together quietly. Chelsea was the first to push her chair back, saying to me, "We're going to watch a movie, if the two of you want to join us."

"Actually," Blair answered, "we already talked about taking a walk after dinner. Maybe we'll join you for the second half."

Chelsea gave me a curious look, but only said, "Suit yourself."

Blair stood and asked, "Shall we?" offering me his hand.

"I can stand on my own, thanks," I told him. He didn't seem surprised or disappointed, just accepted it.

We got our coats from our rooms and then went outside through the rear door leading directly to the patio. The sun had set hours earlier and the sky was hidden by dense clouds. I wondered if we'd get the storm Lydia mentioned a couple of days ago. It seemed like a lot of build up to me, but it was my first winter in Alaska, so what did I know?

We crossed the stone-tiled patio to the wall barring the edge of the cliff. For a minute, neither of us spoke, just stared out into the blackness of the night.

"So, what's going on?" Blair asked finally.

"I wanted to talk to you."

"I guessed that much." There was a trace of the wryness from when I first met him in his voice.

"I think…" I began. "I think I've got a problem."

"With a murderer somewhere in the house, that's a common affliction."

"I'm serious," I said, trying not to snap. "Remember what I told you about Elijah?"

Blair inclined his head. "I'm not likely to forget."

"I thought it'd be okay, as long as I was around the rest of you or Lydia, but…"

I told him what I felt at dinner, about Elijah's eyes on me, even as he went about his work, about how he seemed to be sending me messages with every little gesture. Blair listened without interrupting, but halfway through, he moved a little closer to me. Maybe it was so he could hear me better without asking me to speak up, but I could feel the uneasiness coming off of him.

Blair took out his cigarettes, chose one from the pack, and lit it. The bright flare of the cigarette lighter was dazzling after being in the semi-darkness, and left me seeing stars. He took a long drag from the cigarette, blew the smoke into the air over the rim of the cliff, and said, "Elijah's a mystery. This proves one thing though."

"What?"

"He's human. He finds you attractive, so he's the same species as you and me, at least. I seriously had my doubts. I've never seen a bigger or creepier guy in my life."

I whacked the back of my hand against his shoulder. His coat was thick enough that he probably didn't even feel it. "I'm being serious here."

"So am I." He sucked deeply on the cigarette, making the tobacco embers glow brightly. The faint orange light gave his normally attractive features a sinister look.

"I'm scared of him," I admitted. "I'm almost more afraid of him than I am of whoever killed Jonathan."

"Don't forget Ryan."

"We don't know that!" I snapped, losing patience. "Don't talk like that," I added more quietly.

"Sorry." He drew the cigarette down to the filter in one long pull, then flicked it over the wall and out into space. It spun through the air, falling into the abyss, leaving a vague trail of color in its wake. For a couple of seconds, it looked like a tiny meteorite, streaking towards the earth.

"What do you want me to do about Elijah?" Blair asked. "Do you think I can protect you from him?"

"Do *you* think you can?"

"I don't know." Blair shook his head. "I'd try if it came down to it, but I'd like to have a gun and a few other guys at my back."

"That's not very reassuring."

"Just being honest. Let's move around a little. I'm freezing." He tried to take my hand, but I stepped ahead of him, just out of reach.

Blair caught up in a couple of steps and we walked side by side, without touching, across the shadowed patio. With the moon and stars both covered, the only light was what escaped from the windows of the house, and when we turned the corner towards the wing where the pool was, we were in almost complete darkness.

"I wonder where Lydia found Elijah," Blair said, the first time either of us had spoken in several minutes. "He looks like he stepped out of someone's nightmare, but he's got that surface polish, and his skills are world-class. I don't know much about butlering, but I doubt there are many as good as he is."

"He's more than a butler. He's Lydia's bodyguard too."

Without the cigarette, Blair was just another vague shape in the darkness. I felt, more than saw, his head swivel towards me. "Against what?"

"I don't know, but he told me he would protect me like he's protected her. I guess I don't blame her for wanting one. She's a rich old woman living in the middle of nowhere. He's terrifying to look at and he's as strong as a bear."

"Tame bears can go berserk though. Bite the hand that feeds them and all that."

I shivered and only partially from the cold. "That's not what I'm afraid of. I don't think he'd ever hurt Aunt Lydia. Not for anything."

"Maybe you should relax," Blair said. "He obviously likes you and he said he'd protect you. I'd bet you're safe enough from him."

Anger flared inside me, brighter than Blair's lighter against the night. "Don't you get it? I don't care if he likes me. You're not a woman, so maybe you can't understand, but just the thought of him scares me, especially after seeing what he did to Rick. I can't stand it when he touches me and it's all I can do not to run out of the room when he even looks at me."

Suddenly, strong arms were around me and I could feel warm breath on my cheek. "I can't stand the thought of him touching you either," Blair whispered.

My whole body went stiff, like a cat arching its back against danger, but Blair only held me, and slowly, I began to relax. The way he held me wasn't at all like when he grabbed me and kissed me by the pool. Now, it was more protective than passionate.

"How is the kid anyway?" Blair said. For a second, I didn't know who he meant. "Rick's okay," I told him. "His arm's broken, but I guess he'll be fine in a few weeks."

"Glad to hear it. I kind of liked him."

"Me too."

"Not too much, though, I hope." I couldn't see Blair's smile, but I sensed it.

"He's just a friend. He didn't deserve to get caught up in all of this."

I tried to pull away, but Blair's grip tightened—not hard, just enough to keep me pressed against him.

"Holly, I told you before: I love you. You believe I mean it, don't you?"

"I guess you probably believe it anyway."

"I don't just believe it, I know it. And I know I want to marry you."

"I don't— I mean…" Blackness started closing in around us, darker than the night. It wasn't like when Elijah was holding me, but still I felt trapped. Blair was the only person in this house I thought I could trust. Why was he doing this to me? Was it possible he really did mean it? Even if he did, how could we ever… whether we shared blood or not, legally, we were cousins. We were family.

"Go back home, back to civilization, and wait for me, Holly," he said, right against my ear. "I can ride this out alone and when I do, I'll come find you and we'll be richer than God himself. You'll never have to worry about a thing again."

He leaned down and kissed me. I didn't respond, but I didn't resist either.

"What a charming scene." The voice was sharp as cracking ice, filled with contempt and disdain. Aunt Lydia's voice.

A flashlight came on, blinding me with its brilliance. We sprang apart and I threw up a hand, but it was too late. When my eyes cleared enough to see, I saw Lydia sitting in her chair, down by the far corner. She must have come through the door from the pool and she had wheeled her chair to within ten feet of us. We were so caught up in ourselves, in the discussion and each other, that neither Blair nor I heard her until she called out.

Lydia rolled closer, the wheels of her chair crunching scattered fragments of crusted snow against the patio stones. "I suspected something like this." She sounded so satisfied, she practically purred. "And the two of you cousins." She clicked her tongue against the roof of her mouth in a disapproving way, but it was clear how much she was enjoying herself.

"You object?" Blair asked coolly.

"Far be it from me!" She chuckled. "Young people, thrown together in a stressful situation, cooped up like this... I suppose it isn't surprising at all that you'd want to have yourselves a little fun. I'm almost envious."

"It's more than just 'fun'." The temperature of Blair's tone dropped from cool to icy. "I'd like to marry this woman."

"Well, now, that's interesting." Lydia moved close enough that the three of us formed a triangle, out there in the dark and cold. "The Shaw family are guilty of many things, but incest is a new crime, I believe. I'm sure you'll produce lovely little monsters."

"I'm not really a Shaw," I said quickly. "I was adopted, remember?"

I don't know why I said it, why I was so quick to defend the idea. I didn't have any intention of marrying Blair.

Lydia smiled. "You go right ahead and believe that if it makes you feel good, dear."

It was so obviously meant to provoke me that it had to be a trap. I took the bait anyway. "What does that mean?"

"Oh, sweet child," Lydia said, chuckling again. Her chin dipped against her thin chest and when she looked up again, her eyes were bright in the darkness. Hatred and evil delight were etched across her every feature.

That's what's keeping her alive, I thought. *She's eating herself up inside, but somehow, it keeps her going.*

I saw her at her weakest, after she told me the story of the Shaw family, and after that, I didn't doubt that she was dying, but somehow, she still found strength to play her game, to taunt and torture all of us.

"Did you know your father at all?" she asked.

"I was only four when he died."

Lydia nodded. "You never got a chance to know him then."

She met my eyes. "I knew him very well though. I believe I'm a greater authority on Spencer Shaw than anyone else could ever claim to be. He was the baby of the family, and I admit I spoiled him because of it. He was the most adorable baby; by far, the best-looking Shaw among all of us. Even as a child, he was beautiful, and he had little girls trailing after him almost from the moment he began school. He was a ladies' man by the time he was ten or eleven, and after he realized the power he held over women, he was never without a few on his string. He milked them for whatever he could get and left them by the wayside when he moved on to the next. Why he married, I can't possibly guess, but I'm sure it didn't make a bit of difference in curtailing his habits. He spent much longer developing those than he did married to the woman you called 'mother', after all."

My throat felt thick. I knew Lydia was cruel, but what was the point of tearing down a man dead for more than twenty years?

"Does that, dear Holly, sound like the kind of man who would adopt a child?"

Blair saved me from having to think of an answer. "What exactly are you trying to tell us?"

Lydia turned to him, a leering smile on her lips. "Isn't it obvious? Spencer *was* her father. The devil only knows who her mother was, but I'd wager there was some sort of trouble he couldn't skate out of, and raising his child was the price he had to pay. I can't imagine him accepting the responsibility willingly." She looked back at me. "Whether your 'mother' was more enthusiastic about the arrangement isn't for me to say. I never met the woman." She paused. "Whatever the case, Spencer was taken from her and she was left to raise her husband's child. I'm sure she was a very decent woman."

"There's no proof of any of that," Blair said, angrily.

"I know what kind of man Spencer Shaw was," Lydia countered.

"My mother said…" I broke off. Images of my mother, happy memories, sad ones, painful ones, flashed through my mind.

"Yes?" Lydia leaned forward in her chair, eager to hear whatever I had to say.

I cleared my throat and tried again. "My mom told me that my father was unable to have children because of an illness he had, and that she desperately wanted a baby. She said he wasn't very excited about it at first, but when they met me, they both fell in love." It was embarrassing to repeat that last part, but it's exactly how my mother told it to me.

"A charming story," Lydia said. "Or rather a fairy tale, because I don't believe it for an instant. Spencer Shaw was not the kind to raise anyone else's child, and I've seen enough of you by now to know that you're one of us. You may not look it, but you're a Shaw and if you've got even half the brains I think you do, you'll get one of those DNA tests before you have any more to do with this one." She jutted her head in Blair's direction.

She snapped off her flashlight and then jerked the wheels of her chair viciously, making it shoot forward so quickly Blair and I had to jump aside to avoid being hit. Over her shoulder, she called, "Go back inside before you catch cold, children. That sort of death won't do anyone a bit of good."

We heard her wheels against the patio stones for a few more moments, then the night was silent again, except for the faint noise of a light wind through the trees. Inside my jacket, I was shaking, but with anger rather than from the cold.

"Don't listen to her," Blair said.

"I don't know what to think anymore."

He put a hand on my shoulder. "She's just trying to confuse and upset you."

"Well, it worked. I mean… I never knew my dad at all, and she was basically his mother." I looked up, trying to find his eyes in the darkness. His face was just a gray oval in the night. "I think she probably did know him better than anyone."

"Maybe, but you knew your mom. Was she the kind of woman to lie about something like that?"

"I really don't know," I admitted. "Maybe, if it was a nicer story than the truth."

"It's not true," Blair said. His hand slid down my shoulder and pulled me to him. "I know the Shaw family. I have just as much experience with full-blooded, true-blue Shaws as Lydia does, and you don't act like one of us. You're stronger, braver, and smarter than any of us could hope to be."

"You're just flattering me now."

"Well, think about this then: Aunt Lydia said she liked you, right?"

It was true. She even said she almost wished we could be friends.

Blair went on. "If she really believed that you were her grandniece by blood, she'd treat you just like the rest of us. She isn't the type to actually play favorites. Not when it comes to her revenge."

"Maybe..." It made some sense, but I wasn't convinced.

"Besides, there's something else you're forgetting."

I tilted my head up. This close to Blair, I could just see the outlines of his features through the darkness. "What?"

"You aren't alone out here and Lydia knows for a fact that I'm a dyed-in-the-wool Shaw. She wouldn't want to see me happy, especially not because she brought the two of us together by inviting us both here. I love you, Holly, and just the idea of it must eat Lydia up. Making us doubt each other, splitting us apart, would be just another bonus to her final revenge."

I didn't like that he was assuming that we *could* be split apart, as if we were already together. I liked Blair as a friend, and I *needed* a friend, but I didn't really want to think about him or anyone else in the way he was thinking of me – not until this house and everything that happened here was long behind me.

But his explanation did make a kind of sense. It was a possibility, at least.

Blair leaned down, but I turned my head away. "No, Blair. Stop." I pushed against his chest and he released me.

He held up his hands and backed off a few steps. "Mea culpa."

"I'm going to bed," I told him.

"That's probably a good idea."

We walked back the way we first came, and went into the house.

In the main hallway, Marcus sat on a bench outside of the library. His hair was mussed, and his face was flushed and damp with sweat, as if he'd been running for miles. His eyes were red-rimmed and vacant. His shirt was untucked and unbuttoned halfway down his chest. Seated, his belly bulged over the top of his belt. Despite his size, he seemed soft and helpless. There was a half-empty bottle of liquor next to him on the bench.

"What happened to the movie?" Blair asked.

Marcus looked over at us, then turned away, looking out across the hallway, focused on nothing. "It was my fault," he said quietly.

"What was?" I asked. I shot a look at Blair, but he was watching his brother.

"Jon... Jon's dead and it's my fault." Marcus hiccoughed and it seemed to jar something inside of him loose. Tears formed in his eyes as he groped blindly for the bottle.

Blair squatted on his heels in front of the other man and said, more gently than I ever heard him before, "You can't blame yourself, Marcus."

Marcus swigged from the bottle, gasped, and said, "I'm his brother. I'm the big brother. I should have protected him." He looked Blair in the eye. "I should have protected both of you, but now he's gone. It's too late."

Some of the hardness Blair usually showed his older brother

passed across his face, but faded quickly. "It *is* a little late, yes. C'mon, big guy. We should get you to bed."

Blair put his arm around Marcus's shoulders and tried to lift him, but it wasn't any good. Marcus was too large and he wasn't done talking. "It wasn't any locals killed Jon and it wasn't cuz he was,"—he hiccoughed again—"gay." He shook his big head. "I shouldn't have said that. It was an asshole thing to say."

He lifted the bottle and after he took a sip, Blair intercepted it, taking the bottle from Marcus's half-limp fingers and setting it out of reach. "I won't disagree."

"It was someone…" Marcus hiccoughed again and seemed to get frustrated with his own interruption. "It was someone in this house. Somebody, one of us, killed him. My baby brother." He started to cry, his shoulders racked by huge sobs.

Blair looked at me. "Help me get him upstairs."

It was a struggle, but between the two of us, and with a little help from Marcus himself, we managed to get the big man to the second floor. His room was shut and locked, but when I knocked on the door, Chelsea opened it. She took one look at her husband, threw the door wide, and said, "Put him on the bed."

Once we did, Chelsea tugged his shoes and pants off, then said to us, "Thanks. Goodnight," and ushered us out of the room. The door shut again and we heard the lock click.

"I wonder what set him off," Blair said.

"Isn't it obvious?"

Blair shook his head. "No. I think something happened, something between him and Chelsea. She didn't seem surprised, or at all happy, to see us or the state Marcus was in. Well, it's between them."

"I hope it doesn't happen again. He's lucky it was us that found him."

"Sure," Blair said. "Lucky. I'm going to bed. I'll see you in the morning."

"Okay."

I went into my room and Blair turned down the hall towards his. I locked and secured the door. I was tired, but too many thoughts were jumbled up in my head to make sleep easy. I undressed and showered, then crawled into bed, sifting through everything, trying to sort it all out. I didn't know whether to believe what Aunt Lydia said about my father. I didn't know if I could trust Blair when he said he loved me. I wasn't even sure how I felt about that. Blair was an attractive man and part of me was happy that he found me attractive, too, but whether blood-related or not, we were still cousins as far as I was concerned.

I rolled over in the darkness, trying to find a comfortable position, and remembered what Blair said before, about my going back home and waiting for him. I never did give him an answer. I didn't get a chance. Was he truly worried about my safety or did he just want me out of the house, another rival for Lydia's inheritance eliminated? I thought of Nora and wondered if Blair had a similar conversation with her.

I shifted again, lying flat on my back with my arms and legs spread out, staring up into the blackness. The last thing I remember before drifting off was wondering if you could be both attracted to and suspicious of a man at the same time.

CHAPTER NINETEEN

I slept, but not well, and not for very long. I was up by six thirty the next morning and by quarter to seven, I was doing laps in the pool, the desire to be moving winning out over fear of being alone. Before long, a voice called out, "Another reason I'm sure you aren't a Shaw."

I flipped onto my back and kicked hard, propelling myself to the far side of the pool, away from the voice. I promised myself I wouldn't go swimming around Blair again, so of course, here he was. Normally, he was dressed fairly casually, in sports shirts or polos, but today, he was dressed as if he were going somewhere, wearing the same suit I first saw him in. I wondered what the reason was.

"What's that?" I called.

Blair smiled like the fox who'd gotten into the henhouse. "That body of yours. Shaw women tend to be small, dark, and about as developed as a rail."

"I told you not to talk to me like that."

Blair raised a hand as he moved towards one of the chairs alongside the pool. "Sorry, but it's true. Do you remember ever meeting Aunt Sara?"

"No." I bumped up against the rim of the pool and put a hand on it to steady myself.

"Except for the age difference, she, Nora, and Lydia are pretty much all the same model."

"That doesn't prove anything." I pulled myself from the water and moved to the lounge chair where I set my towel. I could feel Blair's eyes on me every second until the moment I wrapped it around myself.

When I turned back to Blair, he was leaning forward, his shoulders hunched, his hands dangling between his knees, staring into the water. He wasn't fooling me though. He said, "Have you decided what you're going to do?"

"About what?"

He looked up. "Going home."

A flash of the suspicion I felt the night before raced through me. Was Blair really trying to protect me or did he just want to remove another rival? I wished I could talk to Nora, to ask her if Blair said anything similar to her. Maybe I could find a spare moment to slip away from the group later and call her at the motel.

"I haven't decided," I told him. "It's easier to be brave in the morning."

Blair glanced up at the skylight. There wasn't much morning to be seen; the clouds were even thicker today, darker and more menacing. Without the benefit of a clock, it could have been morning or evening. "I wish this damned storm would start so we could just be done with it. I'm starting to forget what the sun looks like."

He stood, looked across the pool at me, and said, "Let's find breakfast. I'm starving."

After I showered and changed in my room, with Blair waiting out in the hall, he knocked on Marcus and Chelsea's door. It opened a crack and Marcus peered out, his eyes bloodshot and crusted with sleep. "What time is it?" he whispered.

"Almost seven thirty," Blair answered. "Feel like breakfast?"

Blair didn't have to ask how his older brother felt this morning. It was obvious that Marcus was still recovering from last night.

Marcus nodded. "Coffee, at least. Hold on."

He shut the door and we heard muffled voices. A moment later, it opened. Holding up a hand, Marcus said, "Five minutes, okay?" The door closed again and we could hear the sound of their shower running.

Blair leaned against the wall and looked me up and down. As dressed up as he was today, I felt like dressing down, just to be different. I was wearing a navy sweatshirt and a light-blue plaid skirt. He didn't say anything, but he seemed to approve.

We were quiet for a few minutes, the only sounds the muted shower a couple of walls away, and the occasional movement inside the room.

Then Blair surprised me. "Suppose Aunt Lydia died in the night?"

It was a terrible thing to say under any other circumstances, but it almost seemed normal in that house.

"I guess we'd hear about it if she did," I said.

Blair nodded and opened his mouth, but then the door swung open and Chelsea stepped through, saying, "That miserable old bitch lied to us from the get-go. She isn't dying." Sparks danced in her eyes like chain-lightning. "I bet she's not even sick. She'll probably live another ten years."

"I doubt that. She's pushing eighty," Blair reminded her.

"So what?" Chelsea spat. "Except for that wheelchair, there's no sign anything's wrong with her at all."

That wasn't true, but I was the only one who knew it. I saw

Lydia when she was exhausted, pale and shaking, from pouring out a story that she probably never told anyone before. Maybe Lydia had good days, or maybe she just hid it well, but I was certain that something was wrong with her. She might really even be dying, like she claimed.

"How much longer do we have to wait?" Chelsea was just upsetting herself, making herself angrier. "I want that goddamned money. I've already put in thirteen years. When do I get something out of marrying that slob?"

"You talk too much, Chelsea," Marcus said from inside the room. He was showered and dressed, his hair wet and pushed to the side, but he still looked hungover and half-asleep. Chelsea gave her husband a sharp look, but stopped talking.

The four of us went down to the dining room. By unspoken arrangement, Blair and I had been sitting next to each other on one side of the table and Chelsea and Marcus together on the other. Today when I sat down, Chelsea hurried to take the chair next to me. Blair raised an eyebrow, but instead of sitting on my opposite side, he pulled out the chair across the table from me and sat. Marcus made no comment, just flopped down next to Blair.

Elijah appeared in the doorway to the kitchen as if summoned by a magic wand, carrying a carafe of coffee and a pitcher of orange juice. He set both on the table, announced that breakfast would be served momentarily and disappeared back into the kitchen. The four of us sat in silence until the food arrived, and when it did, the silence was replaced only by the sounds of our eating.

It was a long time until anyone finally spoke, and it was Marcus, surprising me. "Do you all think Ryan is dead?"

Eyes flicked around the table as everyone tried to gauge the others' responses.

"I hope he isn't," I said, "but..."

"But," Blair agreed.

"That cop, Goddard, is useless," Chelsea sniffed.

"It can't be easy," I said, without looking at her. "From what I understand, he and his partner don't get very much support out here."

Chelsea lifted her coffee cup, but clinked it back down against the saucer. "And that should be our problem?"

"What's everybody got planned for today?" Marcus blurted out. It wasn't like him to play peacemaker, but maybe he was afraid of what Chelsea might say next. He glanced at Blair. "What're you all dressed up for anyway?"

"Can't a man just want to look his best?" Blair lifted his cup and sipped coffee.

"Is that a dig?" Marcus actually looked hurt.

"Not at all," Blair said mildly.

"I want to talk to Aunt Lydia."

Blair met my eyes across the table. "About what she said last night?"

"A little, yes, but there's other things too."

"Want company?"

"Why don't we all go?" Chelsea put in. "Maybe we can shake some sense out of her."

"I wouldn't recommend trying it," Blair warned her. "You've seen Elijah."

"He doesn't scare me," Chelsea sneered.

"He should," I told her, wondering if he was on the other side of the kitchen door right now, listening to us. Lydia and I were probably the only two people in the house who knew just how dangerous Elijah actually was.

"Well, I'm done." Chelsea threw her napkin onto her plate, stood, then lifted her coffee cup and drained it. She said to Marcus, "Are you coming with me or staying down here?"

The big, soft man looked at me. It felt like he wanted to say something, but he didn't. He just stood and waited for Chelsea to make her way around the table and head for the door. Before it closed behind them, I heard Marcus say, "I want to make a call. Can we stop in the library?" If Chelsea responded, I didn't hear it.

"I guess I'm through too," Blair said, just as Elijah came out of the kitchen to begin clearing dishes.

We went out into the hallway. I told Blair, "I'm going up to Lydia's room. Elijah's busy, so now's the best time to talk to her."

"Will she be awake?"

I shrugged. "I'll wake her up, if I have to. C'mon."

Outside of Lydia's room on the third floor, I asked Blair to wait outside. He didn't like the idea, but I think it was more because he didn't want to run into Elijah alone rather than any worry for my sake. I was firm, though, and he gave up quickly.

I pushed the door open and stepped through. I expected the room to be shrouded in darkness, but the curtains were already open and a bedside lamp was lit. Lydia sat up in bed, the various sections of a newspaper spread across the comforter. "Come right in, no need to knock," she said without looking from whatever she was reading. "It's not as if it's my house or anything."

I crossed the room, stopping at the foot of the bed. She spent twenty or thirty seconds more reading, then lowered the paper and looked at me over the top of it. "Oh, it's you, my favorite niece. I suppose that's about right. You're the only one who's come to talk to me, you know."

"I'm not really surprised. You haven't given us much reason to want to talk with you."

Lydia closed her eyes. "Listen to that wind howling." It was true; the wind was stronger than any time since I arrived. "Maybe we'll finally get that storm."

She opened her eyes and smiled without any friendliness. "No, I guess I haven't given any of you a reason to like me. So they hate me. That's just fine; it doesn't bother me at all because I don't like them either – especially that redheaded witch Marcus married. You know, she actually somehow blames her husband for all of this?" She laughed lightly. "As if he was ever responsible for a thing in his life. They had quite a fight about it last night. I couldn't hear it from up here, of course, but Elijah gave me the gist of it, right after he procured a bottle for poor little Marcus."

She shook the section of newspaper she held, straightening the pages, then folded them, and put them aside. "Now, what's on your mind? Still thinking about what we discussed last night?"

I was, but I didn't want to talk about it anymore. Maybe Lydia was telling the truth, maybe Blair's theory was right. I didn't know and it didn't matter then. She brought up Elijah first and I decided that was as good a place to start as any.

"About Elijah…"

"What about him?"

I wasn't sure how to get around to the point I wanted to make. "How well do you know him?"

Lydia made a face as if I was a very slow child asking a very obvious question. "What is there to know? He's been with me for almost twenty years and he's earned my trust. I've never once had reason to regret bringing him into this house."

"He doesn't scare you at all?"

Lydia looked sharply at me. "Why should I be afraid?"

Quickly, the words tumbling out as if I needed to say them before someone could stop me, I told her about what happened in town, about Elijah following Rick and me into the bar and what Elijah did to Rick afterwards. I didn't mention the times he grabbed me or the things he said to me. Those weren't anything I could prove, but Rick's arm was proof of what Elijah was capable of.

When I was through, the old woman batted a hand as if swatting away the entire sequence of events. "Don't be foolish. That doesn't worry me at all. Can't you see that Elijah was protecting you? That Kolit boy is useful for running errands, but he's barely more than a gigolo. He's probably had every lonely woman within a hundred mile radius of this mountain. Elijah just saved you from being the next notch on his belt."

I was shocked, though I shouldn't have been. "Maybe that's true," I began, "but Rick wasn't hurting me. We were having a good time, and I *wanted* to be there. Elijah had no business—"

"Listen to me, Holly Shaw." Lydia's voice was stern, but there was no malice in it. "Elijah is utterly devoted to me and that loyalty extends to anyone I've offered my hospitality to. Whether you realize it or not, he did you a favor. I've known him since he was barely more than a boy, working for my husband over at the refinery, and I've never seen him do any less than his utmost to fulfill whatever he sees as his duties."

Hearing Lydia defend Elijah was strange. I never imagined she was the kind of person to stand up for anyone else. I had the feeling that I'd opened her bedroom door and, like an episode of *Black Mirror*, walked into some alternate universe. But it made me curious.

"So this isn't just a job for Elijah. Was he that devoted to your husband?"

"No." Lydia shook her head slightly. "Elijah hated Piotr."

"Then why—"

"Why would Elijah work for a man he hated?" She breathed deeply through her nose and made a small production of arranging the bedspread around her legs. She began to talk. "Piotr Orlov was a hard man, and he could be a very cruel one. He was miserable to work for—I know that much. When he bought the Foster Oil Works refinery, it was a barely profitable mess. He whipped the business and its employees into shape." She glanced up at me, still playing idly with the bedcovers. "Did I tell you he was given a commendation by the governor?" She didn't wait for an answer. "Piotr expanded the business tenfold, creating new jobs and bringing a lot of money into this area. By global standards, it's a small operation, but even now, close to twenty years after his death, and almost seven since I sold it to a conglomerate, it employs nearly everyone in the area and runs as smoothly as glass."

Lydia looked directly at me. "That's all due to the systems Piotr put in place. He was a hard man, as free with his fists as he was with his words. If he had something to say, he said it, and if someone argued, he was more than willing to put them in their place—physically, if need be. Nobody there liked him, but they came to respect him, and he made a lot of money for a lot of people who previously had very little.

"That success, of course, created new problems. The refinery was constantly in need of men, more than this town or the little encampments outside of it could provide. Outsiders flocked here. The kind of men who were willing to give up everything and work in the middle of nowhere aren't exactly society's finest.

"There was some sort of dispute between the workers and management. I don't know what started it. Elijah, young and hot-headed, elected himself leader of the newer men, and called for a strike. He wanted to meet directly with Piotr. My husband was furious, it was an insult that an employee of his would dare make such a demand—would make *any* demands. He went to that meeting armed with a gun. He didn't even try to hide it. I rarely interfered with his business, because I felt it wasn't my place, but I followed him that day—I still drove then—and when I arrived at the refinery, I found Piotr, all alone except for that gun, facing off against two-hundred men, with Elijah standing right at their head. I don't know what was said, but Piotr was pointing his gun directly at Elijah and shouting in Russian. I put myself between them and somehow, I managed to calm my husband. The senior managers stepped in then and finally worked everything out. I think everyone was scared not to at that point. Before Piotr would sign off on the deal, though, he had one condition: Elijah must be fired. That was non-negotiable."

I tried to imagine Elijah as a young man, idealistic, ready to take on his employer and face a gun for the sake of his fellow employees. I couldn't do it. It was just too out there for me to wrap my head around.

"So how did he become your butler?"

"He is more than a butler!" Lydia snapped. "He is my bodyguard, my caregiver, the head of my household. This place wouldn't run at all if it wasn't for Elijah."

She composed herself and said, more slowly, "I don't know where Elijah came from, I never asked, but Piotr had his way and Elijah lost his job at the refinery. Most people would have simply disappeared, there being nothing to hold them here. Elijah hung around town for months, though, and occasionally I saw him when I went down the mountain or I heard something of him from someone around the town. I gathered that he either had nowhere to go or that he simply *couldn't* go anywhere for whatever reason. When Piotr had his second heart attack, the fatal one, almost nine months after the incident at the refinery, I sent Ned to town to find Elijah and bring him up here. The first thing he did was thank me for saving his life. He was certain Piotr was going to kill him, and I'm sure he was right."

"And that's how he came to work here? You felt you owed each other something?"

"No." Lydia shook her head. "You don't understand at all, but that's not your fault." She took several deep breaths, as if working up to something. "After speaking with Elijah for hours that day, I offered him a job. I admit that Elijah isn't much to look at, but he was strong and willing to work, and... well, I might as well tell you since it doesn't matter anymore."

I was almost afraid to ask. I felt I didn't want to know whatever she was ready to confess. "Tell me what?"

"I told you that Piotr Orlov and I loved each other, and that's a fact. Love and sex were very different things to Piotr, though, things not necessarily related at all. Maybe it's a Russian thing, maybe it was just specific to him. I don't know. I learned very early in our marriage that I couldn't satisfy Piotr. I was a middle-aged woman, completely inexperienced. We never stopped being intimate, but he roamed quite a bit, especially on business trips. At first, I was devastated, but I learned to accept it as just another facet of our strange marriage. As long as I didn't have to see it, I could pretend it wasn't happening. Then he brought Eleonore into this house. She was his last and apparently his favorite. You wouldn't believe it now, but she was once a pretty woman. She was here for close to three years before Piotr passed and I don't think he had another woman besides the two of us during that time.

"After he was gone, I could have thrown her out, I suppose, but she is an excellent cook and for some reason, it seemed like she didn't want to leave. It also would have been next to impossible to replace her, to find someone of her skill who worked for so little and willing to live out here, so I let her stay. Not her brat though; I had enough of children to last me several lifetimes and with this house under my sole command, I made her send him away. Oh, don't look at me like that. I paid for his schooling, down at a boys' school in Washington. He would never have gotten the same quality education here, so it was for both of their benefits as well as mine. Why he wastes it doing odd jobs in this frozen hellhole is beyond me, but that's his choice. I told you to stop looking at me like that, Holly Shaw. I'm not a monster; I just never liked the boy. For all I knew, he was Piotr's bastard, and I didn't want to have to see him around my home any more than was necessary."

"That's horrible," I said.

"Wait until you have a husband of your own before you judge me, my dear. If you're lucky, he'll keep his affairs hidden from you. That's one thing I can say I'm proud of though: I never punished Piotr for his wanderings, and I stayed loyal to him and had no lover of my own until he was gone."

Pieces began clicking together.

"You mean that's why you're so sure of Elijah? Because he isn't just your servant, he's your... lover?"

"Yes!" Lydia sat bolt upright on the bed in her excitement. She was proud that she could tell someone about this relationship. Eleonore and Ned must have known, but I suppose it wasn't the same. "As long as Elijah is in this house, I've no reason to fear anyone or anything. He'd never let any harm come to me."

"I got past him twice now," I said quietly. "He can't be everywhere. When he was clearing the breakfast dishes this morning, I just walked right up the stairs."

The old woman's mouth fell open and some of the color faded from her cheeks. "Y-you," she stammered. "You don't make a damned bit of difference. You're just a girl and you're my own family, besides."

"But you hate your family," I reminded her, "and some of us hate you right back. You're the one who keeps telling me that, aren't you?"

Lydia's eyes clouded over, as if another thought occurred to her—one she didn't like at all. "Get out of here!" she shouted. "Leave me alone. I won't listen to any more of this from you!"

"No, you need to listen to me," I told her, moving closer to the bed. When she was within arm's reach, I lifted a hand. The old woman cringed back against the pillows. It was the first and only time I ever saw her show fear.

"You're in danger, Aunt Lydia," I said. "We all are, but you more than anyone. Elijah's not out there to protect you now and it could have been anyone walking in here instead of me. I want your money as much as the others, but I'd never hurt you or anyone else to get it. I can't say for sure that's true of the others. Whoever hurt Jonathan might just decide that the stakes are high enough now and come after you."

"This is some sort of trick." She hissed it at me, like a spitting cat.

I shook my head. "No, it's not. And I'll tell you something else:

Elijah told me that he'd protect me, just like he's always protected you. I don't know why he'd worry about me in particular, but it doesn't matter, because I don't see how he can protect both of us when our purposes are at odds—"

"Get out!" Lydia shrieked, cutting me off. She jabbed a bony finger towards the door. "Get out! Get out! Get out!"

I already knew what kind of person Lydia Orlov was, but it still hurt being treated that way. She said her husband was a cruel, hard man, but I didn't think she was much different.

I knew what I said hurt her, too, even if she didn't believe it. She wouldn't listen to anything else I had to say now and I couldn't help her if she didn't want me to, so I turned towards the door and slowly went out. I waited a moment, with my hand on the knob, hoping to hear the click of a lock or some movement inside, but there was nothing. She wasn't even able to do that much for herself.

And now, just like Lydia wanted, she really was on her own.

CHAPTER TWENTY

W hen I went into Lydia's room, I left Blair in the hallway and asked him to wait, but now he was nowhere to be seen.

I had a decision to make. I could look for Blair, or for Marcus and Chelsea, or I could go back to my room, lock the door, and hide again.

The idea of hiding was both attractive and off-putting. On the one hand, I should be fairly safe inside my own room. On the other, there was no *guarantee* that was the case. Besides that, I didn't want to be the kind of person who was always running away.

Wandering the house alone wasn't any better an idea though. I would just be making a target of myself for whoever killed Jonathan and maybe Ryan. I wondered where Blair was, why he left. I wished he had stayed put, but I was also worried that something happened to him. He seemed the least likely to be taken in by anyone looking to harm him, but it was always a possibility.

I couldn't stand around outside Aunt Lydia's room

considering my options; Elijah might show up any moment. I compromised by going down to the second floor.

The doors in the guest-room hall were all shut and it was quiet enough that even my soft-soled shoes sent up echoes. Cold pinpricks skittered down my spine as I realized that almost all of the rooms on this floor were empty now. I hugged myself and rubbed my arms, even though the house was always warm enough. I couldn't even consider going back to my room and locking myself inside now. It would feel like climbing into a coffin.

As I returned to the stairs, there was noise from below—small *tmp-tmp-tmp* sounds, like feet moving quickly over carpet, followed by a *thud*, as if something fell or banged into a wall.

"Blair?" I called, afraid it wasn't.

"Yeah," he answered from around the bend in the staircase. He appeared a moment later, favoring his right leg. "I'm here."

I moved down several steps, meeting him halfway. "What happened?"

He shook his head. "I don't have a damned idea." He sat on a step and began rubbing his knee. "I waited for you a while, then I heard yelling down on the second floor. I figured I could check it out and come right back. I wasn't even halfway down, though, when a door slammed and someone went running through the hall and downstairs. I followed, but near the bottom, I tripped over my own two feet." He looked frustrated and maybe a little embarrassed. "I caught myself, but banged my knee pretty good against the wall."

"Who was it?" I asked.

"It has to be either Marcus or Chelsea, doesn't it? And I don't think my brother could run like that. I was coming back up to check their room when you called my name."

"Let's go see."

I started up the stairs, but Blair put a hand on my calf, stopping me. "Do you really want to?"

I looked down at him, letting the irritation show on my face and in my voice. "What does that mean?" I moved up a step, out of Blair's reach.

"I mean that you can get out of this, save yourself any more trouble. We'll find a way to get you into town and you can hop on the plane out of here."

"The next flight isn't for three days," I reminded him.

"I'm sure you could find a way to kill three days, even in a hole like Foster's Place. What about that kid, Rick? He was trying to make you, wasn't he?"

The expression was vulgar, but I didn't know if Blair meant it that way. I let it pass. "I guess so."

Blair nodded. "He probably needs cheering up after what happened. You could play nurse for a couple days and then grab that flight. Since we'll never see any of these people again once we leave, I won't even mind. I'm not the jealous type."

"Don't be disgusting."

Blair lifted his shoulders. "I really am just thinking about your safety, you know."

"Well, don't. Let's worry about your brother and sister-in-law first."

Blair let out a hard sigh.

The door to Marcus and Chelsea's room was ajar. A draft flowed out of it into the hallway. Going first, Blair pushed the door open and stepped inside. When I followed, I noticed two things: there was a suitcase open on the bed, but empty, and one of the windows was open. A stiff, cold breeze rustled the curtains and chilled the room. There was no one inside and the open bathroom door showed that it was empty too.

Blair crossed to the window and stared out of it, his expression brooding. "Looks like we're finally going to get that storm." He closed the window and drew the curtains.

"Do you think something happened to them?" I asked.

"First things first." Blair moved to the door, shutting it firmly, then snapped the lock in place. He turned, saying, "Nobody will think to look for either of us in here, so we should have some time."

"What about Marcus and Chelsea?"

"Chelsea is a survivor. Sometimes, I think she's practically cold-blooded. It would explain why I don't have any nieces or nephews of my own anyway." He lifted his hands. "We already did the room-by-room bit with Ryan and I just don't care to repeat it right now." He moved to the foot of the bed and sat, massaging his knee with one hand. "Want to tell me what Lydia said?"

I told him. He tried to get me to sit next to him, but the room was cold and I felt like I had to keep moving or I'd freeze solid. I paced the floor, arms wrapped around myself, telling Blair about Piotr Orlov and Elijah, and about Lydia and Elijah's later relationship.

Blair let out a low whistle. "Who'd have thought old Lydia was a cougar in her day? She must have been pushing sixty when all of this happened. And that sly dog Elijah. I'd never have guessed."

"I don't want to think about it." Just the idea of Elijah and Lydia engaged in any shared physical act was sickening. Not because of their age difference or their bodies, but because of who they were. They both scared me, each in their own way.

"Well, it explains some things anyway." Blair stood, but only moved to the bathroom doorway and leaned a hip against the frame, working his sore knee back and forth. "I wonder when he found the time to learn his trade."

I sat on the arm of the room's single chair, over by the window. "She still believes he's totally devoted to her. Or at least, she wants to. She actually looked scared when I told her that Elijah said he would protect me."

"The old bitch must be jealous as hell. I'm surprised she didn't try to claw your eyes out right then and there."

"I wasn't that close."

Blair smirked. "Smart girl. So what do we do with this

information?"

"I don't know. I really am worried about Marcus and Chelsea."

"Do you want me to go look for them?"

I frowned. "And leave me alone for Elijah to find? Or maybe for whoever's trying to kill us all off?"

"Come with me then. Two heads are better than one, so I guess four eyes are better than two."

"I'd rather stay here. Lydia's probably telling Elijah what I said even as we sit here talking, and I don't imagine he'll be too happy with me. He won't think to look for me here, though, and if you run into him, you'll be a lot safer by yourself than with me."

Blair made a frustrated sound. "You might be the most inconsistent woman I've ever met. You're worried about my brother, but don't want to look for him. You stir up trouble with Lydia, but then don't want to have to deal with it."

"Look!" I was suddenly angry. "I'm confused, okay? I'm scared, I've hardly slept since I got here, and I'm probably not thinking straight. Aren't you afraid? Your own brother was the first one killed, for God's sake, and it was probably by one of our relatives!"

Blair came to me and put his arms around my shoulders—not really hugging me, just touching me. I didn't want to be touched, but I let him do it.

"I'm sorry," he said softly. "You're right." He leaned forward and kissed the top of my head. A wisp of memory drifted through my mind; my father used to do the same thing when he put me to bed at night. I couldn't reconcile what few memories I had of him with what Lydia told me.

For a minute or so, there was no sound but the wind outside and the faint noises of the house itself. I normally only noticed them at night, and only when I wasn't lost in my own thoughts.

"Lydia's scared now, too, isn't she?" Blair said, picking up an earlier thread of our conversation. He released me and moved back to the window, pulling the curtain aside and staring out at the gloomy, windswept day. "It's about time she had a taste of her own medicine. She's been playing this miserable game, so damned sure that she had the ultimate protection." He turned. "I wonder how this'll change things."

"What do you think will happen?"

Blair lifted one shoulder. "Legally, there are things that could be done to shift the pieces around the board. Will Rick press charges against Elijah for beating him up?"

"No." I shook my head. "He didn't even tell Goddard who did it. I had to. Rick said it was 'just one of those things'."

"Figures. Well, you could try to make a case for kidnapping, since he brought you back against your will."

I didn't exactly protest when Elijah drove me to the house, but I didn't know if that mattered.

"No…" Blair said, walking the length of the room, thinking out loud. "Goddard isn't brave enough to rock that boat. Maybe our best hope here is that Lydia will get so scared she'll just have a heart attack or something and keel over so we can be done with this mess."

"Blair…"

"What?" He turned. "Do you *want* her to live forever?"

"No, but I feel sorry for her in a way. Yes, she's a hateful old woman, but so much has happened to her… She's in pain."

"Have you ever heard of a novel called *She*? By a guy named Haggard."

I shook my head.

Blair said, "It's about a woman who rules over a hidden African kingdom. She's immortal and spends her long life making men do her bidding. The main character's name is Holly, too, by the way, but it's a man and that's his family name. Anyway, my point is, that's how Lydia Orlov has lived the last twenty years: the queen of this isolated little kingdom in the middle of nowhere, with more money than God and a monster to do her bidding."

"What happened in the end?"

"The titular She takes one chance too many and ends up withering and dying. Of course, with her final breath, she promises to return."

"Lydia's not immortal."

"No," Blair agreed. "But there's no telling how long she can hold out."

He moved to the door. One hand on the knob and the other on the lock, he said, without turning, "I better go look for my brother." He glanced back, adding, "Lock it behind me. And stay safe." The lock clicked, the door opened, and he disappeared through it.

I locked the door, then went to the window. The sky was so overcast that the sun was only a vaguely lighter gray behind the heavy clouds. I still hadn't decided if I should stay here or go back home, but the next flight was three days away. A lot could happen in three days.

I don't know how much time passed. I was too lost in thoughts that were black and growing darker, when I heard a shout. I couldn't tell if it was a man's or a woman's, but it sounded angry, rather than frightened or in pain.

I pressed my ear against the door. From somewhere down the hall, closer to the stairs, I heard voices: one male and one female. It must have been Marcus and Chelsea. If they were together and all right, though, why were they arguing out in the hall instead of coming back to their room?

I considered opening the door, but some impulse told me to just keep listening, at least a little more.

I couldn't make out any of the words that were said, but their voices were loud and the tone of the conversation was obviously angry. Lydia mentioned Marcus and Chelsea having a blow-out the night before; that must have been what set Marcus on his drinking binge. They were still upset with one another when I saw them at breakfast and now it was clear that the argument wasn't over, just paused for a while.

Their voices moved closer and got a little quieter. They were still angry, but probably realized that they could be heard throughout the upper floors if they stayed by the stairs. The voyeur in me wished they would come close enough for me to make out the words. I felt a little ashamed for spying, but then reminded myself that this could literally be a matter of life and death.

Wind suddenly whipped at the house, making me jump as it rattled the windows and made sounds like giant fingers scraping across the roof. In the same instant, the bathroom light, which was on when Blair and I entered, flickered. A thought I never considered came to mind: what would we do if the power was knocked out by a storm? Just the idea of being trapped in this house in complete darkness with one of us stalking the rest, made my stomach lurch.

The wind died down and I realized that the voices had stopped. The house was quiet again and after first the argument, then the wind, it seemed very abrupt, as if someone pressed stop on a movie. I put my ear to the door again and thought I could hear muffled sounds, like heavy footsteps moving down the hallway. I guessed that was Marcus, retreating from the fight with Chelsea; she would probably be trying to open the door at any moment. I would have some explaining to do and I wasn't looking forward to it.

A minute passed, and then another, but still the doorknob didn't so much as jiggle. I started worrying. I was sure it was Marcus and Chelsea I heard, but what if I was wrong? What if those heavy footsteps weren't Marcus's, but Elijah's, or even someone unknown? What if Chelsea was out there right now, injured or worse?

My stomach twisted, and my throat grew thick, imagining the absolute worst possible scenario, but I wouldn't learn anything while hiding. I clicked the lock back, twisted the knob, and slowly pushed the door open. Before I had a chance to even glance down the hallway, though, I heard a scream. It was high-pitched and tortured, more a shriek than anything else.

When I was in high school, I found a raccoon on the side of the road. A car hit it, crushing its entire lower body, but not killing it. It managed to drag itself to the ditch, out of the road. I don't know how long it lay there, but I heard it long before I saw it. When I rode up to the spot on my bike, the poor thing's eyes found mine and it screamed in agony. It felt like it was accusing me, just because I was a human being and it knew that humans did this to it. It upset me so badly, I turned around and went right back home. My mom had already left for work, and I didn't know what to do, so I called 911. The operator was sympathetic, but said she couldn't do anything for me and suggested I notify city sanitation to remove the body. I cried for a full hour before I could make the call. It was just so unfair.

The scream I heard was the same as the raccoon's: pain and anger and confusion all jumbled up together. It was dying and it couldn't even understand why. This was more horrible, though, because it was human.

I ran down the hallway without a thought for any danger to myself. The scream didn't come again, but I didn't need it to. Something inside me already knew where it came from: the third floor. Lydia's room.

Pounding up the stairs, I burst out onto the landing and raced to Lydia's door. It was wide open and I didn't hesitate to go in.

I had no idea what I would find, and I was almost to the bed before my brain caught up with my eyes and I realized what I was seeing. Aunt Lydia lay on the bed, the covers thrown back, her bone-white legs exposed, twisted together and so thin I felt sick at the sight of them. Her arms were flung out behind her, grasping fistfuls of pillows, as if trying to find something to anchor herself with. Her face I saw last and wished I didn't see at all; it was as contorted and twisted as her legs, her eyes wide and staring, and her lips peeled back, showing small, white teeth, stained with blood. Her tongue hung loosely from her mouth and I could see where she'd bit it several times.

That wasn't even the worst part though.

Marcus stood next to the bed, one of Lydia's pillows clutched in both hands. His head swiveled towards me. His eyes were unnaturally bright, his face flushed, and his tongue kept flicking out, wetting his lips. Slowly, carefully, he put the pillow down on the bed, as if he didn't want to disturb our aunt.

"She's dead," he said over the blowing wind.

"Marcus, no…" I backed away a step. I couldn't believe what I was seeing. Was Marcus the killer all along? He was distant at first, but last night he seemed genuinely upset by Jonathan's death. Blair might have called it killer's remorse.

"She's dead," Marcus said again. "And Jonathan's gone and Nora's gone and Ryan's gone and now the rest of us, we each get twenty million dollars." He looked at me as if just recognizing me. "We each get twenty million dollars, Holly." His eyes grew even brighter and there was a note of triumph in his voice that sent a fresh wave of horror washing over me.

It didn't last. As I watched him, staring in a kind of fascinated terror, sweat sprung out on Marcus's forehead and the color drained from his skin, leaving him as pale as Lydia. The glow faded from his eyes and in its place was only fear.

I turned and saw what Marcus was so afraid of. Elijah stood in the doorway, his huge shoulders filling its entire width, his head lowered like a bull ready to charge.

For ten or fifteen seconds, no one spoke, no one moved. Elijah and Marcus simply stared at each other, like a predator gauging his next target. The air was thick with violence about to explode.

The spell was broken when Marcus swallowed hard, his Adam's apple bobbing in his unshaven throat. He said just one word, "Please." It could have been to me for help or to Elijah for mercy. It didn't matter. There wasn't either for the man who killed Elijah's mistress.

The huge man stalked forward. He didn't hurry, but his giant feet ate up the distance between them in an instant. Marcus was rooted in place, frozen by fear, only his lips moving, trying to form words, his eyes spinning crazily around the room, as if he was looking for some escape path.

There was no way past Elijah, though, and only one other way to leave the room. Marcus turned on his heel and made for the window, apparently planning to try his chances with a three-story leap.

Elijah was faster. He caught Marcus by the shoulder, swung the other man around, back towards the center of the room. Marcus went stumbling sideways and fell, crumpling to the floor in a heap. Without seeming to exert any real effort, Elijah bent, wrapped his fingers around Marcus's throat, and lifted him until his face was level with Elijah's. Marcus's head nearly touched the ceiling.

Elijah's other hand came up, joined its mate around Marcus's throat, and began to squeeze. I screamed and looked away, the powerlessness Elijah always made me feel surging upward again. Even with my hands over my ears and my eyes tightly shut, I could still hear Marcus choking as the life was literally squeezed out of him. My imagination conjured images that I would probably see in nightmares for the rest of my life, if I didn't do something.

I opened my eyes, and it was worse than I imagined: Elijah held Marcus's throat with both hands, Marcus's feet dangling limply three feet from the ground. Marcus's face was so dark it was purple.

Before I realized I was even moving, I rushed forward to beat my fists against Elijah's broad back, screaming "Elijah! Stop!" knowing it wouldn't do any good, but that I had to try. Elijah barely moved, I only saw a flash of his arm before I was flung backwards. I managed to keep my balance for an instant, then stumbled against the edge of the bed and fell next to Lydia's twisted, lifeless body. The horror of it all caught up with me, and I must have blacked out.

I was probably only unconscious for a few moments, but when I came back to myself, I realized that the room was very quiet, except for the wind and the sound of my own still racing blood pounding against my eardrums. I opened one eye and wished I hadn't.

It was like Elijah was waiting for me, to show off his strength or maybe to warn me about what happened to those who crossed him. He held Marcus's body in both arms, like he carried me from the car to my room. His eyes met mine. There was nothing in them—no hatred, no sorrow, no satisfaction at having his revenge. Then he turned, carried Marcus into the bathroom, and returned a moment later, shutting the door behind him.

Without even glancing at me now, he crossed to the bed and knelt beside it. He clasped his hands together and closed his eyes. His lips began silently moving. The sight of the monstrous butler praying over the body of his mistress was so unreal I couldn't process it properly, but I couldn't stop watching either.

When he was done with his prayer, Elijah stood and gently, delicately, straightened Aunt Lydia's limbs, crossing her arms over her chest, and pulling down her nightgown. He arranged the pillows the way Lydia liked them in life, and pulled the covers up to her chin. That done, his thick fingers found her eyelids, lowered them, and then lightly combed out her hair, putting it into some semblance of order. When he was done, it looked for all the world as if Lydia Orlov died peacefully in her sleep.

It was only then that I noticed the tears rolling down Elijah's scarred, pitted cheeks.

CHAPTER TWENTY-ONE

Trooper Abbott wasn't used to death. I noticed that right away. I didn't see how he acted when Jonathan's body was found, but standing in Aunt Lydia's bedroom, it was obvious how he felt. His eyes were wide, but seemed as if they weren't quite seeing anything, even as his head swiveled to take everything in.

I guess I couldn't blame him. It would probably be a strange scene to anyone, no matter what experience they had. Nothing was changed from the moment Elijah knelt by the bed. The room held an elderly lady who appeared to be resting quietly, peacefully, in bed. There was a giant man beside her, hands still clasped and face grief-stricken and tear-stained—a man who hadn't spoken a word in the forty minutes since he killed Marcus. And then there was the broken, bloat-faced body in the bathroom. Since the door was closed, I had to point out to Abbott that Marcus's body was in there.

When Elijah killed Marcus, I screamed, I cried, I lashed out as best as I could, but now I was numb. While Elijah mourned his lost lover, I backed slowly out into the hallway, and went down to the ground floor to find Blair. He found me first. I told him what happened, then we called the police from the library. Sergeant

Goddard was away dealing with a situation in one of the little clusters of homes a ways north of the town, but Trooper Abbott said he would be out as soon as he could.

Now, Abbott said, "I, ah..." as if lost for words. He turned to me and Blair, swallowed and began again. "I guess this all ties in with everything else that's happened." Slowly, he shook his head and softly added, "Four dead, all over money."

"We don't know that Ryan's dead," Blair reminded him.

Abbott looked over his shoulder at Elijah, who either didn't know we were there or didn't care. Elijah told me he would protect me, like he protected Lydia. I couldn't even imagine what was going through his head now.

Trooper Abbott arrested Elijah, of course.

Abbott was nervous and kept his drawn gun on Elijah as he handcuffed the big man. Elijah didn't exactly resist, but he wasn't cooperative either. His huge limbs were loose, as if boneless, making it relatively easy for Abbott to get the cuffs on him, but it required both Abbott and Blair to get him to his feet. Once Elijah was standing, though, he kept his balance and seemed to listen sullenly as Abbott told him about his rights. Lydia was already dead by the time Elijah attacked Marcus, so technically, he wasn't acting in anyone's defense, Blair explained to me later. It might sound like hairsplitting, but legally, it was an important distinction.

As Abbott guided Elijah towards the door, the giant spoke for the first time. "Wait." He half-turned towards where Lydia lay on the bed and gestured with his head. "Mrs. Orlov... give her the respect she's earned. Don't make her ride with *him*." He nodded towards the open bathroom door. He looked directly at me as he added, "She didn't deserve to die like this."

Abbott seemed uncomfortable, but finally conceded, saying he would ask the emergency services team about making two trips. Elijah wasn't quite satisfied, but he didn't argue.

We followed the policeman and his captive downstairs and

then outside. The wind howled and tiny flecks of snow swirled through the air, stinging where they hit my face. Elijah climbed into the back of Abbott's SUV without argument, though he was so massive it wasn't an easy fit. After Abbott closed the door, Elijah was hunched forward and cramped, but he didn't seem to care at all.

Abbott came back to the porch and told me, "There'll be a lot of paperwork, Miss Shaw. I'll need you to fill out a report—or dictate it to me, if you prefer, and I'll write it up. For now, though, you've been through a lot. The ambulance will be here soon, but you should get some rest."

"Thank you."

Abbott went down the stairs towards his truck as the front door of the house opened and a third person joined us. The trooper looked back at the sound of the closing door. I thought something, a nerve or a muscle, jumped in his cheek, but it might have been my imagination.

He came back, but stopped before climbing the porch and looked up at Chelsea. "Mrs. Shaw," he began.

"I know. My husband is dead," she said with absolute, iron-hard control. Her voice didn't waver, didn't betray any emotion at all. The wind whipped her long, reddish hair around, briefly hiding her face before uncovering it again. "I've been looking at his body."

"Do you..." He looked from her, to Blair, to me, and then back at Chelsea. "Do you know what happened? This isn't easy to say, but your husband apparently killed your aunt." He gestured towards Elijah, sitting in the truck, watching us. "The butler found them and—"

"My husband's aunt," Chelsea corrected him.

Abbott hesitated before asking, "Did you have any idea he planned to do this?"

"I knew he was going to talk to her. He wanted to try and make some sort of deal. I don't know what. He couldn't wait for her to die, so he could get his hands on her money. He wanted to see if he could get an advance on his inheritance. It was a stupid idea and we argued about it. That was the last time I saw him."

"I see." Abbott was at a loss, out of his depth. Chelsea's husband was gone, but she didn't seem especially grieved. It might have been easier for Abbott if she wailed in agony and tore at her hair and clothes. Her icy calm was unnerving. I wished Sergeant Goddard was here, instead of Abbott. I'm sure the young trooper did too.

"What about the others?" Blair asked.

Chelsea turned to him. "What others?" Neither her expression nor her voice betrayed anything. It was as if all feeling was drained out of her with Marcus's death.

"Jonathan and Ryan. If you know anything, you might as well tell us, now that it's basically all over but the shouting."

Chelsea's eyes narrowed. "Marcus wasn't a murderer. I don't believe he killed Lydia. I *know* he didn't kill Jonathan. And we don't even know that Ryan's dead."

"How can you be so sure—about any of it?"

Her blue-green eyes never strayed from Blair's. "I would know. Marcus might have been your brother, but he was my husband. Nobody knew him better than me."

"This isn't getting us anywhere," Abbott put in. All eyes turned to him. "Listen, folks. I need to get the prisoner back to town. I'll get in contact with the sergeant and we'll be back in touch very shortly, I'm sure." He wasn't quite desperate, but it was clear Abbott wanted to get away from all of us. I couldn't blame him.

"Sure," Blair said. "This wraps things up nicely, I guess, if you just want to believe my brother was responsible for everything. The trouble is, Marcus is dead and he can't answer any questions, so we'll never know anything for sure. For example, if he really was the murderer, how do we know Chelsea wasn't his accomplice?"

"Stop it, Blair. Please." I put my hand on his arm. "This isn't the time."

Blair looked at me. He tried to smile, but his eyes were very cold. "Don't tell me—you feel sorry for Chelsea, just like you did for Lydia."

I turned away. Blair was hurting and he wanted to lash out. That didn't mean I had to let myself be his target. He was right that Chelsea might be lying. She might have been Marcus's accomplice, like Blair suggested. It might even have been her idea to kill Lydia. Lydia did say Elijah heard them arguing about her. It just didn't feel true to me though. Marcus might have killed his cousin and aunt, neither of whom he knew very well, but I found it hard to believe he would kill his own baby brother, no matter how much money was at stake. The tears I saw him cry for Jonathan were real.

There was a bigger question now anyway: did any of it even matter? With Lydia dead, the conditions of her will were met and, as Blair said, it was all over but the shouting.

"I better get going," Abbott said. He looked at Chelsea, then said to Blair, "The ambulance will be here soon." He crossed to his SUV, climbed inside, and a moment later, was wheeling down the steep driveway.

Without a word, Chelsea went into the house.

I walked to the edge of the porch and looked up. It was late in the morning, but you would never know it. The snow was light, only the wind making it seem like a real storm, but clouds lowered the sky so it felt like it was right above our heads, almost close enough to touch. It formed a thick, sickly gray barrier that blocked out the sun, casting a veil over everything. A mourning veil. It was smothering.

A hand touched my hip. Blair said, "C'mon. You'll freeze."

I let him lead me inside, trying to convince myself that everything was over, that the house was a perfectly safe place now. Somehow, I couldn't quite believe it.

Dacha Orlov felt like a mausoleum, unnaturally quiet and empty. Outside, the wind picked up, howling like an animal sensing approaching danger, trying to warn the rest of its pack. The temperature in the house was a perfectly comfortable seventy-two degrees by the thermostat in the main hallway, but I felt chilled.

The ambulance came and went. The same two men who picked up Jonathan only three days earlier took both Lydia and Marcus away. They zipped each of the bodies into separate bags, but put them into the back of their van together. Either Abbott didn't tell them about Elijah's request or they didn't care to honor it.

When they were gone, I was at a loss. I had no idea what to do with myself. I just wandered through rooms, wondering what this house must have felt like in happier days.

I found Blair in the den, knocking balls across the pool table. When I walked into the room, he glanced up, moving only his eyes, and then sent the white ball spinning across the green felt, scattering a cluster of four colored balls in every direction.

"Where's Chelsea?" I asked.

Blair shrugged almost imperceptibly, never taking his eyes from the table. "Does it matter?" He sent the white ball barreling across the table, making *cracks* and *thumps* as it moved the other balls around.

I watched him play his solitary game for a few minutes. I wasn't sure how to put what I needed to say into words. Blair was more sensitive than he wanted people to realize—maybe more than he knew himself.

When he spun the final ball into a pocket, I said, "I'm sorry, Blair. For what happened with Marcus and for Jonathan too. I'm not sure if I ever actually said anything to you about how sorry I was for Jonathan. I wish I'd got to know him better."

"He was a good kid," Blair said, without any particular feeling. He began gathering up the balls from the basket beneath the table. "I'm not sure how I feel about Marcus yet."

"That's..." I stopped myself. I didn't know what came next.

Blair saved me the trouble of finding the words. "You don't have to say it. Maybe Marcus got what he deserved. I kind of doubt we'll ever know."

"Don't say that."

He looked at me for the first time in several minutes. "Maybe, if Marcus really did kill the old lady, we even owe him our thanks. Instead of the measly ten million dollars we started with, we'll each get thirty million."

"Not necessarily. We still don't know what happened to Ryan."

Blair placed the black, plastic triangle on the table and began fitting balls inside it. "That's true, but he wasn't here in the house when Lydia died and those were the terms of her will, weren't they? That we had to be here, in her home, when she finally gave up the ghost?"

His blasé attitude was irritating. It made me stubborn. "How do you know he wasn't?"

"You've got a point, but we already looked for him, didn't we? Cousin Ryan's a little too big to fit into a closet or pantry. I suppose he might be in one of the servants' rooms. I can't imagine Eleonore or little old Ned shacking up with him though."

"Well, we won't know until we find him."

"Correct." Blair nodded as he lifted the triangle from the balls. "We need to find him. For accounting purposes anyway."

"Why are you so terrible sometimes?" I asked.

Without looking at me, he answered, "It's that or cry my guts out, and I'd hate to stain this blazer." He picked up the pool stick and took his first shot, breaking up the formation he'd just built.

"Have you ever actually cried for anyone but yourself?"

I turned. Chelsea stood in the doorway. The cold-steel expression was still on her face, but her eyes were red-rimmed.

Blair straightened, holding the stick in one hand like a spear, ready to throw at a charging beast. "Have you?"

Chelsea stepped into the room, but stopped halfway between the door and the pool table. "Why do you hate me so much? Do you really think I helped Marcus kill anyone? Jon was Marcus's brother just as much as he was yours. Was Marcus such a miserable bastard that he would kill his own little brother?"

"He was a miserable bastard, yes," Blair said slowly. "About the rest…" He didn't finish.

I put myself between them, asking, "What good is arguing? Nothing anyone says or does will bring either of them back. There's still Ryan though."

"That's right," Chelsea said, as if just remembering her husband's other cousin. She looked at me. "We never did find him, did we?"

"We should look again."

"Well, let's look then," Blair said, laying the stick across the top of the table. "I can finish the game later."

"Don't be like that, please," I begged.

Blair looked at me, but turned quickly, shaking his head slightly. "You're right. I'm sorry."

I was relieved. There were so few of us left, we had to stick together.

"We've already searched the house though," Chelsea pointed out. "Where else is there?"

"I've been thinking about that, actually," Blair said. "Ryan was too big to hide, but only inside the house. There's a whole wide world out there, and plenty of good spots to hide something you don't want found."

"Or someone," Chelsea added. "Where do you suggest we start?"

It came to me with the memory of Ryan throwing an empty bottle over the cliff.

"Holly's got it."

Blair was watching me. I said, "We should look at the bottom of the cliff, after the storm lets up."

"We should look," Blair agreed, "but I don't think we should wait."

"You can't go climbing down that thing!" Chelsea said. "It's a sheer drop. What did that kid say, when he brought us up here?"

"Three-thousand feet."

Chelsea's chin dipped. "That's right. That's a long way straight down."

"Do you two want to find Ryan or not?" Blair made it a challenge.

I looked at him and said, "But we don't even know how to get down there."

"No, *you* don't. While you were having fun in town the other day, I did some exploring. It's a straight drop down below the patio, yes. That's why the wall is there. Off around the north side, though, it's just steep. It's a slope, not a cliff, so it wouldn't be impossible to make it down there."

"Even so," I told him. "With the wind and the snow and how dark it is, it's dangerous."

"Listen," Blair said.

I started to say something, but he held up a finger.

"He's right," Chelsea said after a moment. She looked from Blair to me. "The wind has died down."

It was true, I realized. I'd gotten used to the sound of the wind so quickly that it stopped registering. Now, though, it was gone and it left a void.

There was no window in the room, so I went into the hall and crossed to the dining room. Pulling aside the curtain from one of the big, floor-to-ceiling windows, I saw that the snow had stopped and the brush surrounding the house was no longer being pushed and pulled by the wind. It was still dark, though; the sky hadn't cleared at all. Did the storm pass by without ever really starting or was this just the calm before it crashed down on us full force?

Blair appeared beside me, wearing his coat and holding a flashlight. I don't know where he was keeping either one of them, but I knew that he planned to go down there all along, with or without Chelsea and me. "Any more objections?"

I tried, but I couldn't think of any.

"Let me change first," I told him.

CHAPTER TWENTY-TWO

Blair was waiting for me at the bottom of the stairs when I came back down, changed into the only pair of slacks I brought with me and the shoes with the chunky heels I was wearing when I first arrived at Dacha Orlov. They weren't at all suited for scrambling down the side of a mountain, but I hoped they'd give me more traction than the soft-soled pair I wore around the house or the dressy shoes I brought just in case.

"Ready?" Blair asked. I nodded and we went out to the patio, through the rear door off the main hallway.

Chelsea stood on her tiptoes, trying to look over the cliff wall, down into the chasm. She turned at the sound of our arrival. "How could Ryan even go over this unless he wanted to? It's so thick I can barely lean far enough to see down there."

Something passed across Blair's face. Ryan was a big man, but so was Marcus. If Marcus was the killer…

But no, there was no point thinking about it anymore. Marcus was gone and we couldn't ask him anything ever again. Maybe it wasn't the truth, and maybe it wasn't fair, but circumstances made him look guilty and that was probably the way it would be officially recorded by the police. It was the easiest, simplest way to close out the files on two murders, after all, and policemen are as human as anyone else.

Without answering Chelsea, Blair turned to me, pointed towards the far end of the patio, and said, "Let's get going, before the storm decides to swing back around our way."

Chelsea followed a step or two behind us to the edge of the patio, around the far side of the house, near where Jonathan's body was found. She stopped following when we stepped off of the paving stones and into the nearby trees. We never discussed her coming with us, but I guess the decision was made just the same.

Under the trees, it was even darker than out in the open. I wouldn't have been able to find my way, winding through trees and brush, but Blair seemed to know where he was going. He did say he spent time exploring.

There wasn't much accumulation of snow around the house, thanks to Ned's efforts, but among the trees, it was uneven, almost random-seeming. In some places, there was almost no snow at all, and in others, it was so deep it came up to my knees. Within minutes, my shoes and pants were soaked and my teeth were chattering. I wished I had a pair of boots and some jeans, but I couldn't have expected a hike like this when I packed for the trip.

Soon, the ground began to angle downward. It wasn't a cliff, but it was still pretty steep, and choked with thick-growing brush and small, stunted trees that seemed permanently bent against the wind, even though it was still at the moment. When the angle of descent grew sharper, the only way I could manage to keep following Blair was to use the brush and trees as handholds to steady myself. It was hard work, and dangerous, but doable. Blair, on the other hand, was so surefooted it was like he was born to this. More than once, he waited to help me through an especially difficult area.

After half an hour or so, we came to a little area that was

more or less flat and Blair called for a break. I sat down right in the snow, so tired I didn't care about being wet or cold.

Blair flopped next to me, looked over and said, "You're a mess, Holly, but I love you whether you're glamorous or not." As if to prove it, he leaned in and kissed me before I could pull away. I let him do it, but I didn't return the kiss.

He leaned back, half-reclined against the snowy ground. "I think you've also got more guts than any woman I've ever met. Probably any man, either, for that matter."

I still hadn't quite caught my breath, but I managed to ask, "What do you mean?"

He glanced over, then looked up at the sky. "I know you still don't quite trust me. You probably have some voice somewhere in the back of your head that thinks I might be the one responsible for all of this." He turned back to me. "Aren't you afraid I'll heave you over the side?" He flashed a mean little boy's smirk.

Sometimes, I thought I had Blair figured out. Others, I really didn't understand him at all.

"No," I told him. "I'm not. Chelsea saw us go into the woods together, for one thing. For another, Aunt Lydia's already dead, and the police know about it, so there's an official record. Even if I died now, you wouldn't get my share of the money."

"True." Blair leaned over and tried to kiss me again, but I ducked away. He seemed annoyed, but all he said was, "Well, for both of our sakes, be careful going down. If you slip and fall, I'll be blamed no matter how obvious an accident it might be."

"I'll be careful," I promised.

The wind began to pick up as we continued down the slope. There was nothing that we could even pretend was a path anymore, and though we could see the bottom of the mountain now, it was still far below. The way was getting steeper and more difficult, and the brush thinner, giving us fewer and fewer handholds.

At just the right time, I looked up and saw a tiny gap appear in the clouds, showing a sliver of blue sky. I wanted to take some encouragement from it, the first glimpse of sky I'd seen in days, but instead, it just felt ominous.

I yelled down to Blair, "I don't think we'll ever make it back up, even if we do get down safely!" His head swiveled upwards at the sound of my voice, but he didn't respond, just continued to climb.

I looked up the slope, back the way we came. I think we were about halfway down the mountain by then, but we'd been climbing for an hour and I knew it would be at least twice as hard going up as coming down. Imagining a fall from this height, I started to get really scared. I damned Blair for first putting the thought into my head.

Blair stood on a tiny outcropping of stone, maybe fifteen feet below where I clung to the side of the mountain. The stone was roughly triangular and must have pushed itself through the surface of the rocky earth at some long ago point in time. I started to move a little faster, hurrying as much as I dared, and a couple of minutes later was standing behind Blair, my back pressed to the angled slope. It was uncomfortable, but the space wasn't big enough that I wanted to chance standing next to him.

Blair's head scanned slowly from left to right and back again, surveying the area. "If a body fell from the very top," he said, "it probably went all the way down."

A gust of wind swept past us, whipping my hair and making Blair stagger. My heart leapt into my throat, but he caught himself and took a step backwards to press his hand against the slope for better balance. "Close one," he said.

"Let's go back up."

He shook his head. "Not yet. The storm's coming back, though, so it'll have to be soon. We won't go any farther down, but this is as good a spot as any to look, so let's just—"

He broke off, his eyes widening. "Look!" He pointed and I

turned, shifting my body clumsily while trying to keep in contact with the mountain.

Almost straight across from where we stood, in the middle of the bare cliff-face twenty-five or thirty yards away, something white fluttered. Standing out from the sheer, almost smooth stone was an outcropping like the one we stood on, but it seemed to be indented, like a bowl. As I watched, the wind plucked at whatever was sitting on it, making the piece of fabric flutter like a flag. It could only be Ryan and a piece of his clothing, maybe torn when it caught on something during his fall.

"See it?" There was excitement in Blair's voice.

"Yeah."

The view was hardly ideal, and it would take a good pair of binoculars to be really sure, but it was good enough for me, and I knew Blair was convinced the moment he saw it. He was already certain Ryan went over the top of that wall and this was proof as far as he was concerned.

Blair's expression darkened. "No wonder we couldn't find him."

"Do you think...?"

Angry eyes found mine. Blair already knew what I was going to say before I finished. "That Marcus pushed him?" His head moved back and forth. "It would take more than a push. That wall is about four feet high. Marcus was a big man, but Ryan was even bigger. If Ryan didn't want to go over, Marcus couldn't have made him."

"Do you think it was suicide then? He was pretty upset."

"Possible, but far-fetched, don't you think? Killing yourself over the death of a cousin you haven't seen since childhood is a little too dramatic. Ryan was a meat and potatoes guy if I've ever met one."

"Well, then someone pushed him. He might have been drunk. He was drunk most of the time the last day or so before he disappeared, wasn't he?"

"Even so, you'd either need a running start to push him hard enough or have to be as strong as an ox to heave him over... and who do we know like that?"

"Elijah? But—"

"But what?" The wind chose that moment to intensify, howling past us and seemingly pulling the words from Blair's mouth and carrying them off into the distance. "Lydia hated us and Elijah loved her. He'd do anything he thought would make her happy, wouldn't he? Especially when she didn't have much time left to enjoy."

Elijah was the only one physically capable of lifting a man as large as Ryan, but it didn't make any sense to me. Lydia may have wanted us dead, but she wanted the pleasure of watching as we destroyed each other. If Ryan was drunk and stumbling though... maybe with momentum, it wouldn't be as hard to get him over the wall as Blair thought.

That wasn't the place or time to consider it though. The wind was steady now and stronger than before, bringing with it little blasts of powdery snow, screaming in my ears and numbing my face.

"Blair, we have to go back."

"You go first." He jutted his chin. "I'll be right behind you."

It took almost three hours to reach the place where we first descended. By the time we did, I was so tired that my arms were numb and I literally couldn't stand. I lay down in the snow, totally oblivious to the cold and wind and the constant flurries that chased us the last hour and a half of the climb. I was so exhausted, I didn't think I'd ever be able to move again.

"C'mon, Holly." Blair stood over me, upside down from my perspective. "You can't sleep here." Grabbing my arm, he tried to lift me into a sitting position. "C'mon, I mean it. You've survived this long; do you want hypothermia to get you now?"

I groaned, knowing he was right.

With Blair's help, I got to my feet. Every part of my body hurt, my clothes were soaked, filthy, and ripped in countless places. Everything I was wearing, including the shoes, would have to be thrown out.

The house seemed very far away, but somehow we made it. Chelsea met us in the main hallway, asking questions: what took so long? Did we find Ryan? Things like that. I wasn't really listening.

I sat on the same bench that Marcus did when Blair and I found him crying over Jonathan's death. I would be perfectly happy to never move again, but Blair was filled with angry energy, even though he must have been just as tired as I was. He ignored Chelsea and went into the library—to call the police again, I guessed. Goddard and Abbott must have been sick of us by then. They probably both wished they'd never heard the names "Orlov", "Shaw" or "Hill".

Chelsea stood in the middle of the hallway. I was sure she wanted to follow Blair, to listen in on his half of the conversation, but she turned back to me. "Are you okay, honey?" she asked with the same uncharacteristically gentle tone she used when Nora had her panic attack.

"I'm just more tired than I knew it was possible to be."

The other woman seemed to notice the state of my clothing for the first time. "You're soaked! C'mon." She put her arms around my shoulders and heaved upwards. "Let's get you into a shower and some clean clothes."

I let her lead me, and a few minutes later, I was standing under hot, stinging needles. Nothing ever felt as good in my entire life. I wished I could stay in the shower forever, but warmed up and clean, my thoughts went back to the problem at hand. Chelsea was just outside the bathroom and while I lingered under the water a little longer, I told her about the climb and what we saw.

"Damn it," she muttered. "I figured, but I still kind of hoped…"

"I know." I stepped out of the shower, wrapping a towel around myself.

Chelsea sat on the edge of the bed. I went to the closet and began dressing. Just as I pulled on a sweater, Blair walked into the room without knocking. Literally any other time, I would have been upset, but I was glad to see him.

"Did you talk to the police?"

He was angrier than I'd ever seen him before. "No, goddamn them. There's a woman answering the phone over there, says Goddard is still dealing with something in Chickaroon, wherever the hell that is. I guess it's a big thing now—they've got state police coming in from other areas too—so he'll be tied up for a while."

"Is Abbott with him?"

He shook his head. "No, and it's weird. She said he hasn't come back."

My breath froze in my lungs. It was close to four o'clock. Abbott left long before noon, with Elijah in tow.

I looked at Chelsea. She was clearly thinking the same thing. Something must have happened to him.

Blair didn't act concerned at all though. "Well, I guess all we can do is wait." He collapsed into the room's one chair. His exhaustion was finally catching up with him. Not even anger could overcome it for long. "Ryan isn't going anywhere and with both murderers out of the house, we should be safe enough."

"No!" Chelsea nearly shouted. She began to cry. "Don't say that. Marcus wasn't a murderer… I know he didn't kill Lydia. He wouldn't. He couldn't have!"

I sat next to her, an arm around her waist, trying to be of some comfort. I wondered what she did, what she thought about, when we left her here alone. None of us had seen Ned or

Eleonore that day and as far as we knew, they were no longer even in the house. Did they simply leave because Lydia was gone? I didn't know. I didn't know either Eleonore or Ned or how their minds worked. The fact remained, though, that they were gone and it simply never occurred to me how hard it would be for Chelsea, being left all alone with her thoughts on the day her husband was both accused of murder and then murdered himself. I felt terribly guilty.

Blair leaned back in the chair and closed his eyes. "We'll never really know."

Disgust temporarily pushed away the guilt. "He was your brother, Blair."

Blair opened one eye. "I know. I didn't want him dead, but I also can't bring him back. You were the one who saw him last, Holly, so why don't you tell me what you think? Did Marcus kill Ryan and Jon?"

"I don't know."

No one said anything for several minutes. Chelsea was quietly crying and Blair might have gone to sleep he was so still. I thought of how Ryan was also very still, but out there all alone in the cold, lying on that bit of stone, the wind whipping at him, while snow worked to hide his body. Sometime since we came back, the storm began in earnest, and now the wind slapped violently against my windows, carrying with it heavier snow and bitter cold that seeped through the glass like a stealthy invader, slowly creeping into the house. The sounds of the storm felt very lonely to me.

"What do we do now?" I asked.

"I don't know what we can do," Blair answered without opening his eyes. "If the Volvo is still in the garage, we could try to find the keys and get out of here, but I doubt it is. I'm betting Ned and Eleonore flew the coop. I don't really want to try driving down the mountain in a blizzard anyway."

He opened his eyes, sat up straighter, and reached into his

jacket, taking from it his package of cigarettes. It was crushed. He gave it an annoyed look and then hurled it into the corner of the room.

"So we just wait?"

Blair looked from Chelsea to me. "I guess. Goddard will have to come back eventually, and when he does, we'll tell him about Ryan. I don't know how they'll bring him up, but they must have a way." He stood. "In the meantime, I'm starving."

I realized I was too. Neither of us had eaten since breakfast and we'd used up a lot of energy.

Chelsea shrugged off my arm and stood too. "I'll make us something."

I reached up and took her sleeve between my thumb and forefinger. "No, you don't have to."

Chelsea jerked away, breaking my grip. "I want to. I can't just sit here thinking about all of this crap anymore. I need to *do* something."

She moved towards the door. I started to argue, but Blair shook his head at me. I gave in.

Blair went back to his room to shower and change. Chelsea and I found our way to the kitchen. The pantry and refrigerator —a big walk-in, like restaurants have—were both well-stocked. The two of us put together a meal and by the time it was ready, Blair was seated in the dining room, a lit cigarette dangling from his lips while he leafed through a book. It was the first I'd seen him smoke that day. He didn't retrieve the cigarettes before leaving my room, so he must have gone back for them.

The three of us ate in silence, the same way we'd shared most meals since coming to Dacha Orlov. When we were through, Blair pushed his chair back from the table and lit another cigarette.

"I wish you wouldn't smoke in here," I told him.

"You're right," he said, pinching out the glowing tip and

setting it on the edge of his plate. "Cancer would be a terrible way to go now that we're all rich."

Chelsea glowered at him. I thought she was going to say something, but instead, she just lifted and drained her wine glass.

"Well, here we are," Blair went on. "Three of the original seven. Or two of the original six, if you prefer," he said, looking at Chelsea, "since Lydia didn't include you in her will."

The stillness that followed was painful, like a huge lead weight pressing down on all of us. Even Blair looked uncomfortable as he sipped his wine.

"Marcus didn't kill Lydia," Chelsea said quietly.

Blair looked straight across the table at her, but she was unwilling to meet his eyes. He said, "It can't be proved either way, and it doesn't matter, so I won't argue."

"I think it can be proved," I said.

Blair looked at me in surprise. "How?"

"Something I remembered. I heard Lydia scream. It was horrible, like a dying animal." The memory of that poor raccoon sprang to mind, overlaid by the image of Lydia, twisted in her bed. "She was definitely in pain."

"I'd imagine so," Blair said.

"Shut up," I told him. "Don't interrupt." He looked taken aback, but kept quiet. "Anyway, it was a scream of pain. I'm sure of that. If she was smothered with a pillow, I couldn't have heard anything, and even if she was scared of Marcus coming into the room and screamed, it wouldn't have sounded like that."

Blair frowned. "That doesn't prove anything."

"No, but what about this: maybe that wasn't her first scream. She couldn't get around by herself without the wheelchair, and I think she only had the one. I never saw it anywhere but down here anyway, and I know Elijah carried her up and down the stairs. And there's something I don't think I told anyone."

I explained the "attack" Lydia had when she told me about her life with our parents, how pained she obviously was and how she struggled against it.

"If she had another one of those 'attacks', maybe she was calling for help before I heard the scream and maybe Marcus heard it."

"And tried to help?" Chelsea asked. There was a very small note of hope in her voice.

"It could be. You said he went to talk to her, right?"

Chelsea nodded. "He said he was going to ask about an advance on the inheritance. He wanted the money so bad, but he really wanted to go home too. He felt trapped here."

"We all do," Blair said.

"So maybe Lydia cried out, Marcus heard it, and went in," I said. "I know her door wasn't locked, because she couldn't have done it for herself."

"Why the pillow then?" Blair asked.

"I don't know. Who knows what Marcus saw? The way her arms and legs were twisted, it looked like some sort of seizure to me. Maybe he was trying to cushion her head so she couldn't hurt herself on the headboard. But when I went in, and saw her so clearly dead, and Marcus standing there holding the pillow..." I paused. "I made a mistake. And Elijah made it, too, when he came running in."

Chelsea was softly crying again. "Are you saying... that my husband was killed because of a mistake?"

"It was a pretty natural mistake to make," Blair said, quickly adding, "I'm sorry. I know that doesn't help."

"No." Chelsea sniffed. "It's better than thinking he was a murderer someone took revenge on."

"Whenever we get to talk to Sergeant Goddard again," I said, "I'm going to insist they do an autopsy on Lydia. If whatever disease or illness she had killed her, I'm sure they'll be able to prove it."

My gaze found Chelsea's across the table. The redness of her eyes set off the blue-green irises, making them brighter and more striking. She really was a beautiful woman, and she had her flaws, but she was a very strong woman too. I hoped Marcus had known how lucky he was to have been with her.

"If they can prove Lydia died naturally," I told her, "Marcus's name will be cleared."

She hesitated a moment, then left her chair, came around the table and hugged me tightly. "Thank you, Holly."

Blair watched us, a tinge of jealousy in his eyes.

Outside, the wind continued howling.

CHAPTER TWENTY-THREE

The snowstorm hit hardest just as we were hoping the worst was over. The wind howled for hours, sending gusts of snow pelting against the windows, and at times even making the big house creak. About eight o'clock, though, the howling became a roar and the swirling snow turned to machine-gun blasts of hard, icy particles that rattled against the walls and windows so strongly you could almost feel the vibrations in your body.

The three of us were in the library, which seemed to be the sturdiest room in Dacha Orlov. I don't think any of us really believed the house would come apart, but the small gas fireplace, the big overstuffed chairs, and the shelves crammed with books were comforting and made the house seem a little cozier on a dark, miserable night.

I was curled in a chair by the fire, reading a dog-eared copy of *The Lion, the Witch, and the Wardrobe*, a book I hadn't even thought about since elementary school. Somewhere, Blair found a Monopoly set, which seemed strange in this particular house, even if Lydia did say a child once lived here, however briefly. He and Chelsea played a half-hearted game on the library table in the center of the room, barely speaking as they rolled the dice and moved pieces around the board. I knew how they felt. As much as I loved Lewis's fantasy world, I was having a hard time losing myself in it the way I wished I could.

A little past nine, the phone rang, startling all of us. Blair looked at it like it was something foreign that dropped out of the sky, so I rushed over and picked up the receiver, hoping to hear Sergeant Goddard or Trooper Abbott's voice. Instead, it was Rick.

"Holly!" He sounded both excited and worried. "You guys all okay?"

His worry was infectious, and it must have shown on my face. Blair asked, "What is it?"

"It's Rick," I told him, not bothering to cover the mouthpiece. Into the phone I asked, "Why wouldn't we be?"

"Listen." He was breathing hard, as if he'd just run a long way. I wondered if pain from his broken wrist was causing it. "Elijah's on the loose."

"What?" Hearing my tone, Chelsea's face took on a sudden look of concern. "How?" I asked.

"Don't know, but it's all over town. Nobody heard from Mike Abbott in so long that Marie—the girl who runs the desk at the station—sent her husband and brother to go look for him. They found his truck off the road near the bottom of the mountain, the rear windshield all broken out, and no sign of Elijah." He paused. "Abbott was dead, his head smashed in."

My whole body went numb. We thought everything was over, that we were finally safe. We should have known this nightmare couldn't end so easily.

"Holly, you there?" Rick asked.

I tried to swallow a cold lump in my throat. "Y-yes, I'm here. What about Sergeant Goddard?"

"Still way up north. With the storm, who knows when he'll be back?"

I looked towards the library's one, huge window. The curtains were drawn against the night and the cold, but outside, the storm raged. The last I saw, nearly a foot of snow must have accumulated around the house and all in just a few hours. I didn't have to ask to know that no help would be coming. We were trapped.

"Listen." Rick's voice crashed into my thoughts. "Lock the doors and stay put. I'll try to get up there. I know that road and the Explorer has handled the mountain a thousand times."

"Don't you dare try with that broken wrist," I ordered.

Whatever Rick might have said in response was lost. There was suddenly nothing but silence on the line.

"Hello? Hello?"

It was useless; the phone was dead, knocked out by the storm —I hoped. I didn't want to consider alternatives.

"What's wrong?" Blair asked.

I replaced the handset. "What isn't?"

I told them what Rick said. Chelsea's face went stark white and lost all animation. She sat limp and boneless in her chair, not speaking, not really seeing me or Blair.

"Do you really think Elijah will come back?" I asked Blair.

"We have to assume he will." He stood. "You two stay here. I'm going to have a look around the house real quick."

"For what?"

"Piotr Orlov definitely owned guns. We've all seen the hunting pictures scattered around the hallway. I'm hoping there are still a few around the place."

I moved to Blair and took his arm in both hands. "Be careful, and don't be long." He gave my cheek a quick peck. "Fast as I can." Then he went out of the door and was gone.

I put a hand on Chelsea's shoulder. When I said her name, she started. A ripple seemed to go through her body, like every muscle contracting and releasing in turn, then she took a deep breath. She looked up at me. "I'm fine. Thanks."

"Are you sure?"

"No, but what else can I say?"

I couldn't sit still. I paced the room. Chelsea put the Monopoly board back into the box, taking a long time over the individual pieces. She examined each one as if looking for something, and when she was done, there was a thoughtful look on her face. "A hotel in some far-off place with a beach." She sighed. It sounded nice, but I wasn't in a dreaming mood.

Blair came back into the library, shaking his head hopelessly. "If there's a gun in this house, it's well-hidden."

"Maybe hiding is all we can do too."

"No. Elijah must know this place like the back of his hand. There's nowhere we can hide that he wouldn't find us."

"So what then? We just wait and see if he comes back?"

"I guess so. I really don't want to fight him, unless it's absolutely necessary."

"How could you even fight someone that huge?" Chelsea said, speaking for the first time in quite a while.

"Well, there's this," Blair said, drawing a long, thin knife from behind his back. It was at least twelve inches long and serrated. As Blair's hand moved, the blade caught the light and bounced it back in a brilliant flash. "I got it from Eleonore's kitchen. Against anyone else, I'd feel better, but it seems pretty inadequate for dealing with Elijah."

"It's better than nothing."

"Do you think he'll actually come back here?" Chelsea asked. "He killed Marcus and now that policeman, Abbott, too. If he has any brains at all, he should be running for the hills." She sounded sick of everything, like she couldn't care less what happened next so long as we could just get it over with.

"You forget," Blair said, like a teacher to an unruly student, "that we're on the biggest hill around. You forget, too, that whether it's true or not, Elijah believes my brother—your husband—killed his mistress and, at least at one time, lady love. He got his revenge on Marcus, but he might be interested in the man's wife too. For all Elijah knows, you put Marcus up to it."

Chelsea's face was still, but stress lines appeared around her mouth and eyes, and her breasts rose and fell as she began to breathe more heavily. "He can't possibly believe that," she said at last.

"No, he's right," I told her. "We don't know what goes through Elijah's head."

"We know one thing." She turned to me. "From what you've said about protecting you, Holly, I'm pretty sure he wants you. Maybe if it comes to it, you could at least distract him."

"Cut it out," Blair said sharply. "We're not sacrificing anyone."

"It was a joke," Chelsea muttered.

The incessant noise outside the house took on a new tone, sounding now like screaming jets rocketing over the house, bathing it in the backwash from their engines. The snow and sleet pounded against the library window with thousands of fists, demanding to be let in. Safe in my own bed back home, I might have enjoyed the sounds of a night like this once in a while, but now, all I could think of was that if Elijah was out there, we would have no way of knowing. He could be creeping up to the house as we stood here speaking. He might even have found a way in already.

"Listen," Blair said, holding up a hand.

I was focused on the wind and snow and my own thoughts, but now, I could hear something else, a sound that didn't belong to the storm. It was a small sound, muffled by distance, the walls of the house, and the storm, but it was a definite thumping noise, repeated at regular intervals. If Blair hadn't noticed it first, I probably wouldn't have at all. I glanced at Chelsea and saw she heard it too.

I exchanged looks with Blair. "What do we do?" I whispered, as if Elijah was in the room with us.

"We should stay down here, maybe barricade the door. If we

go wandering, we'll just end up running into him sooner or later, and if we go upstairs to our rooms, he'll pick us off one by one. We've got to stick together, that's the important part."

"What if he breaks in?" Chelsea asked.

Blair answered, "Look, he's huge, but I'm betting all three of us are faster. If it comes to it, we run. The house is big enough that we can make like a *Scooby Doo* montage for a while if that ends up being our only option."

Chelsea was about to make an angry retort when a tremendous sound of splintering wood and shattering glass interrupted the conversation, seeming to shake the entire house. I clapped my hands over my ears and screamed, not realizing what I was doing until it was done. I was embarrassed, but it was too late to take it back.

The three of us stood staring at one another for several seconds. The noise of the storm made it hard to decide just where the crash came from. There was another smashing sound, smaller but closer, making it more menacing.

"The dining room," Blair said. He looked from me to Chelsea. "The biggest windows on the first floor are in there. I made sure all the doors were locked when I was gun-hunting, so that's his best bet to get in."

We all heard it then: heavy footsteps crossing the main hall. An instant later, there was a *thump* against the library door.

Chelsea's eyes went wild and she lunged towards one of the big leather chairs, trying to shift it towards the door. "Help me!" she yelled. "Before he gets through!"

"No!" Blair grabbed her arm. "It's too late. Elijah knows where we are now, he'd just go around to the window."

Something hard and heavy slammed against the library door so powerfully that I could feel the vibration in the floor. Chelsea jumped involuntarily, then turned angry eyes on Blair. "What do we do then? Just wait for him to break down the door and tear us apart?"

Blair looked at me. "You and Chelsea keep off to one side of the door as far as you can get. I'll stay right where I am. When Elijah breaks through, I'll be the first one he sees and then…" He brandished the knife. "Well, you just make a run for it."

"He won't go after you," I said, seeing the flaw in his plan. Another thump against the door was accompanied by the sound of cracking wood, making me wince. "He doesn't care about you. You'd have to attack him first and if he gets even one hand on you—"

Wood splintered and the door flew inward so hard it bounced off the wall, swinging back around so that it half-closed again. Elijah pushed it open and strode through, leaving a trail of slushy puddles to mark his passage. When Abbott arrested Elijah, nobody thought to get the black parka he wore when he went into town and now he was soaking wet, dripping melted snow. His clothes were torn and dirty and his hair was matted to his head. A deep gash across his forehead still looked wet and shiny, but didn't seem to be bleeding. It only made him more terrifying, like a giant out of a fairy tale who can't be killed except with some magical weapon. And all we had was a kitchen knife.

Elijah stepped deeper into the room, his eyes on Blair; they burned with what I could only describe as hatred. I knew then that Elijah didn't only blame Marcus for Lydia's death—he blamed all of us, the entire Shaw family. In a way, he was right to: if we'd never come to this house, Lydia Orlov might still be alive. She was the one who had invited us, though, and it was her game that cost so many lives.

Several feet from Blair, Elijah paused as if unsure of what he was supposed to be doing. Maybe the head wound was more serious than it looked or maybe he was just trying to decide who to kill first.

Either way, it probably only meant seconds' delay, but it was an opportunity. Blair took it.

"Run!" he shouted, pulling his arm back over his shoulder and whipping it forward. The knife flew from his fingers, arcing end over end towards Elijah, but hitting him grip first and bouncing uselessly off of his huge chest.

It was only a distraction, but it was all we had. Half-pulling Chelsea behind me, I dashed towards the door and out of the room. Blair followed an instant later with desperate speed, knowing Elijah would be right behind him.

In the main hall, my head swiveled back and forth, unsure of where we could even go. Should we find another room to hole up in? Should we just keep moving? There was no time to decide.

"This way!" Blair yelled, waving us towards the front of the house. He couldn't mean to go outside and the only other thing in that direction was the pool.

Like lightning, memories flashed through my brain and inspiration struck. "Blair," I panted, as we ran. "The pool—"

"Yeah," he huffed. "If we can just get it between us, we can stay away from him and keep moving."

"The pool is perfect! I don't think Elijah can swim!"

"Even better." He tried to grin, but it was more of a grimace.

Almost as one, we crashed through the door at the end of the long hallway, coming out into the warm, wet air of the pool-house. The water's surface shimmered as if calling to us. We were almost there, but we weren't safe yet. We charged forward and dove, slipped, and even fell into the pool without bothering to remove clothes or shoes.

I was conscious of water closing over my head, and for a moment, I did nothing but let it hold me. It seemed peaceful beneath the water and infinitely preferable to anything I would find up on the surface. I didn't have a chance to take a breath before falling in, though, and my lungs began to burn. My choice was drown or face whatever was happening above.

Still beneath the surface, I pushed off the side of the pool, making for the deeper part towards the middle. I was so tired and my chest hurt so badly, I only managed three or four strokes before I had to surface.

When I did, everything was calm. The room was quiet, damp, and pleasantly humid. The overhead lights were out and the skylight was as black as pitch, but the dim, wavering light from the tiny bulbs at the bottom of the pool filtered upwards, giving the area and everything in it a shimmery, dream-like quality. I imagined this was what it was like inside the womb.

Blair and Chelsea shared my instinct. Both were treading water a short distance away. We saw one another and came together in a tight cluster, almost exactly in the middle of the pool. If what I suspected was true, this was the only really safe place we would find in the house.

None of us spoke. There were no sounds but the gentle lapping of the water against the rim of the pool, our breathing, and our limbs churning, keeping us afloat. No one dared say a word. Elijah stood in the doorway to the house, backlit by the long corridor's overhead lights. His shoulders rose and fell in silhouette with his labored breathing. His arms hung at his sides. A long, thin black line that could only be the blade Blair gave up dangled from his right hand. He moved forward and disappeared into the shadows along the outer areas of the room. The noise of the wind was louder thanks to giant windows and the skylight, and with the snow still beating against the house, his feet made no sound at all once on the tiles. He completely disappeared.

"All we have to do is keep treading water," Blair said, turning in a slow circle, trying to spot Elijah. "We might have to do it for quite a while, though, so we should all strip."

"What?" Chelsea spluttered, her chin just barely above the level of the water. Blair and I swam together a couple of times, but we were the only ones who used the pool. Seeing Chelsea now, it was clear that she wasn't as good a swimmer as either of us.

"Your clothes," I told her. "They make you heavy and make it harder to swim."

"Take them off," Blair ordered. "There's no time for modesty."

He was right. I only caught a glimpse of Elijah as he darted closer to the edge of the pool, then faded back into the shadows again, but he was out there and we all knew he wouldn't be satisfied until he had his revenge against the family he blamed for Lydia's death. I already kicked off my shoes and as Blair was telling Chelsea we had no choice, I shimmied out of my pants and pulled the sweater over my head. I wished I'd put on a bra earlier, but it wasn't the most important thing now.

In the low light, panic and confusion showed in Chelsea's eyes as she struggled in the water. She wasn't a strong enough swimmer to keep her head out of the water while she undressed. Blair finished with his pants and then the two of us came to her rescue. I unzipped her dress, Blair pulled it over her head, leaving her in bra and panties. Blair tossed the dress away, but soaked as it was, it didn't go far. It landed with a small, flat *splat* against the water before spreading out and floating away like a lily pad in a pond.

We clustered together again, back to back, trying to keep watch from all sides. Elijah was a moving piece of darkness just outside the uncertain light from the pool, prowling around, looking for a way to reach us.

"I don't know how long I can keep this up," Chelsea said after several minutes.

"If you feel yourself going under," Blair told her, "you can wrap your arms around my neck and take a breather."

"But—"

I cut off any protests. "Just do what he says. Blair's a great swimmer, he can help if you need it." I looked over my shoulder, trying to see her face, but she was turned away. "Only if you have to though. We'll all be tired before long."

"Yeah," she said quietly.

I was worried about Chelsea, but I would let Blair keep an eye on her for now; all of my focus was on Elijah, somewhere out there in the darkness. I was scared, and I was already tired, but I was glad for one thing: it looked like I was right about Elijah not being able to swim. He seemed wary of the water the other times I'd seen him near the pool. The way he was now, I'm sure he would have chased us right into the water if he was able to, but all he did was endlessly stalk around the pool, looking for an opening.

Slowly, I treaded water, conserving my strength as I tried to get inside Elijah's head. The man was almost completely a mystery, even after learning about his shared past with Lydia. I knew he was loyal to her, but how far did that really go? And why was he so disturbed now? He was devastated, but calm when Trooper Abbott arrested him. Rick said the trooper's SUV was found off the road, the rear windshield smashed out and the trooper dead. Was that really Elijah's doing? Did Abbott say something to Elijah that set him off? Or was the crash just an accident that Elijah took advantage of?

There was no way to know and my energy was better spent elsewhere, like considering how Elijah might try to get at us. Somewhere, there must be a drain or a pump to empty the pool, but that would be a slow process and Elijah had to know he didn't have forever to get his revenge. The people in Foster's Place were alert to his escape and sooner or later, help would come. It was only a matter of time.

But while time wasn't on Elijah's side, it wasn't on ours either. How long had we been in the water already? The minutes passed more slowly than any I ever experienced. My arms and legs were already starting to stiffen, and Chelsea must be even worse off. Elijah could see her struggle, and he would know she was the weakest of us, that she would run out of strength before Blair or I did. Chelsea was the one who would drag us down. It was almost inevitable. When she just couldn't keep swimming any longer, and Blair couldn't support her without going down himself, she would have to get out of the pool. When she did, the rest of us would need to go with her or leave Chelsea on her own. All Elijah had to do was stay patient and he would get his chance.

A chair flew out of the darkness, sailing over our heads and splashing into the water before sinking to the bottom. Chelsea shrieked and Blair swore violently. Maybe Elijah wasn't as patient as I thought. Even so, we had to hold out. Sergeant Goddard might already be racing up the mountain to our rescue. It was a thin hope, but I held on to it.

We braced ourselves, but no second chair was thrown. Elijah might have just wanted to scare us, hoping we would panic and climb from the pool. It had the opposite effect; our cluster got tighter, until we were practically in each other's arms, and we all grew even more alert.

At least an hour passed. Maybe two. Help still didn't come.

Several times, I called out to Elijah, hoping to reason with him, reminding him of what he said about wanting to protect me, but it was useless; he never spoke a single word in return. Finally, Blair said, "Save your breath, Holly. You need it." He was right. It was clear that Elijah just wasn't interested in talking.

More than once during that hour, Chelsea had to cling to Blair for minutes at a time to keep from sinking. That took its toll on Blair too. He tried not to show it, but the weariness was in his eyes and even his movements were slowing.

"Next time you need a break," I told Chelsea, "lean on me." She was so exhausted, she didn't react at all. I wasn't certain if she even heard me.

"No," Blair said, the strain in his voice now. "I've got a better idea." He pointed at the far side of the pool, the deepest end. "Elijah's over there somewhere. I just saw him. One of us swims to the other end, hangs on to the rim and rests. As soon as we see that bastard running towards them, the other two make for the side he just left, grab ahold and rest. The person at the far end rests as long as possible, right up until the moment he reaches them, then swims back to the center, and the other two do the same."

"If it works, we might be able to keep that up a while."

"Let's hope," Blair said, kicking towards the far end of the pool, volunteering himself as the first bait. I took Chelsea by the shoulder and pushed her ahead of me in the other direction.

The plan worked—but only once. Elijah saw Blair break away from the group and came out of the shadows at a dead run only to pause when he noticed that Chelsea and I were heading for the opposite side of the pool. He only had a moment of indecision, though, and went after Blair. He knew that Blair did the most to support Chelsea in the water and that without him, neither she nor I would last long. Because of that, Blair only had a few seconds to rest before needing to escape back to the deeper water in the pool's center.

"Let me help Chelsea," I said once we regathered.

"You'll both drown," Blair panted.

I looked at the other woman and was afraid he was right. Chelsea was moving so slowly that she kept sinking. Each time, the water crept further up her face, covering her mouth, then her nose, and when it did, she jerked as if coming awake and had to struggle to make it back to the surface, choking and spluttering.

"We have to do something." My voice sounded high and whiney and desperate and that was just how I felt.

"Stop thinking about it," Blair scolded. "We know the plan works. This can't go on forever."

That's what I was afraid of—how it ended.

Without thinking about what I was doing, I kicked for the side of the pool opposite where we last saw Elijah. I could feel his eyes on me, like searchlights striking out of the gloom, but I just swam harder, pushing myself like I never did before.

"Are you nuts?" Blair yelled, but I ignored him.

When I reached the edge, I tried to climb out of the water, but

I slipped and fell back with a little splash. I was even more tired than I realized.

I threw a glance down the length of the room and saw Elijah slowly emerge from the shadows. He was watching me, but he made no move and I took it as encouragement. I lay my forearms flat against the rim of the pool and slowly, painfully, wriggled up, inch by inch, until I could turn around and sit on the edge. The air was humid, but after so long in the pool, it was cold against my skin, making me shiver. Until that moment, I forgot that I was practically nude. I was sure that Elijah hadn't though. The pressure of his gaze was almost tangible.

I watched Elijah for nearly a minute. He shifted the knife from one hand to the other, but didn't come any closer. Slowly, ready to dive back into the pool at an instant, I levered myself to my feet. I knew the chance I was taking, but something needed to be done to break this stalemate.

"Rest whenever you can," I shouted to Blair and Chelsea. He said something back, but I couldn't hear him over the sounds of the storm and my wet feet slapping against the paving stones surrounding the pool as I started moving.

My eyes on Elijah the whole time, I ran to the far side of the pool, moving as fast as I could while still being as careful as possible. If I slipped and fell, I might break something or knock myself out, or even fall into the pool and drown. Even if none of that happened, Elijah would catch up to me before I got back to my feet.

He must have thought the same thing, because suddenly he rushed around the curve of the pool, putting himself on a course to meet me along its length. Blair was wrong before: Elijah was just as fast as he was strong, and he was amazingly agile too. I had to move around pool chairs and loungers, but Elijah simply leapt over them.

Just before it was too late, I turned on my heel, lurching sideways to catch my balance and faced back the way I came. I was slower than Elijah, I knew that now, but as long as I kept enough distance, I could give the others at least a couple of minutes to rest.

I didn't dare look back, but when I took the corner around the edge of the pool, leaning far over to make use of momentum, I caught sight of him. He had already closed most of the gap between us. My heart lurched in my chest as fear clawed at my insides. It was enough to upset the rhythm of my stride. My foot slipped, went out from under me, and I fell, landing hard, the jolt racing all the way up from my backside into my head, leaving me dizzy.

My vision blurry and my body aching, I silently screamed at myself to get up, to keep going. My legs were like jelly from the exertion and I wasn't sure I'd ever be able to stand again. By some instinct, I felt rather than saw or heard Elijah and I knew there was no more time. I twisted and rolled over the edge, landing in the pool with a *plip* noise. The water revived me a little, enough that I could move. I swam desperately away from the rim, not caring where I went, as long as I was out of Elijah's reach.

"That was incredibly stupid," Blair said. I looked up and realized I'd somehow made it back to the center of the pool.

"I know," I wheezed. "I'm about to pass out."

I couldn't though. We were all exhausted, but I refused to be the one who ruined us.

Chelsea continued to tread water, one hand on Blair's shoulder, her eyes closed like she only wanted to sleep and waking up didn't matter. Blair was barely able to hold his own head out of the water now. I knew he was fit and a good swimmer, but he was basically supporting both himself and Chelsea. He was a much stronger person than I ever realized.

Along the rim of the pool, Elijah paced back and forth. I heard him talking to himself, but I couldn't be sure of the words. After all the patience he showed, even he was at his limit. Maybe almost having caught me pushed him over some line. Or maybe he sensed that his time was finally running out. Oh, God, how I wanted that to be true.

"I'll drown before I let him lay a hand on me," Chelsea said near my ear. Her eyes were open now, but huge and blank, staring off into the darkness without actually seeing anything. "I saw what he did to Marcus."

"Shut up," Blair said, without any heat or energy. "Nobody's drowning. Just keep it together. If we help one another, we'll make it. We just have to hold on a while longer."

How long is a while? I wanted to ask, but wouldn't. Blair was doing his best. We all were. Fatigue and dullness and even a kind of apathy began to creep over me though. I was so tired and every single part of my body ached like it was ready to fall apart. The temptation to just stop moving, to just close my eyes, sink to the bottom, and let it all end was strong. Maybe drowning wouldn't be painful if I didn't fight it. As the thought occurred to me, I slipped under, swallowing a mouthful of water before I bobbed back to the surface by pure reflex. I wasn't quite ready to give up after all, I guess.

"I can't... I can't..." Blair said under his breath, barely loud enough for me to hear.

"Can't what?" I asked, glad for any distraction at all.

One of Blair's hands was around Chelsea's arm. She'd stopped moving entirely; he was the only thing keeping her from sinking. I wasn't sure if she was even conscious.

Blair looked at me. "I can't keep this up anymore. If I don't let her go... we'll both drown."

I pushed myself forward, moving around him. "Let me take her then."

"No," he said. "She'll just drag you down instead, and if only one of us gets through this, I want it to be you. I know you don't... believe me, but I love you, Holly."

The words didn't really register. Across the big room, I saw something. It caught my attention without my understanding what I was seeing. At first, it was only a lighter place in the darkness, moving through the deeper shadows behind where Elijah stood, his chest heaving as if he, too, was utterly exhausted. Hope soared inside me, thinking at first that it might be the white STATE POLICE across Sergeant Goddard's protective vest, but died when I realized it was too low to the ground. Goddard was a tall man and it wasn't close to his chest height.

I couldn't take my eyes from whatever it was though. It was an unknown and it might be our salvation or it might finally be our end. I lifted a hand and wiped water from my face, squinting, trying to see better in the uncertain light.

The white spot moved closer to the pool and a vague shape formed around it. The shape, the height of the lighter-colored object... I knew what I was seeing. Rick's cast!

I didn't believe him when he said he would try to make it up here to us—not really. Rick was a nice boy, but what could he do? Elijah had already beaten him soundly once, breaking Rick's wrist in the process. Maybe if he had others with him or a gun or both, like Blair wished for earlier, he could help, but alone and injured? He wouldn't even be able to occupy Elijah long enough for us to escape from the pool and find someplace to hide.

Something clicked inside my brain and before the thought was completely formed, it was leaving my mouth. "He can't swim! Push him in!" Every ounce of strength I had left was in that shout; I needed to make sure Rick heard me over the howling of the storm and the rattling of snow and ice against the windows.

After so much time spent literally just treading water, hoping only to make it into another moment, what came next seemed to happen at a lightning pace. Rick didn't hesitate for even an instant. If he did, Elijah might have been able to defend himself. Instead, the white blob in the darkness moved like a meteor streaking through the night sky. There was an audible impact as

Rick threw his entire body against Elijah, sending the much bigger man stumbling forward and hurtling into the water.

Where Elijah went in, the pool was more than eight feet deep and he instantly started shouting wordlessly and thrashing wildly, churning water like a huge fish and sending spray in all directions. Blair and I kicked for the shallow end of the pool, Chelsea held afloat between us, dragging her along.

Rick ran to the head of the pool and as I reached the stairs, he splashed into the water to his knees, bent and helped me, one-handed, up and safely away from the water. Then, with Rick's aid, Blair pulled Chelsea out and lay her down. Her eyes were still closed, but her chest moved with her breathing and there was no longer any chance of her drowning.

Only when all three of us were safe did anyone think to look back to the far end of the pool. Elijah's shouting didn't last long, but the thrashing was growing weaker now too.

"Can we really just… let him drown?" I asked.

Breathless, Blair asked, "Are you insane? He wanted to kill us all."

I knew he was right, but it didn't make watching someone die any easier.

Soon, the seething water began to calm. A collective sigh went through everyone at the thought that this time, everything was really over.

Elijah surprised us though; his head briefly broke the surface, then a hand. I jumped back, startled, afraid the horror would begin again, but both head and hand quickly disappeared beneath the water. For at least four or five minutes, all of us just watched. Elijah didn't appear again and the water was completely still. Only then did I start to feel safe at last.

"We should pull him out," I said quietly.

"Leave him for Goddard," Rick said.

I realized that Rick's good arm was around me, supporting me, keeping me upright. I remembered, too, that I was nude, except for my panties. I found it hard to care. All I wanted was to lie down and sleep for a long, long time. My whole body was a quivering mass of exhaustion. I never imagined it was possible to be so tired.

I felt my eyes drooping and then...

CHAPTER TWENTY-FOUR

A small fuel tanker was parked next to the little commuter jet, a hose between them like an umbilical cord, pulsing as the plane drank its fill. When fueling was done, it would take us south to Fairbanks, where we could catch a larger plane down to Seattle before going our separate ways.

It was cold outside, but warm in the building that served as the terminal. The snowstorm ended the day before, leaving behind low temperatures, but clear, blue skies. The sun was shining and already the snow piled up around the edges of the airport's faded asphalt was melting, leaving sparkling rivulets everywhere. It was a beautiful day. It felt like Alaska was trying to make up for everything that had happened, trying to leave us with one final good impression.

A hand touched my lower back. I turned. Blair had joined me by the window. He was wearing a plain, white T-shirt beneath one of his blazers. Over that, he wore his winter coat, unzipped and hanging loosely. He was a little paler, and seemed thinner than when we first met. It gave him a different air, but he was still attractive. Now that we were both millionaires, I supposed it didn't matter what he looked like—there would always be people attracted to money.

"I wish they'd hurry up," he said.

"I never want to see snow again," Chelsea added. "Instead of going back to Chicago, maybe I'll try Los Angeles. Somewhere on the west coast anyway. Or Florida, maybe—a nice resort hotel right on the Gulf."

Chelsea was changed too. After first losing Marcus, and then our last night at Dacha Orlov, she could have been a total wreck without anyone finding fault in her. Instead, she was a woman who survived the worst possible ordeal of her life and came out the other side a new person—stronger and excited to start living again. Rest and Blair's and my promise to share what would have been Marcus's piece of the inheritance with her helped immensely, I was sure. She wore a deep-blue, almost purple dress that hugged the curves of her body, and a brand-new, fur-lined jacket that she bought at the one clothing store in town. She looked younger, fresher, and more vital than I ever saw her. If she mourned Marcus, it was only in private. She barely said his name the last two days.

Nora, as quiet as ever, but looking healthy and happy, was with us too. She and Chelsea talked, exchanging stories and chit-chat about all sorts of things. Blair and I decided we would each give her some of Aunt Lydia's money too. She may have left the house, giving up any claim by the terms of the will, but she made the right decision for herself. It wasn't fair to punish her for it. I was actually even glad that she stayed in town the last several days—I couldn't imagine how differently the night of the storm would have gone if there were four of us.

There was a fifth member of our group, and he was the only one who wasn't excited about the plane being nearly ready. Rick was waiting for us at the tiny Foster's Place airport when we arrived, driven by a different local, doing a favor for Sergeant Goddard. He greeted us warmly and wished us a safe trip. He even had souvenirs for us: small, carved-ivory figures called Billiken that supposedly brought good luck. Rick knew as well as the rest of us that we'd probably used up our entire allotment of luck in a single night.

"A guy from Saint Louis invented them," Rick confided in me, "but we've kind of made them our own up here." He was cheerful as he chatted, but there was a sadness lurking behind his eyes—and something else too. Something I couldn't quite identify. No matter how big he smiled or how loudly he talked, he just couldn't hide whatever was simmering beneath the surface.

I was glad he came to see us off though; he was our savior, after all. Still, it depressed me a little. Rick was a nice boy, and it was plain how he felt about me. He drove up a mountain one-handed in a raging blizzard, and then fought a monster to save my life. And that was the *second* time he fought Elijah. He risked his life and was seriously injured for my sake. It was the kind of grand gesture a lot of girls dream about.

I appreciated everything Rick did for me, and for Blair and Chelsea, too, but it didn't make me love him. I just wasn't wired like that.

The morning after that last night in Dacha Orlov, I woke up in a bed at the Bird Creek Motel. After hearing from Chelsea how Blair drove all four of us—himself, Chelsea, me, and Rick—down the mountain in Rick's Explorer, and briefly talking to Sergeant Goddard about what happened, I went back to bed and slept for another twelve hours. When I opened my eyes the next day, I felt rested and relaxed, knowing that I was really, finally through the nightmare this time.

There was another issue I would have to deal with before I could put all of this behind me though.

Acting like I just wanted a better view through the window, I stepped away from Blair.

I liked Blair. He was a friend, and a member of my family, and someone I knew I could rely on when push came to shove. But I didn't love him any more than I loved Rick, and no matter how much he claimed to love me, to want to marry me, no matter what he promised about the future, I knew that I could never love him back, regardless of whether we actually shared Shaw family blood or not.

Since that night in the pool, it wasn't an issue. Blair was distant, always seemingly lost in his own thoughts. We barely spoke and when we did, it was only necessary things, arrangements about going home and so forth. He never once spoke of any future plans, with or without me. Was it his way of giving me space after everything we went through? Or did something change his mind about how he felt?

Part of me wanted to let sleeping dogs lie. If Blair didn't say anything, did I have to? It was entirely possible that we would never see each other again. After all, we went twenty years between our first and second meetings. Did I want that though? Wouldn't putting a definite status on the relationship between us be for the best?

Pete, the manager and jack of all trades of the airfield, disconnected the hose from the small jet. The hose was reeled back up behind the tanker truck, then he climbed into the cab and drove it out of sight, off behind one of the hanger buildings. I glanced at my watch; the flight was scheduled for 9:35 in the morning and it was just now 9:15. Despite how casual everything seemed, Pete ran a pretty tight operation.

In a few minutes, we would be boarding. A boarding staircase was rolled up to the plane. A moment later, Pete came into the terminal building through a side door, announcing the flight could be boarded now. Our luggage was already aboard, and there were only four other passengers for this flight—including Charlie Shelton, Lydia's attorney, who didn't say so much as a word to any of us while we waited—so it wouldn't take long.

The five of us, plus two men who looked local, and Miriam, the woman on my first flight, walked out onto the landing field.

A light breeze played with my hair and flipped Blair's down onto his forehead, making him look younger and somehow giving him a shy quality that he didn't really have. Shelton managed to put himself first in line to board and as he scrambled up the rolling stairway, the *whoop-whoop* of a police siren turned everyone's heads.

Sergeant Goddard's white-and-black, blue-streaked Ford Explorer flashed its lights and whooped its siren once more before it came to a halt by the terminal building. The tall, lean man unfolded himself from the driver's side while an unfamiliar, stocky woman climbed out of the passenger side. She was also wearing a state police uniform, and I guessed she was Trooper Abbott's replacement. A little twinge went through me; he didn't deserve what happened to him.

Goddard approached us. Blair moved to meet him, putting out a hand. As they shook, he said, "Thanks for coming to see us off, Sergeant."

Blair tried to withdraw his hand, but Goddard held him firmly. He looked over Blair's shoulder to the rest of us and said, "Thought you folks would want to know that we brought Ryan Hill's body down from the side of the cliff this morning."

Nora let out a sob and turned away. Guilt washed over me. When I first woke up in the motel, I talked with Goddard about finding Ryan's body, but I realized I hadn't thought of my cousin since then. A lot happened to occupy my mind, and I did spend almost twenty-four hours asleep, but it wasn't any excuse, not when it came to a man's life.

"Another body to transport," Blair said as if all the weight of the world was solely on his shoulders.

"That's true," Goddard said, "but it's not the reason I rushed over here. All that can be handled by phone, if it's necessary."

When none of us took the bait and asked, Goddard continued. "There are two things, actually. First—" He turned to me. "Miss Shaw, you were correct: Mrs. Orlov died of natural causes. The coroner tells me that a seizure, triggered by stress and the tumor in her brain, was the cause of death—not suffocation."

Chelsea's face lit up, her belief in her husband vindicated, but before she could say anything, Goddard added, "And Mr. Shaw, Marcus Shaw I mean, was right too."

The confusion I felt was reflected on Chelsea's face and in Blair's eyes. "Meaning?" Blair asked.

Goddard said, "Miss Shaw saw Elijah Breaux kill Marcus Shaw with her own eyes. That's not in doubt. And neither is Mike—Trooper Abbott's death. Ryan Hill and Jonathan Shaw are another matter."

"I don't understand," I told him, looking around at everyone else's reactions. That was the question that we never answered. We feared and suspected one another, thinking that a family member must have killed Jonathan because of the money. Logically, we were the only ones who had anything to gain from his death. Money is a powerful motive for anyone. We never seriously considered any other possibility—not until Elijah tried to kill the rest of us, seeking revenge for Lydia, probably thinking it was what she would have wanted after living with her hatred of the Shaw family for so long.

"Didn't Elijah kill Ryan and Jonathan too?" I asked. "Because he thought it was what Aunt Lydia wanted."

"He must have," Blair said. "Ryan was a big man, and Elijah was the only one who could have tipped him over that retaining wall around the patio."

"That's not evidence," Goddard countered. His face turned hard, but he wasn't looking at any of us; he was focused on something else. "This is." From a pocket on the front of his vest he produced a plastic bag. He held it between two fingers, so its dangling contents were plain for everyone to see.

It was Rick's big, gold watch. The watch I noticed was missing just before we ran into Elijah in town. Did he have it when I first saw him that day? Or at the restaurant where we had breakfast? I couldn't remember. I thought of the five-hour nap I took in Rick's truck though. I was exhausted. I slept like a log. He would have had plenty of time to drive to the house and push a probably drunk Ryan over the wall while I slept. If Ryan was sober, only Elijah could have sent him over the wall, but if he was stumbling around drunk…

And the whole time, I was with Rick, unknowingly giving him an alibi if he needed one.

"This," Goddard said slowly, "was found in Ryan Hill's hand when we recovered his body. He must have grabbed it as he was being pushed over the wall."

At some unspoken signal, the female trooper came forward and arrested Rick. As she was reciting his rights to him, he shouted hoarsely, "My name should have been Orlov! That house, the money—it should be mine!"

"Another heir," Blair said, awe in his voice.

Lydia told me that Eleonore was Piotr Orlov's lover, that her son might even have been Piotr's. That was why Eleonore's child was sent away. The school in the states was a rationalization, but getting rid of him was the real reason. I couldn't imagine letting anyone separate me from my child, if I had one. What made her do it? The job couldn't have meant that much to her, not after Orlov died. I suppose the opportunity for Rick to get out of Foster's Place and make something of himself was too good for her to refuse. But then, at some point, Rick came back home and worked odd jobs, anyway—just to see his mother? Or for an excuse to be in that house again? I couldn't understand it. It wasn't my life, but just thinking about it hurt. I wouldn't have lived it for all of Lydia's fortune.

I looked at Rick, but he turned his face away.

We didn't escape Foster's Place that morning. The flight left without us, but Blair and I each had more than enough money to arrange for pick-up from a private jet coming out of Anchorage —the same one that Marcus, trying to impress everyone, chartered for their trip in. We would leave the next day instead. Ryan, Marcus, and Jonathan's bodies would come with us.

The extra day gave everyone time to wrap up loose ends from the new developments. That morning, I thought of Rick as a loose end I could just leave hanging, but after learning what he did, I wanted to be done with him in a way that was definite and final.

The last time I saw him, his face had a grayish tone and he looked worn out and sad, like he was abandoned by the whole world. His surroundings probably contributed to it. He was still wearing his street clothes, but the drab green walls and iron bars separating us were not a good look for anyone. When he saw me, though, his eyes were still dark and warm, and I could see that even if nothing else he said was true, he really did care for me.

For several minutes, we didn't speak. I wasn't sure how to say what I wanted to and Rick must have known that nothing he said would ever make me forgive him.

Finally, I asked, "Did you plan to kill us all?"

"No. I thought one would be enough." He lifted his shoulders. "I thought, get rid of the one, the rest'll get scared and go home. Then my mom, and Elijah, and Ned would split the estate when Mrs. Orlov died."

"The will wasn't even written like that."

Rick looked at his feet and shrugged again. "I didn't know that then, and I thought that this was the only chance. The more I thought about it, the angrier I got, and then I just—"

He lowered his head, shaking it slowly. When he raised it again, he looked right through me, as if he was seeing another place entirely. "I let it get to me, the idea that it should have been my house, my home, and it was just supposed to be the one. I thought I could live with that, if that's what it took. And Jonathan was easy to get to. He was a lonely guy." He paused. "Anyway, when the rest of you didn't pack up and leave, I thought I'd have to do it again." His eyes met mine. "I didn't like it, but…" He trailed off and looked away.

My eyes began to itch and my vision was blurry. I wiped tears away with the back of my hand. "Just tell me why, then."

Rick moved to the far side of the small cell. He looked out of the mesh-covered window, his profile to me. I was wrong when I said the bars weren't a good look for anyone. Even behind them, Rick was a very handsome boy.

"If you hate us all so much, why did you fight for me?" I asked. "First in town, and then you came all the way up the mountain in a storm, with your arm broken. I'd be dead, we'd *all* be dead, if it wasn't for you. That's what I want to remember about you, not…" I couldn't decide what to call it. "Not this."

Rick was silent for so long that I thought he wasn't going to answer. Finally, he turned from the window, leaned his shoulders against the concrete wall and said, "I wouldn't let you die for all the money in the world. You've got some kind of spark, Holly. I think everyone sees it, and I'd be a real monster if I was the one to let it go out."

I was crying openly then, not caring what it looked like or who saw me. I didn't know how I felt about any of this and it would be a long time before I could sort it all out.

Then Rick was at the bars, his good hand holding one of mine. "Don't. I'm not worth it."

———

Blair was waiting for me outside of the police station. He didn't ask what Rick and I talked about. Instead, when we were halfway to the Bird Creek, he asked, "Did you like him?"

"I don't know. He was handsome and fun to be with, but I don't think I ever really knew him at all."

"If I can say one thing for myself, it's that at least I'm not a killer." He tried to take my hand, but I slipped away and hurried a little, outpacing him.

With some distance between us, I turned. "I know, but that's not enough."

Lydia told me not to settle and I intended to take her advice. Rick gave me a bad feeling when we first met, but I brushed it aside because of how he acted, how he looked. In the end, my instincts turned out to be right, but it was too late to do any good. I wasn't afraid of Blair—in fact, I knew I could trust him— but I also knew that he wasn't right for me. I didn't want any more relationship with him than being his cousin. Putting aside all of the money I'd inherited from Aunt Lydia, maybe, after everything that had happened, learning to trust myself was the most important thing I could take away from this place.

I walked the rest of the way back to the motel by myself.

THE END

A NOTE FROM THE PUBLISHER

Thank you for reading this book. If you enjoyed it please do consider leaving a review on Amazon to help others find it too.

We hate typos. All of our books have been rigorously edited and proofread, but sometimes mistakes do slip through. If you have spotted a typo, please do let us know and we can get it amended within hours.

info@bloodhoundbooks.com